Samantha Towle is a *New York Times*, *USA Today*, and *Wall Street Journal* bestselling author. She began her first novel in 2008 while on maternity leave. She completed the manuscript five months later and hasn't stopped writing since.

She is the author of contemporary romances, The Storm Series and The Revved Series, and standalones, *Trouble*, *When I Was Yours*, *The Ending I Want*, *Unsuitable*, *Wardrobe Malfunction*, and *Sacking the Quarterback*, which was written with James Patterson. She has also written paranormal romances, *The Bringer* and The Alexandra Jones Series. All of her books are penned to the tunes of The Killers, Kings of Leon, Adele, The Doors, Oasis, Fleetwood Mac, Lana Del Rey, and more of her favorite musicians.

A native of Hull and a graduate of Salford University, she lives with her husband, Craig, and their son and daughter in East Yorkshire.

Keep up with Samantha and her upcoming releases at www.samanthatowle.co.uk, find her on Facebook: www.facebook.com/samtowlewrites or follow her on Twitter: @samtowlewrites.

By Samantha Towle

Standalone
The Bringer
Trouble
When I Was Yours
The Ending I Want
Sacking the Quarterback (with James Patterson)
Unsuitable
Wardrobe Malfunction
Breaking Hollywood

Revved Series
Revved
Revived

Storm Series
The Mighty Storm
Wethering the Storm
Taming the Storm
The Storm

Alexandra Jones Series
First Bitten
Original Sin

BREAKING
HOLLYWOOD
SAMANTHA TOWLE

HEADLINE
ETERNAL

First published in Great Britain in 2017
by HEADLINE ETERNAL
An imprint of HEADLINE PUBLISHING GROUP

1

Cataloguing in Publication Data is available from the British Library

ISBN 978 1 4722 5144 2

Offset in 11.5/14.65 pt Sabon LT Std by Jouve (UK), Milton Keynes

Printed and bound in Great Britain by CPI Group (UK) Ltd,
Croydon, CR0 4YY

Headline's policy is to use papers that are natural, renewable and recyclable
products and made from wood grown in sustainable forests. The logging
and manufacturing processes are expected to conform to the environmental
regulations of the country of origin.

HEADLINE PUBLISHING GROUP
An Hachette UK Company
Carmelite House
50 Victoria Embankment
London EC4Y 0DZ

www.headlineeternal.com
www.headline.co.uk
www.hachette.co.uk

BREAKING
HOLLYWOOD

Chapter One

Ava

DON'T CRY.

Don't you dare cry, Ava Simms.

You've gotten through harder things than losing your job.

I've lost my job.

Shit. I've lost my job.

My boyfriend left me a month ago. I'm homeless as of tomorrow. And, now, I have no job.

Okay. I'm going to cry.

My lip wobbles, and tears start to run from my eyes.

With my heels clicking loudly across the tiled floor of the lobby, I speed walk out of the building, ignoring the receptionist's curious eyes on me.

Pushing through the rotating door, I'm out of there. Head down, I rush around to the side of the building where my car is parked.

I climb in, shutting the door behind me, and toss my

bag on the passenger seat. I jab my key in the ignition and turn the engine on.

I just want to go home.

But I don't have a home anymore. Not after tomorrow.

And here comes the serious waterworks.

Tears are pouring down my cheeks. I swipe a hand over my eyes, not even caring that I'm probably smudging my makeup.

It's not like I have anyone to impress anymore.

I slam the shift stick in reverse and hit the gas.

A second later, I go over a small speed bump.

I don't remember speed bumps being down here.

My head whips around, and I see a body vaulting away from my car.

Oh, shit.

It wasn't a speed bump.

It was a person.

I just hit a person with my car! Could this day get any worse?

Scrambling out of my car, quickly drying my eyes with my hands, I rush around to find a guy on his ass on the sidewalk, holding his right foot, cursing, and groaning in pain.

"Oh my God! I am so sorry! Are you okay?"

"No, I'm not fucking okay!" he barks. "You just ran over my foot!"

His voice sounds vaguely familiar, like I've heard it somewhere before.

I can't see his face properly, as his head is down, just a head full of dark hair.

"I think it's broken," he groans. "Fuck, it hurts."

I get to my knees beside him, tugging my skirt down to cover my thighs. I knew I should've gone with pants this morning.

"What can I do to help?"

"I think you've already done enough," he snaps.

His head lifts, and he stares straight at me.

Oh, Jesus, fuck no.

I recognize those penetrating dark eyes and that brooding, gorgeous face.

Gabriel Evans.

Hollywood's resident bad boy and my current celebrity crush. I've had a few celebrity crushes over the years, but I'm all about the Italian Stallion nowadays. Not that the press calls him that. I just do in my head because he's part Italian, and I like to think he's a stallion in the sack.

And he's stunning to look at. He has a smoking body and that whole badass thing going on. I just love him.

"No," he says.

"No?" I echo, puzzled.

"No, you can't have my autograph, and you most definitely cannot take a selfie with me."

"I wasn't going to ask for your autograph."

"Just a selfie then?"

"What? No!"

"You always blush when you're lying, Speedy?"

Speedy?

"I'm not lying!" My hands automatically go to my cheeks. They're on fire. That's what I get for thinking about how hot he is.

"Sure you're not."

"I'm not! I swear! And people really do that? Ask

you for a selfie after they've run you over? Because that's a really shitty thing to do."

"You'd be surprised what people would do for a picture with me. But I've never been run over before. This is my first time, so I'll have to get back to you on that."

"I don't want a selfie! Honestly! If I did, I would have asked for one when we met before. Six months ago." When he blankly stares at me, I fill in, "We met at a club. My friend Charly Michaels is dating Vaughn West. Vaughn introduced us."

"I don't remember."

Oh. I can't deny that I'm disappointed. I always hoped that, if I did ever get lucky enough to see Gabriel again, he'd remember me.

But then, why would he? He meets tons of people all the time, and most of them are probably women.

Well, he'll definitely never forget me now.

Way to get your movie star crush's attention, Ava. Run over him with your car.

"Well, no worries." I smile. "My name is Ava—"

"You could be called Candy and strip off all your clothes right now, and I wouldn't give a fuck. Right now, I just need you to help me get my shoe off because my foot is hurting like hell!"

"Do you think that's a good idea? I remember when my brother broke his foot when we were kids. He pulled his sneaker off straightaway, and he was in agony. He couldn't walk. My dad had to carry him to the car and take him to the hospital. He cried all the way there. The doctor said his sneaker held his foot together, and if he'd left it on until he got to the hospital, he wouldn't have been in as much pain. He broke four bones in his foot. Had to have surgery. He was in a cast for months."

"That's a cheery story. Did you break your brother's foot as well?"

"No! Of course I didn't. He broke it after falling out of our tree house."

"I don't give two shits how your brother broke his foot! Did you not hear me say, my foot is fucking hurting? I don't think it can get any worse! Now, will you just take my goddamn shoe off?"

"Okay. Jesus. You're so damn testy."

His response is a growl.

I untie the laces on his shoe and very gently start to ease his shoe off.

"Ah, fuck! That hurts!"

"I told you this wasn't a good idea. Do you want me to stop?"

"No, just keep going."

"Should I do it like a Band-Aid?"

"What?"

"Should I just rip it off like a Band-Aid?"

"No! Just take my shoe off like a normal fucking person takes a shoe off. No ripping off anything."

"I didn't mean that I'd literally rip it off. I just meant, quick, like a Band-Aid. God, you're prickly, and you do curse an awful lot."

His dark brows come together in an unfriendly frown. "You just ran over my *fucking* foot, and you're complaining that I'm prickly and I curse too *fucking* much? How about this, Speedy? I'll get in my car and run over your foot, and then we'll see how that goes for you."

"Jeez, I was only saying," I mutter. "And please stop calling me Speedy."

His lips tighten, his brows rising.

"Okay. We can discuss the use of nicknames later. Let's just get this shoe off, and we can assess the damage on your foot. One . . . two . . . three."

I give it a good tug, and the shoe is off. All the while, Gabriel yet again curses like a sailor.

"Motherfucking cunt of a son of a bitch!" he yells.

"Does it hurt more?"

He pauses, giving me a dark look. "What the hell do you think?"

"Well, I told you—"

"Don't you fucking dare say *I told you so*."

"I wasn't going to." *I so was*. I press my lips together. A beat later, I ask, "Do you want me to take your sock off as well?"

"No, I can do it."

I sit back on my haunches and watch while he carefully peels off his sock.

"Ah, fuck," he groans.

"Ooh, that does not look good at all." I move in close, looking at his foot, which is a spectacular shade of blue. "It shouldn't be that color and not this quickly. I definitely think it's broken." I glance up at his face.

God, he's pretty.

"No shit, Sherlock," he mutters.

And he's an ass.

I stare back at his foot. "I don't think that bone should be sticking up like that." I point at it with my finger.

He bats my hand away. "Don't touch it!"

"I wasn't going to touch it! I'm not stupid."

"You sure about that?"

"Hey!" I lean back, affronted. "That's not nice! I know I ran over you with my car, but it was an accident. I didn't mean to. I've never run over anyone with my car before. I have crashed into another car before, but I'd call it more of a bump, and it was the other driver's fault, not mine. He'd pulled out in front of me. And there was this one time when I clipped this dude's side mirror, and he was pissed, but if he'd parked his car better and not left it sticking out in the road, then I wouldn't have hit it. It's not my fault there are incompetent drivers out there."

Gabriel is gaping at me.

"What?" I ask, a little self-conscious.

"Do you actually hear yourself when you're talking?"

"Of course I do." I frown. "I'm not deaf."

"Good. Because, for a moment there, I was wondering if you were actually aware of the crap that comes out of your mouth."

Ugh. Asshole.

He starts to get to his feet—well, foot. I stand and offer him a hand because I'm a nice person, unlike him, but he ignores my offer, choosing to struggle instead.

So, I watch as he gets up, balancing on one foot, his hand resting on the roof of my car for support.

He's so tall. Six-four, according to his website. I'm only five-three. He's a whole foot taller than me. Even with my heels on, I still have to crane my neck to look up at him.

His face is pinched in pain.

"We need to get you to a hospital. I think Presbyterian is closest."

He lets out a hard laugh. "No, thanks."

"Why? What's wrong with Presbyterian?"

"Nothing's wrong with Presbyterian. It's you that's the problem. No fucking way am I getting in a car with you."

"Hey now! There's no need for that. Seriously, Gabriel, you're close to hurting my feelings."

"Am I? Oh God, I'm so sorry." He slaps his hand on his chest. "Because I would hate to hurt your feelings after you so kindly ran me over with your fucking golf cart of a car and broke my fucking foot!"

"It was an accident! And my car is not a golf cart!"

"It was not an accident! You didn't see me because you were too busy bawling your eyes out to notice I was even there!"

Shit. He saw me crying.

I feel so embarrassed. It stains my cheeks.

"What happened? Did you have a fight with your boyfriend?" he prods sardonically.

"No," I bite. "I don't have a boyfriend." *Anymore.* "And, not that it's any of your business, but I was just fired."

"Did you run over your boss as well?"

Ugh. Asshole.

The urge to stamp on his good foot with my stiletto, taking that one out of action as well, is strong. But I won't do it because I'm a better person than he is. He is so off the top of my celebrity crush list.

"You are not a nice person, Gabriel Evans." I fold my arms over my chest.

"And you're a danger to people everywhere. I should call up the DMV and have them take your license away because whoever gave it to you must've been fucking high."

"Mr. Anders was not high! He was a nice old man! God! Why don't you just skip the DMV and call the police to report me for dangerous driving? I'm sure they'd happily take my license away from me!"

Ah, hell. Why did I say that?

From the smirk he's now wearing, I'm guessing he didn't think of calling the police.

I am so going to jail.

I swallow down.

"As nice a thought as that is, you wouldn't last five minutes in jail, Speedy. Call this me being nice, as I'm keeping your pretty ass out of jail by not calling the cops."

Is it sad that I'm stuck on the fact that he called me pretty? Well, he called my ass pretty, but whatever.

God, I seriously need a slap across the face.

"You're welcome," he snips.

Then, he pushes off my car and starts to hop. I kid you not; he's hopping away.

"You forgot your shoe and sock," I call out to him, spotting them on the sidewalk.

"You can keep them as souvenirs," he calls back as he hops toward a fancy-looking silver Audi parked a little further down on the other side of the road.

I bend down and pick up his sock and shoe.

I told him that he wasn't a nice person, but there must be a little nice in him. He could've called the cops. He probably should have, but he didn't. And I didn't even thank him.

Sock and shoe in hand, I start to walk over to Gabriel,

who's just made it to his car and opened the driver's door.

By the time I reach him, he's inside, and the engine is on.

I rap on the window. He turns his head and stares at me.

"I brought you your sock and shoe." I hold them up for him to see.

He rolls his window down, and he takes them from me without a word, tossing them on the passenger seat.

I awkwardly stand there, biting on my lip and twisting my hands together. "I should have said thank you. For you not calling the cops. I do appreciate it. And I am sorry about running over your foot. Really, I am. And I would totally understand if you changed your mind and wanted to call the cops. So, I can give you my cell phone number in case you need to—"

"Are you hitting on me right now? Because I've gotta say, that's just straight up inappropriate if you are. You broke my foot, and now you're trying to get in my pants. Bad form, Speedy."

"What? No!" I step back in shock, my hands going to my face. "I-I was just-just—" I splutter, shaking my head. "I am not trying to get in your pants! I was trying to be a good person! I can't believe you think I was hitting on you!"

"Weren't you?"

"No!"

"Well then"—he scratches his chin—"I don't know whether to be relieved or offended." He looks me up and down. "I'll go with relieved."

"Ugh! God, you're a . . ."

"What am I?" he goads.

Be the bigger person, Ava. Do not take the bait. It's clear that he loves an argument. Don't give him what he wants.

I take a few deep breaths in and out and then change tack. "Are you sure you can manage driving?"

He blinks back at me like he was expecting me to argue back. And I swear, I see a spark of disappointment because I didn't.

"Of course I can," he retorts. "It's an automatic. I only need one foot to drive it."

"Your right foot, and that's your injured foot. I really don't think you will be able to drive. You can't even put weight on it. And, if you do somehow manage to drive, you could cause more damage to your foot than there already is."

"Are you a fucking doctor now?" he bites. "Of course I can drive my goddamn car. Now, will you disappear, so I can get to the hospital?" He dismisses me with a flick of his wrist.

"Fine." I raise my hands and step back. "I'll leave. But don't say I didn't warn you, Hoppy."

"What did you just call me?"

"Nothing." I smile innocently. "You drive safe now." I turn on my heel and walk back over to my car.

I hear the rev of his engine.

When I reach my car, instead of getting inside, I lean against the driver's door and watch as he tries to drive his car, which I know he doesn't have a hope in hell of doing.

It moves slowly at first and then jerks forward, like he went heavy on the gas. The car stops, then jerks forward again, and then stops.

"Motherfucker!" he yells, slamming his hands on the steering wheel, which sets off his horn.

I have to hold back a laugh. "You okay there, Hoppy?"

He doesn't even look at me. He gives me the middle finger.

Asshole.

But, instead of getting annoyed, I laugh, knowing it will vex him more.

The engine loudly revs again, and then, suddenly, his car lurches forward and jumps the curb, right in the direction of a street sign.

Holy crap!

He quickly swerves off the curb and slams hard on the brakes.

His hands are curled around the steering wheel, his face taut and angry.

I open my car door, reach in, and grab my bag. Then, I lock my car up and walk over to Gabriel.

He's still sitting there, staring angrily at his steering wheel.

"I told you—"

Laser eyes turn to me, cutting me off mid sentence. "If you fucking say *I told you so*, I'm calling the cops, and then I'll have them drive me to the hospital while you sit in the back of the patrol car in handcuffs."

I bite my lip to keep from laughing. "So, does that mean you want me to drive you to the hospital?"

"No," he growls.

Then, he yanks his seat belt off and jerks open his car door. I jump back just in time to avoid being hit by it.

I watch, confused, as he hops his way around his car.

Then, he opens the passenger door, gets inside, and slams it shut.

"Are you driving me to the fucking hospital or not?" he hollers from inside the car.

Okay. Guess I'm driving the cantankerous superstar to the hospital.

Without a word, I climb in his car, shut the door, and drop my bag on the backseat. I adjust the seat forward, so I can reach the pedals, and then I put my seat belt on.

"I'm taking you to Presbyterian?" I check.

"Yes. My brother's a doctor there. He'll see to me."

I didn't know he had a brother, let alone that he was a doctor.

I wonder what kind of doctor he is. Do they look alike? God, I hope so.

Gabriel might be a monumental asshole, but he's a good-looking one.

I'm not holding my breath that his brother is nice though. I thought Gabriel was a nice guy after our first meeting, and look at how wrong I was about that.

I'm just about to shift the car into drive when I see Gabriel reach into the pocket of his pants. He pulls out a small silver hip flask. He unscrews the cap and takes a drink of whatever's in there, and I'm guessing it isn't water.

"Should you be drinking?" I ask.

He frowns. "It helps with the pain."

"I have some Advil in my bag," I offer.

Ignoring me, he takes another drink from the flask.

"Fine." I sigh. "Let's go." The sooner I get him to the hospital, the better.

I put the car in drive, and then I double-check and then triple-check the mirrors before pulling off.

Gabriel opens up the central console and gets out a pack of cigarettes and a lighter.

I didn't know he smoked.

He rolls his window down, gets a cigarette out of the packet, puts it between his gorgeous lips, and lights it up.

Even though he looks seriously sexy and kind of badass with a cigarette, smoking is gross and really bad for your health.

The smell of the smoke filters through the car, even with his window open.

Ugh, God, it stinks.

I let out a loud, exaggerated cough and roll down my window.

"Problem, Speedy?"

"Did you know passive smoking kills thousands of Americans every year?"

"I didn't. Did you know that irresponsible drivers kill tens of thousands of innocent Americans in road-traffic accidents every year?"

He gives me a pointed look and takes another long drag of his cigarette, letting the smoke filter slowly out of the corner of his mouth.

God, he's so sexy.

Stop it, Ava. Focus on the matter at hand.

"Mine was by accident. And I didn't kill you."

"Just broke my foot. And I'm not killing you."

"But you're purposely putting my life at risk with your cancer stick." I jab a finger in its direction.

He puts the cigarette between his lips, leaving it there, dangling.

Dear God. He looks like James Dean or a young Marlon Brando. All beautifully bad and cool.

Ugh. Why does he have to look so good with the grossest thing in the world hanging from his mouth?

"Don't worry, Speedy," he says, cigarette still between his lips. "I'm sure you're far more likely to kill yourself in your golf-cart car than die from the inhalation of my smoke."

"Well, if I do die of lung cancer by smoke inhalation, then my death is on you."

He takes another long drag of his cigarette and then removes it from between his lips. Holding it between his thumb and index finger, he flicks the ash out the window. "I'm sure I'll find a way to live with it."

Ugh. Bastard.

"Not when my pissed-off ghost comes back to haunt your smoking ass, you won't."

"Did you just make a dirty joke, Speedy?"

I run my words back through my head, hearing them how he heard them, and my face floods with embarrassment, my cheeks burning.

"You think my ass is smoking hot?"

I have nothing, so I do what any grown woman would. I flip him the bird.

He laughs. It's deep and sexy, and I feel it *everywhere*.

"I'll take that as a yes."

"Take it as a no. A big fat no. Now, will you be quiet and let me drive? I'd hate to have another accident."

I flick a glance at him and find him grinning at me.

"Sure thing, Speedy." He winks at me. Then, he puts his cigarette between his lips and takes another drag, looking every bit the gorgeous movie star that he is.

And my girlie parts shimmy in response.

Uh-oh.

Chapter Two

Ava

TWO MORE CIGARETTES, THREE mints, four drinks from his hip flask, and what feels like five years later, I pull up outside of Hollywood Presbyterian Medical Center.

Who knew being stuck in a car with my celebrity crush could be so painful? Especially when I was aware of every single thing he did, down to every inhalation of breath he took.

I bring the car to a stop in the patient drop-off zone.

I'll leave it here, help Gabriel inside, and then come back out to move it to the parking lot.

I take my seat belt off at the same time as Gabriel.

I open my mouth to speak, but he beats me to it.

"You can just leave my car here. I'll have Tate move it. And here's some money for a cab back to your car."

I hold up a hand, stopping him. "I don't want your money for a cab. I can pay for my own cabs." *For now at least.* "And, as much as I'd like to leave you here, my conscience won't allow it. I have to make sure you're okay."

"I'm okay. There. Your conscience is eased."

"Funny. I didn't know you became a doctor in the five years it took to drive here."

"That's weird because, the speed you drove, it felt more like five seconds to get here."

"I did not speed! I stuck to the speed limit the whole way. And I got you to the hospital in one piece, didn't I?"

He eyes his broken foot with a raised brow.

"That doesn't count because it was already broken before I got in the car with you."

"Your logic is screwed up."

"It is not! God, you're so annoying." I glare at him.

"And smoking hot, Speedy. Don't forget that."

Argh!

"I never said you were smoking hot! I said I would haunt your smoking ass! As in the fact that you smoke— which is a disgusting habit, FYI—and I was using the word *ass* as an insult, you ass! I do not think that your ass is hot! Seriously! I would rather kiss a toad's ass than ever think that your ass is hot! I do think that you're vain, crude, argumentative, and seriously annoying though!" I break off, breathing hard. I'm pretty sure I have steam coming out of my ears.

Jesus, I barely know him, and I want to strangle him! No one has ever annoyed me more than he does. And it's so disappointing because I thought he was awesome. That was before I got to know him, of course.

"Has my hair gone gray?" he asks, pressing a hand to his head.

"No." I frown. "Why?"

"Because I feel like I just lost twenty years of my life after listening to your little rant. Seriously, Speedy, you should consider getting help with that verbal diarrhea that falls out of your mouth. I know a good vocal coach who might be able to work on it with you. He normally just works on accents and word pronunciations, but he should be able to help you learn to speak properly."

"Ha-ha. You're hilarious. And twenty years? You'll be lucky to see another ten if you keep smoking your nicotine sticks at the rate you do."

"I'll outlive you, Speedy. The way you drive, especially in that golf-cart car of yours"—he rubs his chin in thought—"I give you two years. Three, tops."

Eyes narrowed, I tip my head to the side. "Want to bet on that?"

A grin spreads across his face. "Oh, I'm all for betting, Speedy. But you wouldn't like the stakes. And, also, there'll be no satisfaction in my winning because you'll be dead, and I won't be able to claim my win or flaunt my victory in your face."

I give him a smart smirk. "You keep telling yourself that, Hoppy. And, as nice as this conversation is, we can't sit—sorry, I mean, I don't want to sit here all day with you. So, let's get you inside and to your brother."

"I told you, I don't need your help."

"And I told you, I'm coming. So, unless you want me to take out your other foot as well, you'll stop arguing with me and get out of the car."

"Fine," he grunts. "Just let me get ready before we go in."

"Aw, do you need to do your hair and makeup before

we go inside in case you get papped?" I laugh at my own joke.

"Ha. You're a comedian," he says in a droll voice. "No, I need to put on my ball cap and sunglasses just to prevent me from being recognized."

I watch as he opens the glove box. He pulls out a pair of Ray-Ban sunglasses and slips them on, followed by a Lakers ball cap, which he fits on over his hair.

"Ready?" I ask.

He nods.

I climb out of the car. When I make it around to his side, he's already out, resting on his good foot, holding on to the car with his hand.

"How are we going to do this?" I ask him.

"If you don't know the answer to that, then I can't do this with you."

I look up into his face and see the smile edging his lips. Surprisingly, I find myself smiling back.

"I mean, you're the size of a giant, and I'm normal-sized, so—"

"I am big; that's true. But you're not normal or normal-sized. You're under-sized."

"I am not. I'm a normal size for a woman. And, anyway, didn't anyone ever tell you that the best things come in small packages?"

"No. Because it's a lie. Big is better. Just ask all the women I've fucked."

"Jesus Christ!" I scowl. "Do you have to be so crude?"

"It's not crude. It's called being honest. You're just a prude, Speedy."

"I am not a prude." My hands find my hips. "And

sorry to burst your bubble, but not all women want big."

He barks out a laugh. "Yes, they do. They just say they don't to make their small-cocked boyfriends feel better about themselves."

"Well, maybe the women who told you that you were big only did so to make you feel better about being tiny."

"You're hilarious. And they definitely didn't. I'm more than happy to prove it to you."

His hand goes to his zipper, and I slam my hands over my eyes.

"I don't want to see your . . . thing!"

"Cock. And you can uncover your eyes. I wasn't actually going to get my big cock out in front of the hospital."

I slide my hands from my eyes and give him a dirty look.

"Speedy, as much fun as this is, can we get moving? I'm in agony here."

I see the pinch of pain around his mouth and feel a shot of guilt.

"Shit, of course."

I move beside him and slide my arm around his back. Even with my heels on, he's still ridiculously taller than me. Next to him, I must look like a toddler playing dress-up.

"Okay, put your arm around my shoulders, and then put your weight on me."

"If I put my weight on you, we'll go down like dominoes. You weigh, what? One twenty?"

"One thirty, and I'm stronger than I look."

"Yeah, well, I'm as heavy as I look."

"Stop arguing with me, and let's do this."

"But I'm enjoying arguing with you. It's almost like foreplay."

I look up at him. He's not smiling this time. His eyes look darker. Lustful. A thrill runs through me.

"You're hilarious. Now, put your arm around my shoulders, and let's get moving."

He drapes his arm over my shoulders, and it's heavy. God knows what the rest of him weighs.

"Ready to move?"

"Yep."

We start to walk, and, Jesus, he wasn't kidding. He weighs a freaking ton, and I don't think he's putting much of his weight on me.

But it's a ton of pure muscle.

Under my fingers, I can feel the ridges of those muscles in his back.

I bet his stomach is like a washboard that I would want to scrub my face all over.

And he smells good. So good.

The annoying thing about this is that I can smell the cigarette smoke on him along with the mints he ate in between smokes and the clean scent of his aftershave. Somehow, mixed together, it just works. I want to hate it, but I can't.

It's making my girlie parts tingle with excitement.

He smells exactly like I'd want to after a night of amazing sex.

I have a flash of being in bed with him. Him hovering over me as he moves inside me. My fingers digging into the hard muscles in his back, like they are right now.

And, now, I have a sweat on, and it's not from lugging him around.

Great.

We reach the main doors. They whoosh open, and we walk straight into the busy reception area.

I feel Gabriel tense.

"You okay?" I ask him.

"Yeah, I just don't want to get noticed."

"Okay, let's keep moving. Where's the emergency care department?"

"We need Pediatrics, on the fifth floor."

I stare up at him. "Pediatrics?"

"That's where Tate works."

"Tate's your brother?"

"Yes."

"He's a doctor for kids?"

"What gave it away? When I said he worked in Pediatrics?"

"Funny, Hoppy." I pull a face at him. "God, I hope your brother is nicer than you," I add as I steer him in the direction of the elevators.

"He is. A lot nicer. And don't call me that."

"What? Hoppy?"

"Yeah. It sounds like something a cartoon character would be called. It's very emasculating."

I laugh. "And Speedy is so flattering."

"I mean it in the nicest sense of the word."

"Sure you do. Okay, I'll make you a deal. You stop calling me Speedy, and I'll stop calling you Hoppy. What do you say?"

"Fine," he grumbles.

And it makes me smile.

Reaching the elevators, I hit the button, ready to wait, but luckily, the doors to one of the cars open immediately. I usher Gabriel inside, and using the railing, he shifts and leans back against it.

I push the button for the fifth floor and move to stand next to him.

"I need you to do me a favor when we see Tate," he says as the elevator starts moving.

"What's the favor?" I turn my head to look at him and get an eyeful of his shirt-covered chest. Straightening up to my full height, I still have to tip my head back to look into his face. The height difference is very annoying.

"When Tate asks how I broke my foot, tell him a tank ran over it."

Laughter bursts from me. "A tank? You want me to tell your brother that I was driving a tank when I ran over your foot? Somehow, I don't think he'll believe that."

He pulls his sunglasses off and hangs them in his shirt pocket. Cool brown eyes stare back at me. "I don't care if he believes it. I just don't want him knowing that your golf-cart car did this. If he knows, I'll never hear the end of it."

"Wouldn't it be more believable if you just told him that I was driving a big car, like, I don't know, a truck or something?"

He purses his lips in thought. "You know, Ava, you're smarter than you look."

Ava.

That's the first time he's said my name. It does something strange to me. It makes my heart beat a little faster, and my stomach flips.

"I think there was a compliment in there somewhere, Gabriel."

His eyes warm, crinkling at the corners. "Call me Gabe."

"Gabe, it is."

His brown eyes seem to turn a shade darker, and all of a sudden, it starts to feel a hell of a lot warmer in here.

I look away. "So, Tate. Is he older or younger?"

"Younger."

"How many years?"

"Five."

"My brother's four years older than me," I tell him.

"You close?"

"Yeah, we talk on the phone all the time, but Jayce lives back home in New York. He's a corporate lawyer, and he consults for a lot of big firms, so he travels quite a bit with work. I don't get to see him as often as I'd like."

The elevator reaches the fifth floor. Gabe slings his arm around my shoulders, and I put my arm around his back.

"You know"—I tip my head back to look at him—"that's the longest we've had a conversation without arguing or hurling insults at each other."

His eyes meet mine. "Felt really weird, right?"

"So weird." I grin.

"Okay, as soon as we're out of this elevator, we resume our normal bickering."

"Definitely," I agree.

The doors slide open, and we step out of the elevator.

Chapter Three

Gabe

"**B**ITCH."

"Jerk."

"God, that felt good," I faux groan. "Did it feel good for you, Speedy?"

"So good," she moans.

And the sound reverberates through my chest.

I wonder if that's the sound she would make if my head was between her legs.

"But we made a deal, remember?" Her tiny finger pokes my chest. "No more calling me Speedy."

"Oh, yeah, I forgot." Like hell I did. I just like calling her it.

It's perfect for her. Not just for the fact that she drives like she's trying to beat the land-speed record. She is the definition of a motormouth. She can talk at speeds I didn't know were possible. I've seriously never heard anything like it. She doesn't even stop to breathe. Run-on sentences actually exist in speech. She must have the lung capacity of a whale, which could come in handy for some serious deep-throating.

Yes, I want to fuck her.

Sure, she's annoying as hell. But, when her mouth is shut—or, if I had my way, full of my cock—she's incredibly fuckable.

A total babe.

I wanted to fuck her the moment I saw her. And I don't mean today.

I remember her from the club. Of course I do.

You don't forget a woman who looks like her.

She's stunning. A mane of long brown hair, which is sadly tied back into a ponytail today. But, man, does it look soft as fuck. I want to pull that hair tie out and slip my hands into all that gorgeous hair, getting my fingers tangled up in it, while I fuck that tight body of hers and stare into those smoky-blue feline eyes, watching her lose control as she comes.

I would have made a move on her that night in the club, but before I even had the chance, she mentioned a boyfriend, so that was the end of that. And, even if she hadn't had a boyfriend, she got totally trashed that night, and I never screw a drunk woman. I would have just waited until the morning when she was sober, and then I'd have banged her.

Of course I would have taken her home with me. Look at her; she's fucking gorgeous.

But it didn't happen.

And, since that night, I never thought of her.

Until, out of nowhere, there she was, leaving the studio building, tears running down her pretty face.

I had the urge to follow her and find out what or who had made her cry.

But I didn't follow.

And then I saw her walk off down the street from where my car was parked.

So, I made the decision to go over to her car and knock on the window to check if she was okay, which is not like me at all. I don't like it when women cry. It makes me uncomfortable, so I avoid crying women at all costs.

I'm kind of an asshole if you haven't guessed.

But something drew me over to her, and I was just approaching her car when it suddenly moved, and she ran over my foot.

And that was when everything went to shit. And, after that, no way was I going to admit that I remembered her.

Admitting I remembered her would have meant that she had had an impact on me even if it was only a small one. She didn't need to know. Knowing that would give her the upper hand, and when it comes to women, I need to be on top every time. Literally and figuratively.

"Well, that was your last chance, Gabe." Her voice pulls me back. "Call me Speedy again, and you'll see what happens."

She's so argumentative.

Seriously, I'm not used to women giving me shit like she does. They're usually all, *Yes, Gabe. Whatever you say, Gabe. Put it in whatever hole you want to, Gabe*, no matter how I speak to them.

But not Speedy. She doesn't take my shit. She's

quick-witted and feisty. Different. And, oddly, I like that about her.

It makes her even hotter.

"And what are you gonna do if I call you it again?" Of course, my tone is mocking. Gotta bait if I want to get a bite.

It's like a game of verbal chess.

Waiting to see what barb she'll say next, it's entertaining as fuck. Has my heart beating faster and my dick getting harder. Who knew insults turned me on so much?

Her small body tenses under my arm. "Guess you'll find out if you call me it again." Her tone is edgy.

Oh, yes.

And, obviously, because I can't help myself and I seem to have developed the mentality of a teenage boy when I'm around her, I say, "Bring it on, *Speedy.*"

She huffs this cute little growly sound that has me grinning from ear to ear.

"You're an asshole."

"Is that my punishment?" I mock. "Because I thought you had more in you than that, Speedy."

"Ha! That wasn't even close to payback, *Hoppy.*"

She scowls up at me, and I want to kiss it off her face.

"Gabriel! Oh my word! What have you done?"

We're interrupted by Agnes, one of the nurses who works here with Tate. Out from behind the reception desk, she comes barreling toward me.

I love Agnes. She's my favorite. She always showers me with affection and feeds me cookies when I'm here. And it's not just because of who I am or because she wants on my cock. It's because she genuinely likes me.

And, also, she's been married to the same guy for forty years, and her kids are older than me.

"She ran over me with her car and broke my foot." I thumb in Speedy's direction.

I hear her gasp, and I grin.

God, I'm a dick. And I love it.

"Why on earth did you do that?" Agnes frowns at Speedy.

"I-I ... it wasn't on purpose," Speedy splutters to Agnes. "It was an accident."

"I don't know, Agnes. I think she did it on purpose," I stage-whisper.

I glance at Speedy, and her face is all pinched and angry. She looks like she wants to murder me in my sleep.

Sexy as fuck.

"Never! No one would hurt you on purpose. You're adorable." Agnes takes my face in her hands and smushes my cheeks like I'm a little kid.

And I fucking love it. I'm an attention whore. What can I say?

"Yeah, I guess you're right." I give a dramatic sigh. "She must just be a really bad driver. Apparently, she didn't see me, but it's not like you could miss me. Right?"

I can feel the rage emanating from Speedy. It's taking everything in me not to laugh.

"Of course! You're unmissable, sweetheart. She must be a really bad driver." Agnes cuts another dirty look to Speedy.

Then, she extracts me from Speedy, and I go willingly.

Agnes is built a lot sturdier than Speedy. I felt bad about putting my weight on Speedy, so I was bearing the brunt of it, even while my foot was in agony, but I don't feel too bad about leaning on Agnes because I know she can take it.

"Let's get you in a chair."

Agnes moves me over to a waiting wheelchair, and I sigh with relief the moment my ass hits the seat.

"Better?" she asks.

"Much."

"Right, I'll just page your brother. I'll be back in a moment. You want me to bring you some cookies?"

"What do we have today?"

"Your favorite. Triple chocolate and salted caramel."

"Agnes, you are a modern miracle."

"And you're a charmer." She chuckles before heading back to the reception desk.

Speedy is still standing in the same spot as before, looking a lot uncomfortable and a little lost.

I get a pang in my chest. "You okay over there?"

Her eyes turn to me. She still looks like she wants to kill me. "You're asking if I'm okay?"

"Yes," I answer carefully.

She stalks over to me, stopping in front of me. "You just made me look like a really bad person in front of that nice lady, so, no, assface, I'm not okay!" she hisses.

"I was just playing. Agnes is cool. She doesn't think you're a bad person."

Her arms fold over her chest, pushing her tits up. I can't help but look at them. But then I force my eyes back up to her face.

She still doesn't look happy.

"Come on, Speedy. I was just yanking your chain."

"It's fine to yank my chain when it's just between

you and me. I don't appreciate being made to look bad in front of someone else."

"Okay, point taken. Won't happen again. But it was the truth. You did run over me with your car."

"Not on purpose!" She stamps her foot, little hands clenched in fists at her sides.

"Okay, okay. Simmer down there, tiger. We're on a kids' ward, remember?"

She glances around, taking in her surroundings.

Agnes reappears with a plate piled with cookies and hands them to me.

"Thank you." I give her my best smile. I pick up a cookie and moan around it.

"Good?" Agnes asks.

"Amazing," I say.

And she beams.

"You want one?" I offer the plate to Speedy.

She reaches over and takes one. "Thanks."

I watch as she takes a bite and chews. Then, she moans, her eyes closing.

And my dick starts to get hard, and Agnes is standing right there.

Down, boy.

"Tate said to put you in his office, and he'll be with you soon."

"Thanks, Agnes."

She wheels me toward Tate's office. Speedy follows, still eating the cookie and still moaning.

It's like torture.

"This cookie is amazing," she says to Agnes. "Just so good."

"Thank you, honey."

Not that Agnes hasn't heard the praise before. She's famous in this hospital for her cookies.

If my brother ever stopped working here, I'd still come just for Agnes's cookies.

Whenever I need to be away to work on a movie, Agnes always packs me up a box of cookies to take with me.

"Right, I'll leave you here." Agnes parks me in Tate's office. "Got rounds to make. You want me to get you some painkillers before I go?"

"No, I'm good. Thanks, Agnes."

She closes the door, and then it's just Speedy and me. Alone. In a doctor's office.

If I weren't in so much pain right now, I'd ask her if she wanted to play doctor and nurse.

Speedy sits in a chair, opposite me, and crosses her legs.

She has great legs. Tanned and toned. They'd look fucking amazing, stretched up, with my hands on them while I pumped in and out of her.

I put the plate of cookies on Tate's desk, and then I stretch my own leg out, trying to move my injured foot.

I hiss at the pain. *Fuck, that hurts.*

"You should take something for the pain," Speedy says.

"I did."

"Alcohol does not constitute a painkiller."

"It's nature's very own painkiller."

"Yeah, whiskey brewed in a factory is nature's way of easing pain." She rolls her eyes.

"How do you know it was whiskey I drank? It could've been water."

"Was it?"

"No."

She laughs.

I get a sharp pain in my foot. My brows pinch together.

I get my flask from my pocket and take another drink of whiskey.

"Just take some pain medication if it hurts that much."

"No."

"God, you're stubborn."

"God, you're annoying."

And I'm five years old again. *Why exactly do I act like a child around this chick?* I'm three seconds away from pulling her hair and pushing her to the floor.

But, even still, I like arguing with her. It's fun. And kind of hot.

"Speedy?"

"What?"

"Will you argue with me? It's what's been distracting me from the pain this whole time."

"So, you'd rather argue with me than take pain pills?"

"Yes."

"Why?"

"Because I'm odd."

"I already figured that. I'll make you a deal. You tell me why you won't take pain pills, and I'll argue with you to your heart's content."

No way am I telling her that. I don't tell anyone anything about myself because, if I did, I'd be reading about it on *Radar Online* an hour later.

"Forget it." I pull my ball cap off, toss it on Tate's desk, and run my fingers through my hair. Then, I shut my eyes, tip my head back, and breathe through the pain.

"Your last movie was shit, by the way."

A grin spreads across my face.

I open my eyes and look at her. "As shit as your driving?"

She holds back a smile. "My driving could never be as shit as your acting."

"So, you're saying that all my movies are bad. Yet you've watched them all."

"I never said I watched them all. I said, your last one was bad."

"You've so watched them all. I bet you have them all on DVD and watch them every day. Especially *Bonjour*. I bet you know that one scene by heart—when I'm buck naked and fucking Annette Channing on the Pont de l'Archevêché."

"I do not!"

Her cheeks are as red as the blood currently pumping through my veins and down to my cock. And I know she's watched that scene multiple times. Probably gotten off to it.

I lean forward. "You want to know something about that scene?" I leave the words teasing, tantalizing.

And, like a fly to my web, she leans in closer, moving forward in her seat. I don't even think she's aware she's doing it.

Her eyes are focused fully on me.

As mine are on her.

The scent of her perfume fills my nostrils. She smells

like summertime and apples. And I want to take a big bite out of her.

"You know how the press reported that it was real? That I really screwed Annette in that scene?"

She moves even closer, ass on the edge of her seat, hanging on my every word.

"I didn't," I whisper. Then, I grin big.

Chapter Four

Gabe

Speedy's eyes narrow. "Jerk."

"Perv."

"I am not a perv!"

"You so are." I laugh, sitting back. "You were practically salivating at the thought of knowing that it was real. Just admit it. There's no shame in being a pervert, Speedy."

"I am not a pervert!" she snaps, righteously crossing her arms over her chest.

And, of course, my eyes go to her tits again. I can see her cleavage pushing up through the top of her shirt, practically bursting to get out.

I bet she has great tits. They look amazing under her clothes. I can only imagine they are fan-fucking-tastic in all their naked glory.

"Unlike you," she growls. "Hey, pervert! My eyes are up here."

Busted.

But I take my sweet time in raising my eyes. And, when I meet hers, I give her a cocky smile.

"I know exactly where your eyes are, Speedy. You just have great tits. It's hard not to look at them, especially when you insist on drawing my attention to them." I point at her cleavage.

She looks down and drops her arms. "God, you're crass and disgusting and crude and-and . . ."

"You at a loss for words, Speedy? That's a first. Hang on, let me get my camera out to capture the moment." I pretend to reach for my phone.

"Ugh! You're a pig!"

"Who's a pig?" Tate asks, walking through the door.

"Me, apparently."

"Well, that's nothing new."

Tate's eyes go to Speedy, who has swiveled around to look at him.

Then, a thought dawns on me.

Tate could like her. She's definitely his type. Well, she's everyone's type.

And she could like him.

Sure, he's not as hot as I am, but he is a good-looking bastard.

We have the same dark hair, except Tate wears his a bit shorter than mine. And I'm taller by a couple of inches. Our skin has the same olive tone to it. But, apart from that, we look completely different.

I look like our dad, whereas Tate looks like Mom.

And Tate is a better person than me. He always has been. He takes care of sick kids, for fuck's sake. I read lines that someone else wrote, and I'm good at fucking. That's about the extent of my abilities.

Tate has so much to offer. And I have literally nothing.

As I watch the interaction between them—which feels like it's lasting forever when in fact it's mere seconds—I feel my chest tighten.

But it's definitely not jealousy because I don't get jealous. Especially not when it comes to Tate.

I'd do anything for him. I always have, and there's nothing that will ever change that. Especially not some hot chick who I want to get balls deep in.

If Tate likes Speedy, then I'll step aside. Easy. I mean, at the end of the day, all I want to do is spend a little more time arguing with her and winding her up before eventually fucking her and then sending her on her way.

I have never been good at sticking with just one girl.

Still, I find myself holding my breath as he walks over to her, watching his face for signs of interest.

"I'm Tate, Gabe's brother." He holds his hand out to her.

She gets to her feet and shakes it. "Ava Simms. I ran over your brother's foot with my car and broke it—his foot, not my car. He wanted me to lie and say it was a tank. But, actually, it's a Mercedes Smart car. If you're not familiar with them, they're, like, super small. Tiny. Light as air, in fact." She glances my way, a smirk spread across her face. "Honestly, I don't know how it could have broken his foot. He must have really weak bones. Or tiny feet, and you know what they say about a man with small feet."

She's evil. Pure evil.

I'm going to kill her. No doubt about it.

Forget worrying about if Tate likes her. I'm going to strangle her to death and then drop her body off at the hospital morgue. And I'll wear a smile on my face the whole time.

"Agnes said that someone ran over your foot. But it was seriously one of those miniature cars? And your foot's broken?" Tate chuckles.

"It wasn't a tiny car. It was a tank."

"He's lying. It was my super-small and ultra-lightweight car that broke his weak foot," Speedy tells Tate. "How small are your feet anyway?" she asks me, laughing.

"As big as my dick, which is eye-wateringly huge."

"He wears a size ten," Tate tells her.

"Ten and a half!" I yell.

"Isn't that small for a guy who's as tall as you?" she taunts.

"I wear a twelve, for clarification purposes," Tate says.

"Fuck off, Tate. And you, Speedy"—I angrily eye her—"you are the actual devil. I'll never trust you with anything ever again."

"Oh, my heart is breaking." She slaps her hand to her chest. "It's your own fault. I told you I'd get you back, *Hoppy*."

The look of triumph on her face would be sexy if I didn't currently want to maim her.

It takes me a second to get what she means, and my eyes nearly bug out of my head. "You ratted me out because I called you Speedy? That is in no way comparable!"

"Who cares? I told you I'd get you back. And, honestly, the whole perving on my breasts only upped the ante and made it totally comparable, jerkface."

"You bitch," I scowl.

"That all you've got?" She laughs. "I thought you could do better than that."

"Should I come back when you two are done?" Tate asks.

I say, "Yes," at the same time as she says, "No."

Screw my foot. I'll get that sorted after I've sorted out the devil here.

"You just wait, Speedy. I'm gonna come at you with some serious payback when you least expect it."

"Ooh. I'm shaking in my heels," she mocks.

"I can't believe a Smart car broke your foot." Tate's smile is getting wider by the second.

"Shut up. And we don't know it's broken for sure yet," I counter.

Tate comes over, crouches down, and lifts my foot, examining it. I hiss at the pain from the movement.

"I'm pretty sure it's broken, brother." He looks up, a big-ass smirk on his face. "And it was broken by a baby car."

"Fuck off. Those cars are not as light as they look. And she was sitting in it as well." I jerk my head in Speedy's direction. "That car is, what? A couple thousand pounds at least. Add on another one fifty from hefty over there, and you're looking at some serious weight. Enough to break even the hardest man's foot."

"Hey!" she squeals. "Hefty? That's just mean! I'm not hefty! And what the hell happened to 'You weigh, what? One twenty?'" She mimics my voice.

I glare at her. "She gained thirty pounds when she ratted me out."

"Asshole."

"Shrew."

"Ooh, you got a new word. You're getting better at this, Hoppy."

"Bite me, Speedy."

"Jesus, how long have you two known each other?" Tate asks, getting to his feet.

"Too long."

"An hour," she says, ignoring me. "Although we have met before, but your superstar brother doesn't remember that."

"Bitter much? Does it hurt your feelings that I don't remember you?" I taunt. "Did you bitch at me that night, too? Maybe that's why I can't remember you. I blocked out all the nagging. And, actually"—my eyes go to the clock on the wall—"it's been an hour and a half. The *longest* hour and a half of my life."

"Aw, you're counting our time together, Hoppy. So sweet."

And, like the grown-up that I am, I flip her off.

"As much fun as this has been—and, trust me, it's been entertaining—I need to get you down for an X-ray," Tate says. "Cover up, so you don't get recognized. But security is down there just in case you need it."

I sigh.

That's the part of my life I don't like—having to hide in public—but it comes with the territory.

I forgo my sunglasses and just put my ball cap back on.

"How long will he be?" Speedy asks Tate.

"Thirty minutes, max."

"I'll go move his car. I left it in the drop-off bay."

"There's a parking garage just across the street," I tell her. "You can just leave the keys at the main reception if you want. Save you from coming back up here."

I don't want her to go. Even if she is the devil. But I'm not going to ask her to stay.

"I'm not going yet." She frowns, a cute little pucker forming between her brows.

And I hold back a smile.

"I already told you, I'm here till the bitter end."

"You're so sweet," I tease.

"You know it." She throws me one last smile. Then, she turns on her heel and heads out the door.

"Well, that was interesting," Tate says as he moves behind the wheelchair and starts to wheel me out of his office.

"*Interesting* is a word for it."

"She seems nice. Angry but nice."

"Mmhmm. You like her?" I ask, testing the waters.

"Do I like her?"

"Do you think she's fuckable?" I clarify.

"She's hot for sure." He muses. "But she's not my type."

"No? She looks like your usual type."

"Unlike yours, which is anything goes."

"Variety is the spice of life, baby bro."

We reach the elevator. Tate presses the button and comes to stand in front of me.

"So, you don't want to ask Ava out?" I check.

He laughs. "No. She's all yours."

"I never said I wanted her."

"Sure you don't."

"I don't. I just want to fuck her." Even if she is the most infuriating woman I've ever met. I'll just gag her when we finally do it.

"Isn't that the same thing?"

"Definitely not, brother. Have I taught you nothing?"

He laughs again. "Sorry to tell you, Gabe, but sex is going to be the last thing you'll want to do when you're in a cast. It's uncomfortable as hell. Add that in with the pain you'll be in. And I know you don't like to take painkillers."

Yeah, because I know how easy it is to get addicted to that shit.

I frown down at my foot. Christ, I didn't think of not being able to have sex. I've clearly been too obsessed with thinking about screwing Speedy. I didn't even consider the fact that I might not be able to. And it's not like I'd be able to show my amazing bedroom skills off to her with my foot like this.

That means I can't have sex with her until I'm fully healed.

"Exactly how long is my foot going to take to heal?" I ask Tate just as the elevator doors open.

"Depends on what the X-ray shows," he says as he maneuvers me. "But six weeks at least."

"Fucking hell," I groan.

Six weeks.

Six fucking weeks to wait before I can get inside Speedy.

Well, that sucks.

The doors on the elevator close.

"So, a Smart car did this to your foot?"

"Tate . . ." I growl.

"Ah, come on." He laughs. "You know, if this were me, you'd be giving me shit for months about it."

"Fine," I sigh. "Get it off your chest."

"Fuck, this is so exciting. I don't know who to tell first."

"Anyone but that fucker Vaughn West because, the minute he hears, I'll never live it down."

Tate goes silent behind me.

I crane my neck to look at him. He's on his phone.

"What are you doing?"

He lifts his eyes from his phone and grins at me. "Texting Vaughn, of course."

Chapter Five

Ava

I WALK OUT OF THE hospital, car keys in hand.

Gabe might be a monumental pain in the ass and wind me up like nobody's business, but I put him in this position with my carelessness, and I should do everything I can to help him.

Probably not bickering with him would be a good idea, too, but, honestly, in an odd way, it's actually fun, sparring with him.

If not a little surreal.

If you'd told me a few months ago that I'd be single, homeless as of tomorrow, and jobless and that I would hit Gabriel Evans with my car, break his foot, and spend a few hours verbally sparring with him, I would have laughed in your face.

Funny how life can change in the blink of an eye.

Or, as in my case, go to shit in quick succession.

"Ah, crap!" I complain, grabbing the parking ticket off the windshield of Gabe's car.

Add parking fine to the damage I've done to him.

"Just fucking great," I mutter to myself as I stuff the parking ticket into my bag and get in the car.

I move it into the parking garage and pay for the parking.

Heading back into the hospital, I get two black coffees from the cafeteria and some creamer and sugar in case he takes them. I'm a black-coffee girl myself. The stronger, the better.

Just how I like my men—dark and strong.

Not that Jeremy, my ex, possessed those traits. Well, he had dark hair. But strong? No way. Weak asshole? Definitely.

I had known he was difficult and selfish, but I didn't realize how bad he was until after he was gone.

Don't get me wrong; I was gutted when he told me he'd gotten an acting job in Australia, that he was leaving in a few days, and that he didn't want me to go with him.

He said our breakup had been coming for a while.

He was right. It had been coming. And I know I'm better off without him. He was stifling me.

I've always been a strong person, but with him, I allowed myself to be weak. I let him boss me around and tell me what to do and be an asshole to me because I was afraid of losing him when losing him was exactly what I needed to do.

My only regret is that I wasn't the one to end it.

I might have lost my job and my home, but I'm freer than I ever was when I was with Jeremy.

Things will work themselves out. I know they will.

They have to.

I take the elevator back up to Pediatrics. Unsure of whether to go back to Tate's office or not, I decide to sit in the reception area and wait there.

I haven't been waiting for long when Gabe arrives back in a wheelchair, Tate pushing him.

"What's the verdict? Is it broken?" I ask Gabe.

But Tate answers, "First and second metatarsal. Clean breaks. And some tendon damage. It's hard to break the first metatarsal, so you got him good."

I wince. "Jesus. I'm so sorry, Gabe."

He shrugs. "It is what it is. And, hold on, did you just apologize to me? Wait, I need to get it on camera that you did actually apologize to me once."

"Hey! I've said sorry to you plenty of times since I ran over your foot."

He grins at me, and I just shake my head, annoyed.

"Gabe, I'm gonna go sort out getting a boot fitted for you," Tate tells him.

"Boot?" I ask.

"It's instead of a cast," Gabe tells me as Tate walks away.

"Oh, right."

"One of those mine?" Gabe nods in the direction of the coffees on the seat next to me.

"Yeah, sorry. Here." I hand his coffee over. My fingers touch his in the exchange, and my whole hand heats. "I got it from the cafeteria downstairs," I tell him, like he really needs to know. "Do you want creamer and sugar?"

"Creamer and three sugars."

"Three?" I frown.

"It keeps me sweet."

I raise a brow. "*Sweet* is hardly a word I'd use to describe you. But I only brought two sugars, as normal people have one or two."

"I'm not normal."

"Clearly."

"Two will have to suffice."

He puts his hand out for them, and I drop the sugar packets and creamer in his palm.

I sip my coffee, watching him pour all that crap into his coffee, ruining a perfectly good drink.

"How can you drink it with all that crap in it?" I ask as he takes a sip.

"How can you drink it without it?"

"Have you ever tried it black?"

"Yeah. It was one of the worst moments of my life. What about you? Ever tried it with creamer and sugar?"

"Nope."

"Wanna try mine?"

I consider saying no, but then the prospect of getting to put my lips where his have just been is too good of an opportunity to turn down.

He might be annoying, but he's still hot as hell.

My future sex daydreams about him will just now have to involve putting a gag over his mouth.

"Sure. Why not?" Putting my own coffee down, I take his from him. I put the cup to my lips and take a sip. "Ugh! That's disgusting." I hand it back to him. "It doesn't even taste like coffee. Just hot milk and sugar."

I quickly take a drink of my own coffee to get rid of the taste, and Gabe chuckles.

"Did you move the car? Thinking you probably shouldn't have bothered, as I'll be done here soon."

"Oh, yeah. About that . . ."

"You didn't smash up my car, did you?"

I give him a look. "No, of course I didn't."

"Run over some other innocent person?"

"No! Shut up, will you? You got a parking ticket."

"You mean, you got me a parking ticket."

"Well, no. I only parked there so you would be closer to the hospital and wouldn't have to walk too far."

"And I'm only in the hospital because of you."

"Fine." I throw my hand up in the air. "I'll pay the damn parking fine."

"No, you won't."

"Yes, I will."

"No."

"Yes! And why are we arguing about this exactly?"

He stares at me for a long moment. "If you haven't figured that out yet, Speedy, then you never will."

Huh?

I open my mouth to ask what the hell he's talking about, but Tate reappears, interrupting us.

"I'm going to take you down to the fracture clinic and have the boot fitted there," he tells Gabe.

"Should I wait here? Or come with you?" I ask.

"Come along," Tate tells me. "Gabe's going to need a ride home when he's done. Would you be okay driving him? I'm on shift until ten tonight; otherwise, I'd take him."

"I am here," Gabe pipes up.

"Of course I'll drive him," I answer Tate, ignoring Gabe.

"I can get a cab," Gabe says to me. "You don't have to drive me."

"You don't want me to drive you?"

"Well, I do quite like living, Speedy, but that's not what I meant. I've taken up most of your day. I'm just saying, you don't have to give up any more of your day for me."

Hang on. Was he just being nice?

"Was that you . . . being nice . . . to me?"

His brows draw together. "Maybe."

"Okay"—I shake my head—"I'm not sure what to do with that. But I want to drive you. It's the least I can do after breaking two bones in your small foot with my tiny car."

He gives me the middle finger, and I'm back on steady ground, which was shaking a moment ago from shock at his niceness.

Tate wheels him over to the elevator, and I follow, my coffee in hand.

We all get in, and Tate presses the button for the first floor.

I feel like I've spent too much of my day in this elevator. I'll be ready to never see it again.

"You're going to need some help around the house," Tate says to Gabe. "Is Donna away?"

"Yeah, she's on vacation, but playing nursemaid for me isn't part of her job description as my PA. And, anyway, I'll be fine. I can manage."

"No, you're going to need help. I don't want you on your foot at all for the first few weeks, so I'm putting you on crutches. Getting around is going to be tricky. I can try to take some time off to help you, but—"

"I can help," I hear myself saying.

What?

Two sets of dark eyes swivel to me.

Me and my damn guilty conscience.

Well, I've said it now, so I can't take it back.

I clear my throat. "I mean, if you need help while you're stuck, Gabe, I can help you. After all, you are in this position because of me, so the least I can do is take care of you."

"No way," Gabe says at the same time as Tate says, "That'd be great."

"What?" Gabe jerks his gaze up at Tate.

"It would be a big help, Gabe. I can't be there all the time to help you out. You know what my shifts are like. I'll only be worried about you being there on your own. Having Ava take care of you would ease my mind."

"I'm a fucking grown-ass man. I don't need you to worry about me, and I definitely don't need a goddamn babysitter." He looks at me when he says that last part.

Babysitter? Asshole.

Also, I'm trying not to feel too insulted that Gabe's first response to my offer was, "No way."

Sure, I know we argue, but I'm not a bad person. I'm actually a good person to have around. And I kind of got the impression that he liked arguing with me. Clearly, I was wrong.

"I'm not suggesting I babysit you." I frown down at him. "I'm just offering to help you out when you need it. I've got some free time at the moment"—*thanks to being fired*—"so it's not a problem."

"Sounds perfect," Tate says.

The elevator reaches the first floor. The doors open.

"Sounds like hell," Gabe mutters as Tate starts to push him out of the elevator.

I rear back at his words. "What did you just say?" My body is bristling, as I know full well what he said, but I want to hear him say it again, so I can tell him that he can go fuck himself and that my offer is officially rescinded.

That was mean and uncalled for. I was trying to do something nice, but then he had to go and say that. I'm actually hurt.

I wait for Gabe to respond, but Tate speaks before Gabe does, "He said it sounds like heaven. Didn't you, Gabe?"

Gabe swivels his head to look at Tate. I see Tate frown at him and then flick his eyes in my direction.

"You know what? Forget it. I heard what he said."

I get Gabe's car keys from my bag and toss them at him. He catches them.

"Sorry that I broke your foot, and I'll pay for the parking ticket. It was really nice to meet you, Tate. Wish I could say the same thing about you, Gabe, but it wasn't."

I turn on my heel and head for the stairs. The last thing I want to do is get back in that damn elevator again.

And now my eyes are stinging with tears, which is stupid. I don't even know why I'm upset.

I guess it's just been a butthole of a day, and it's only going to be worse tomorrow when I have no home.

God, my life sucks monkey balls.

I always try to stay positive, but life is really testing my positivity at the moment.

I push open the door to the stairwell.

"Speedy."

The sound of Gabe's deep voice stops me.

I glance at him over my shoulder. Whatever he sees on my face makes him wince.

He's alone. Tate's not with him. He must have wheeled himself over here.

"What do you want?" I let go of the door and turn to face him.

"That was an asshole thing to say. I don't know why I said it . . . except that I'm an asshole."

"Yeah, you are."

"And . . . I'm . . . sorry." It sounds painful for him to say.

Of course I'm going to milk it. "Can you say that again? I didn't quite hear you. And wait while I get my phone out, so I can get this on camera."

"Ha. Very funny. Don't push your luck, Speedy."

I smile, and so does he. Then, silence falls between us.

"It was a really shitty thing to say." My words are quiet.

"I know." He sighs. "I just have a hard time with accepting help. I don't like to feel useless. I took that out on you. I shouldn't have."

I meet his eyes. "You're forgiven."

His eyes smile back at me. "So . . ."

"So, what?"

He scratches his cheek, looking uncomfortable. "Well, if the offer's still there . . . I'd really like to take you up on it."

"Oh, I don't know . . ."

"Please, Speedy. If you don't, Tate's gonna hire some scary-ass nurse called Big Bertha to come and take care of me."

I laugh.

"I'm not kidding. He just threatened me with it. And, apparently, she's mean as hell."

That makes me laugh harder. "I don't know, Gabe. I think Big Bertha is just the punishment you deserve for being an asshole."

"Please, Speedy." He grabs my hand, his gorgeous brown eyes pleading up at me. "I need you."

Well, if that doesn't get me, nothing will. My heart-beat has tripled in time. And he's still holding my hand, and my skin is on fire.

But I play it cool. "Fine"—I sigh—"I'll come take care of you. It's not like I have anything better to do right now anyway."

He smiles. "You're awesome."

"I know. Now, come on, let's go get your foot sorted, so we can get you home."

Chapter Six

Ava

G ABE LIVES IN WEST HOLLYWOOD, so we're actually heading back in the direction of where I left my car, which I'll need to pick up later.

He directs me to his apartment building, and he tells me to park his car in one of his two allotted spaces in the underground parking lot.

I help him out of the car, and he allows me to, which is a miracle in itself. He's been a lot more cordial since his apology earlier. We've still bickered, of course. It would be weird if we didn't.

I hand him his crutches, and we head for the elevator.

He's got a boot on, which goes up to just below his knee. It seems a little extreme to me for a broken foot, but I guess the doctor knows best.

And Tate wants him to keep his weight off his foot for the next few weeks, so no walking on it—hence the crutches.

He looks kind of funny and not just because of the

boot and crutches. But Tate had to cut off the leg of his pants so the boot could be fitted. So, he has one leg of his pants cut above the knee while the other is still long.

We go inside the building and step into a huge lobby area to reach the elevators.

Gabe lifts his hand in greeting at the older man behind the security desk. "Hey, Harry."

The man stands and comes around the desk. "Evening, Mr. Evans. What on earth happened to your leg?"

"Oh, she broke my foot." He jerks his head at me.

For the love of God, I wish he'd stop telling people that! Even if it is true.

The security man's eyes briefly come to me, and then a smile appears on his face. "Did you deserve it though?" he asks Gabe.

Gabe laughs. "Yeah, probably."

"Thought so." Harry chuckles. "You need me to do anything for you?"

"No, I'm good. Speedy's going to be taking care of me for a few days. So, you'll see her coming and going."

"Shall I add her to the approved list?"

"Sure."

"My name's Ava, not Speedy," I tell Harry.

"Ava. Got it. Good to meet you, Miss Ava."

"You, too." I smile. "And Ava's just fine."

The elevator pings its arrival, and the doors open.

"Catch you later, Harry," Gabe says.

"Bye, Harry."

Once we're inside the elevator, Gabe puts a key in the control panel, turns it, and then presses the button for the penthouse.

Figures.

We ride up in silence, and I have a sudden bout of nerves.

I'm going to Gabriel Evans's apartment.

Gabriel Evans!

I keep forgetting just who I'm with when I'm arguing with him. He just seems like this normal, regular guy.

He is a normal guy, dummy.

Who just happens to be adored by millions.

Me included.

And, now, I'm heading up to his apartment.

It feels a little more than surreal.

And, when the elevator doors open into his apartment, I'm reminded once again of exactly just who he is.

And not just because of the framed posters of some of his movies that hang in the huge foyer, but—*Holy shit, this place is amazing.*

It's a movie star's home.

"Wow," I say to him. "Your home is beautiful."

I walk into the living space, which is the size of my whole apartment. It's wall-to-wall windows, and I can see all of Hollywood from here. Dusk is just setting in. I bet it looks stunning at night when the city is all lit up.

I walk over to the window. "You have a terrace and a pool?" I turn to face him.

"Yeah."

He empties his pants pocket of his cell, wallet, the key he just used in the elevator, and his hip flask, which I'm pretty sure must be empty from the way he was drinking it on the way back. Honestly, if I drank that much liquor, I'd be flat on my back right now. I've always been a lightweight.

He tosses his stuff onto the wooden coffee table in front of him, which looks like it probably cost more than my car.

Then, he sits down on the massive white leather sofa that faces the view, putting his foot up onto the footstool. He sets his crutches next to him. "I'm just gonna sit a minute, and then I'll show you around."

"No need. You sit and relax. I'll show myself around. I can snoop better if you're not tailing me."

I grin, and he chuckles.

"Have at it." He rests his head against the back of the sofa.

"You need me to get you anything?" I ask, walking over to him.

"Nah, I'm fine. Just gonna rest a sec." He closes his eyes.

I look at his face. His full lips are pressed together. Enviably long lashes sweep his high cheekbones. His hair is all mussed up.

Lord, he's pretty.

"Speedy, are you staring at me?"

I almost jump out of my skin. *Busted.*

"No! Of course I'm not," I squeak. I step away, my heels suddenly sounding a lot louder on the marble floor.

He chuckles darkly.

I'm glad his eyes are still closed, as my face is flaming.

"Right, I'm going to look around. Be back in a few." I drop my bag on the floor by the sofa.

"Don't go looking in my underwear drawer, Speedy."

"Why? What's in there?"

He pops open one eye. "My underwear."

"Funny." I stick my tongue out at him and then head for the door on the other side of the room.

"You're gonna look now to see if there is actually anything else in there, aren't you?"

"Of course I am."

His laughter follows me as I walk through the door and into a hallway.

I discover a sublime, large kitchen that looks like it's never been used, and a utility room. Two bedrooms, both with en suite bathrooms. I guess which bedroom is Gabe's right away. Aside from the fact that there are dirty clothes tossed on the chaise, it has framed movie posters of *Raging Bull, Taxi Driver*, and all The Godfather films up on the wall. And there's a photograph of him with Robert De Niro.

Must be a De Niro fan.

There's also a framed picture of him and Tate on his nightstand. No picture of his parents though.

And there's a Stephen King novel with a pair of reading glasses next to it.

It somehow seems sweet that he wears glasses for reading.

His bathroom is gorgeous. It has one of those freestanding claw tubs and a walk-in shower with one of those massive showerheads.

I salivate at the thought of using both. My soon-to-be ex-apartment only has a shower, and the water pressure sucks.

Also, there's an office and a home gym.

I manage not to go snooping through drawers and cupboards even though the temptation is great, and when my self-tour is done, I go back into the living area.

"That dildo and lube in your nightstand are for personal use, right?" I tease as I walk over to him.

I know he's sleeping right away. Not only because I didn't get a rise out of him, but his mouth is slack, and an unlit cigarette is dangling from it.

He must have been exhausted if he fell asleep before he could even light his cigarette.

He looks so adorable. I'm tempted to snap a picture, but that would be super creepy.

I gently remove the cigarette from his mouth and the lighter from his open palm. I put the cigarette back in the pack, which is on the sofa beside him.

God knows where he got that pack of cigarettes. He probably has boxes stashed all over his apartment. He'd need to with the way he smokes.

I leave them next to him in case he wants a smoke when he wakes up.

I grab a blanket off the other sofa and lay it over him, covering him up.

Then, I head to the kitchen, thinking I'll cook some food, ready for when he wakes up.

Only I open the fridge, and it's empty, except for bottled water, beer, and what looks to be an old carton of Chinese food.

I try the freezer and get vodka and ice cream.

I look in the cupboards, and they're bare, except for chips, cookies, and peanut butter.

Does this guy not eat?

Looks like I need to go to the store.

I grab a bottle of water and head back into the living area.

I put the water next to Gabe, so he'll have a drink if he wakes up before I get back from the store.

I grab his key from the table and get my bag, and then I head for the elevator.

Harry's at the security desk when I get down there.

"How's Mr. Evans doing?" Harry asks me.

"He's sleeping at the moment," I tell him. "I need to go to the store, as it's like Old Mother Hubbard's cupboard in his kitchen."

Harry laughs.

"Do you know where the nearest store is?"

"Take a right out of here, and there's a store on the corner of the block. Couple of minutes' walk. It'll have everything you need."

"Brilliant. Thanks."

I head out onto the street and take the directions Harry gave me, and I find the store, no problem.

I grab a cart and fill it up with groceries. Then, I pay and pack my stuff up into a few bags.

Thank God I'm not too far from his building, as I've got a lot of stuff.

I lug the bags back to his building.

Harry rushes to open the door when he sees me. "Do you need a hand getting these upstairs?" he asks, taking a couple of bags from me.

"No, I'll be fine. If you could just get me in the elevator, that'd be great."

Harry puts the bags on the floor in the elevator for me, and I climb in.

"You sure you don't want a hand?"

"No, I'll be fine. But thank you." I don't really want him to come up with Gabe sleeping on the sofa.

Using Gabe's key, I get the elevator moving.

It opens up, and I grab all the bags. My heels click on the floor, so I kick them off. Barefoot and being quiet, I carry the bags through the living area, heading to the kitchen.

Gabe is still sleeping.

I dump the bags on the counter and then start unpacking the food.

When I'm done, I start on making some soup for Gabe when he wakes.

I hope he likes carrot and ginger soup. It's one of my favorites.

I love cooking. I used to cook for Jeremy all the time. It's not so much fun though when you're only cooking for yourself.

I make up the vegetable stock I bought. Then, I chop up the carrots and boil them in water to soften them. I pour the stock into the sparkling clean blender. Add in the carrots, ginger, turmeric, cayenne pepper, sour cream, and some wholemeal bread, and I blend the whole thing together. Then, I pop it in a pan on the stove and heat it through.

When I'm done, I head back into the living room.

The smell of cigarette smoke tells me that Gabe's awake.

"Hey," I say, walking over. I open the door to the terrace to let in some fresh air. "You sleep okay?"

He rubs the palms of his hands over his eyes. "Yeah. Guess I needed it."

I walk over, pick up the ashtray on the coffee table, and hand it to him.

"Thanks."

I perch on the sofa next to him. "I made soup. I hope you like carrot and ginger."

"I wondered what that nice smell was."

"Surprised you could smell it over the stench of your nicotine stick."

"Surprised you can cook."

"Hey!" I shove his arm with my hand.

God, his biceps are big.

He chuckles. "Just kidding, Speedy. Where did you get the food from?"

"This crazy place called a store. You heard of one before?"

He gives me a look. "Of course I have."

"I wouldn't have thought so with how bare your cupboards were."

"I always order in. Or eat out."

"Well, you have an amazing kitchen back there that was in serious need of use. So, I went to the store and bought you some food. You owe me a hundred and twenty bucks, by the way."

"Did you buy the whole store?"

"Just the essentials and enough to feed you for the next week."

He leans his head back against the sofa and takes a drag of his cigarette.

I'm mesmerized by the set of his lips around that cigarette and then the way the smoke flows out of his mouth before curling up into the air.

Smoking is gross. But, somehow, he makes it seem sexy.

"Thank you." He turns his head to look at me. "I appreciate you cooking for me."

The way he's looking at me, warm brown eyes on mine, I can feel his stare in every part of my body. And it feels good.

"So"—I clear my throat, looking away—"do you want to eat now?"

"Shower," he says. "I feel gross."

"How is that going to work?" I ask.

He stares down at the boot on his leg. "Fuck if I know. Guess I can take it off while I shower."

"Nope. Tate said under no circumstances are you to take it off. So, it's shower with the boot on. Or would a bath be easier? I could keep the water low, and you could hang your leg out of the bath. Rest your foot on a stool."

"Sure, I guess that could work." He shrugs.

"Okay. I'll go run you a bath."

I head off to his bathroom and get the bath going. I find some bubble bath that says it helps with muscle relaxation and pour it in.

I need something for him to rest his foot on while he's in the tub.

There's a stool under the vanity unit. I pull it out and set it next to the bath.

Perfect height.

The bathroom has started to steam up, and my shirt is sticking to my skin.

I hear the sound of Gabe's crutches on the wooden floor of his bedroom.

I shut off the taps.

"It's ready," I tell him.

"Thanks," he says, coming into the bathroom.

"So . . ." I twist my hands in front of me. "Will you be okay getting in . . . or do you need my help?"

"I'll be fine."

"Okay. Right then. Just holler if you need anything."

I back out of the bathroom and close the door behind me.

I hear the swoosh of his clothes being removed, and I try not to think about Gabe getting naked behind the door.

He's naked in there.

Lord help me.

Squeezing my eyes shut, I force all thoughts of naked Gabe away. Then, I take myself out of there and into the kitchen where I give myself a much-needed infusion of coffee.

Chapter Seven

"**S**PEEDY!"

I hear the urgent call of my name, so I come running from the kitchen.

"You okay?" I call through the bathroom door. I don't want to just go barging in there.

"Where have you been? I've been calling you for ages."

"Ages? How long?"

"Well, I yelled your name, like, three times."

"Three times is hardly ages, Gabe. And I was in the kitchen. What's up?"

"Will you come in? Talking through the door is annoying."

I push open the door, and there he is, in the tub, in all his naked glory. Leg hanging out of the bath. Cigarette in hand. Bubbles covering the important part. Olive skin as far as the eye can see. A smattering of dark hair on his ripped chest.

Dear God.

He looks sexy as hell.

My heart starts thumping, my pulse skyrocketing through the roof. My girl parts shimmy with pure joy.

Gulp.

I look away, lifting my eyes to stare at the wall, because, if I keep looking at him, I might do something crazy, like climb in the tub with him.

"I can't believe you're smoking in the tub." My mouth has gone dry. I run my tongue around it.

"What else am I supposed to do in here?"

"I don't know." I cross my arms over my chest. "Relax."

"I am relaxing—with a cigarette."

My eyes come down to the ashtray perched on the edge of the bath. "It already has two cigarette butts in it."

"Or three. I was bored, and you took ages to come."

"Good Lord." I lift my eyes skyward. "So, what can I do for you, Smoky?"

"I need help getting out of the bath. Seems getting in was easy—well, not easy, but easier. Getting out, not so easy."

My eyes flash down to him. "But . . . you're *naked*."

"Naked is how people usually are when in the bath, Speedy."

"B-but I can't help you get out. I mean, you're naked. I'll see you naked."

"You've seen me naked before."

"I have not," I gasp.

"You've watched my movies. You've seen me naked before. I'm not shy, Speedy."

"No shit."

"Are you a ... prude?" His voice is teasing, but there's a definite challenge to his tone.

"No, I am not a prude!"

"Then, what's the problem?"

"Well ... I mean, sure, I've seen you naked in your movies, but this is real life, and your thing ..." I nod my head in the direction of his southern region.

His eyes go down. "My cock?"

"Yeah." I swallow roughly.

"Say it."

"What?"

"Cock, Speedy. Say it."

I frown at him, my hands unfurling from my chest and finding my hips. "Cock. Cock. Cock. Cock! Better?"

"Much." He grins, eyes flashing at me. "So, you're afraid of seeing my cock. It's not gonna bite you. Not unless you ask nicely."

"Ugh. God, you're such a pig."

He snorts. "And you're so easy. Look, if you're that worried about seeing my massive cock, then hold up a towel. I just need a hand with getting out and making sure I don't get my boot wet, is all."

"Fine," I huff. I grab a towel from the rack.

The thing is, I'm not afraid of seeing his cock. I'm more afraid of what my reaction will be if I do see it.

I walk over to the bath. He stubs his cigarette out in the ashtray.

I pick it up to move it out of the way and put it on the vanity unit.

"So, how are we going to do this?"

"Honestly, I'm not sure."

"Okay, so how about I move the stool, you sit up, and I help you stand in the bath as you keep your boot out? Then, I'll quickly wrap the towel around you to stop the water from running down your body and soaking the boot."

"Sounds like a plan."

I toss the towel over my shoulder. Putting my hand under his leg, I move the stool away.

"Okay?" I ask him.

"Yeah."

"Right, well, sit up, and we'll get you out of here."

He sits forward. I keep a hand on his leg, and I realize the logistics don't seem as straightforward as I thought. I thought I'd be able to pull him up with my hand, but I don't think it'll work.

He's going to have to put his arm around me.

Dear God.

I squeeze my eyes shut.

"You okay?" he asks me.

"Yeah." I open my eyes. "You're gonna have to put your arm around me, so I can get you up."

A smile glimmers in his eyes. "I'll get you wet."

I bite the inside of my cheek. "It's fine."

"Okay. If you say so."

Taking the towel off my shoulder, I tuck it between my thighs, and I lean closer to him. He puts his arm around me.

Sweet Jesus.

He smells so good, and he's all wet and soapy and hot as hell.

This is torture. I swear, I'm in hell.

The best kind of hell.

"Can you push yourself up, using your hands on the edge of the tub?"

"Sure can." His words whisper over my neck, setting off goose bumps everywhere.

"Okay. Count of three. One . . . two . . . three . . ."

As I lift myself, Gabe pushes himself up, lowering his leg to the floor. His wet side presses against me. And I know I'm dangerously close to his cock.

It takes everything in me not to look.

Look at the wall. Not the cock. I repeat, not the cock.

I need to cover him. I grab the towel from between my legs, keeping my eyes high, and I shake it out. Holding it up, I press it to his chest.

"Dry off," I tell him.

"You mean, you're not going to do it for me?"

I give him a less than amused look. "Funny."

He starts drying his chest and stomach to stop the water from running down to his boot. I avert my eyes.

My shirt is soaked. I'll have to change it. Maybe he has a T-shirt I can borrow.

"You dry?"

"Yep."

"Okay, let's get you out of the tub."

I look at him, and he's got the towel wrapped around his waist.

I grab his crutches from beside the tub and hand them to him. He sets the crutches on the floor and tucks them under his arm. I can see the strain it puts on him as he gets his good leg out of the tub and onto the floor, putting his weight on it.

"Okay?" I ask.

"Yeah."

"Let's get you dressed then."

We head into his bedroom, and with his directions, I get him some boxer shorts and a T-shirt to wear.

I help get the boxer shorts on over his boot, up to his knee, and then I let him do the rest himself, turning my back to give him privacy.

"Do you have a T-shirt I could borrow? My shirt's a little wet. I'll bring it back tomorrow."

"Knock yourself out. Top drawer of the dresser."

I walk over to it and grab the first T-shirt I lay my hand on. It's black, and the material is really soft.

"I'll just change in the bathroom. You finished with your towel?"

"Yep."

I take the wet towel in the bathroom with me and close the door. After I hang it up, I remove my wet shirt and pull Gabe's T-shirt over my head.

It almost hits my knees, and it smells of him. I'll just ignore that fact.

I tuck the T-shirt into my skirt and go back into the bedroom, taking my wet shirt with me.

Gabe's sitting up against his headboard. His hair is still damp from the bath. The TV that's mounted on the wall is on with what sounds like sports on it.

His eyes go to me. Something flares in them.

"This shirt okay to borrow?" I check.

He nods slowly, eyes still on me.

Okay.

"You hungry?" I ask him.

"Yeah."

"I'll get you some of the soup I made and bring it through."

"Can you grab me a beer as well?"

"Sure."

I go to the kitchen, dump my shirt in my bag, and reheat the soup. I pour some into a bowl and grab some bread, a spoon, and a beer. I put it all on a tray and carry it through to him.

"Dinner is served." I rest the tray on his lap and take a seat on the edge of the bed.

"You're not eating?" he asks.

"I'll get something at home. Will you be okay if I head off soon?"

For a brief moment, I actually think he looks disappointed, but if it was there, it's gone now.

"Sure I will. I'm a grown-ass man, Speedy. I can take care of myself."

"Just can't get out of the tub on your own," I tease.

He tears off some bread, dips it into the soup, and puts it in his mouth.

I watch as he chews.

"This is good," he says, a moan of appreciation in his voice.

And it's embarrassing how much I light up at the compliment.

"It's just soup," I say, downplaying it.

"It's good. You made this?"

"Yep."

"I've never had homemade soup before."

"Your mom not a cook?" I ask.

"No." His abrupt answer tells me not to ask anything more.

"Both my parents are chefs. They have a restaurant. Jayce and I were cooking before we were walking. The soup is just a quick, basic meal. I'll rustle you up something a little fancier tomorrow."

"I look forward to it." He meets my eyes for a brief moment before he goes back to eating.

"Right. Well, if you're okay, then I'm gonna go. I need to pick up Sunny."

"Sunny?" His brows draw together.

"My car."

The frown quickly turns into a smile. "You named the golf cart Sunny?"

"Don't start," I warn him, pointing my finger.

He grins. "As if I would ever give you grief about naming your golf-cart car Sunny. I mean, that's totally normal to name your car Sunny."

"You're a big jerk. And I'm going." I get to my feet.

"Aw, don't be like that, Speedy." He laughs. "Take my car. It's getting late. Pick Sunny up tomorrow." He grins.

"I don't want to leave her there overnight."

"I'm pretty sure she won't get stolen."

"I just need my car tonight. Thanks for the offer though. I'll just grab a cab, get my car, and then go home."

"Get Harry to call you a cab when you get downstairs."

"I'll order an Uber. It'll be quicker. You got your cell phone?"

"Why?"

"So I can put my number in it in case you need me."

He hands me his cell, and I put my digits in his Contacts.

I hand it back to him. "Call me if you, I don't know, fall down or something. Or just need me for anything.

And I'll come right away. Just try not to move too much. Rest as much as possible." I pick up his crutches from the floor and stand them by the bed for easy access for him. "And just leave the tray on your nightstand. I'll clear it away in the morning. I'll be back first thing."

"Speedy, I plan on finishing my soup, drinking my beer, and then watching sports on TV until I fall asleep."

"Okay, good." I turn and head for the door.

"Ava?"

This is only the second time he's said my name today. And my body has the exact same reaction as it did the first time.

I turn back to him. "Yeah?"

His eyes are warm and serious on me, and my insides heat.

"Thanks for all your help today."

"Gabe, you really don't have to thank me. You wouldn't be in this situation if it wasn't for me. This is the least I can do."

"Well, either way, I just want you to know I appreciate it."

"And I appreciate you not calling the cops on me."

I smile, and he laughs.

Then, his face goes serious. "Can I ask . . . why did you get fired?"

I wrap my arms around my chest. "Cutbacks."

"You worked for the studio?"

I tilt my head in question.

"I was in the building for a meeting and saw you coming out."

"Oh, right. Yeah, I worked in wardrobe."

"That's how you know Charly?"

"Yeah, we worked together in New York first. That's where I'm originally from. Then, I moved here to be with Jeremy."

"He's your ex?"

I nod. "I got a job with the studio as a wardrobe assistant but got promoted to wardrobe mistress. I was working on Vaughn's film, and I hired Charly to come work with me."

"So, because of you, they met."

"I guess." I shrug. "Anyway, I should go." I thumb over my shoulder.

"Sure. See you tomorrow. And don't worry about the job front. Someone will hire you in no time."

"Yeah." I smile, but it feels weak. "Okay, see you in the morning."

I order an Uber before I leave Gabe's apartment. I wait only a few minutes before it turns up.

The Uber drops me back at my car.

I get in, start the engine, and drive toward my apartment, stopping at the deli on the way. I grab a sandwich and a bottle of wine from the liquor store next door.

I let myself in my apartment, and Gucci is at the door, waiting for me.

"Hey, baby! Sorry Mama was out for so long. It's been a butthole of a day. You hungry?" I pick her up and hug her.

Gucci is a pygmy goat. She's four months old, and I just adore her. She's the cutest thing ever. Little gray and white thing with a black patch on her head. Some might think that a goat is an odd pet to have, but she's awesome. So full of life and happiness. And she's just so spunky and really loving.

I walk into my bare apartment. I avoid looking at the empty space and go straight into the kitchen to sort her food out.

I put some of her favorite alfalfa hay in her bowl along with some chopped up vegetables. And I fill her water bowl up.

Then, I sit at the breakfast bar while she eats, and I have my sandwich. I open up the wine and drink straight from the bottle.

I don't have any glasses. All of my stuff has either been sold or is in storage. All I have here are my clothes, shoes, toiletries, a pillow, and a sleeping bag, which has been my bed for the last four days, as I sold my bed and my sofa.

It's not so bad, sleeping on the floor. Could be worse. I could be sleeping in my car.

But that's what Gucci and I will probably be doing tomorrow if I don't get something sorted fast.

I can feel tears pushing at the corners of my eyes.

Don't cry. It'll be fine. You'll figure something out. And, if not, you can just go back home to New York.

I take a big swig of wine.

Gucci pushes against my leg with her head.

"You need some air, baby? Come on, let's get you outside."

I pick her up, and taking the wine bottle with me, I leave my apartment and head up to the rooftop garden.

I'm really going to miss this place.

I put Gucci down, and she has a wander around, sniffing the plants that Mr. Goodman keeps up here.

I sit down on the bench and drink some more wine.

When the bottle's half-empty and I'm feeling sleepy, I get Gucci and wobble back down to my apartment.

I lock up and get ready for bed.

Then, I shut off the light and climb into my sleeping bag. I set the alarm on my cell for seven a.m. and put it on the floor next to me.

Gucci comes over and lies beside me, like she does every night, so I open up my sleeping bag and let her inside.

She snuggles into me.

"It's gonna be all right, Gucci. I'll find us somewhere to live. I'll get a new job, and we'll be just fine. I promise. Things can only get better, right?"

The silence echoes around me.

The tear that leaves my eye soaks into the pillow.

I hug Gucci closer, shut my eyes, and wish for a better tomorrow.

Chapter Eight

Gabe

"**M**ORNING, SUNSHINE."

That voice. So soft and sweet and sexy.

I went to bed alone last night. I was sober, which is a rarity for me, so I definitely know I was alone.

"I made you some breakfast."

Speedy.

She came back.

What? You thought she wouldn't? She isn't you, asshole.

"What time is it?" I scrub my hands over my eyes. When I move them away, the first thing I see is her face.

Her hair is down and tousled. And she's wearing this fitted gray dress that basically looks like an oversize tank top.

Her tits look spectacular in it.

Fuck, she's stunning.

Now, that is a fantastic sight to wake up to.

"It's nine," she answers. She puts the tray of food in

her hands on the bed beside me and sits down. "How are you feeling?"

"Okay." I push myself to sit up, resting my back against the headboard. My foot starts to throb. Ignoring the pain, I ask, "You just get here?"

"I got here at eight. Cleared away your dishes from last night and washed them. Then, I made you breakfast. Blueberry pancakes okay?"

I glance down at the tray with freshly brewed coffee and a plate filled with pancakes and maple syrup. I pick up the fork, cut off a piece of a pancake, and put it in my mouth.

"Fuck me," I moan. These are amazing. The taste of blueberry is bursting on my tongue. "You made these?"

She nods.

"So good." I chew, swallow, and take another bite. "Anyone ever tell you that you're a fucking awesome cook?"

Her cheeks flush, and she chews on her lower lip. "Not in a while."

"Well, you are. Can I keep you?"

She laughs, but I'm only half-kidding.

"I'll leave you to eat." She gets up from the bed, heading for the door.

I want to ask her to stay while I eat, but it seems weird to do so, so I say nothing and let her go.

She stops in the doorway. "Oh, I used your washing machine. I washed your T-shirt that I borrowed yesterday. It's drying at the moment. My washing machine is, um ... broken. But I didn't want to return it dirty. I hope that's okay."

You could have kept it if you wore it every day.

There's just something about seeing a woman in your clothes, and when I saw her wearing my T-shirt yesterday, my dick was so hard, it could have cut glass. If I didn't have this stupid fucking boot on my leg, then I would have gone over to her and taken her like I wanted to. I'd have fucked her with my tongue and then my cock.

I clear my throat at the memory. "You didn't have to wash it."

"I like to return things I've borrowed as I found them." She shrugs.

"Baaahhh!"

I pause mid bite. "What was that?"

"What?"

"That noise."

"Baaahhh!"

"There it is again." I sit forward, listening. "It sounds like a . . . sheep. You hear it?"

"It must be the TV in the living room. I was watching a nature program. Enjoy your breakfast." She quickly closes my bedroom door, disappearing off.

I stare at the door. *That was weird.*

I shrug it off and get on with eating my breakfast. When I'm done, I get up, using my crutches, and take a piss. Pissing and balancing on crutches is not easy, as I've discovered.

Neither is trying to brush your teeth. Who knew having a broken foot would be such a pain in the ass?

I look at the shower with longing. I'm dying to get in it, but it just seems like too much hassle right now. I'll have to get another bath soon. Have Speedy get me out again.

God, that was so much fun yesterday, watching her get all flustered. Not so much fun when her shirt got all wet. I could see her lacy bra through it, and my dick started getting hard.

I go back into my bedroom and grab a fresh pair of boxer shorts, a tank, and a pair of athletic shorts.

Getting dressed is a pain as well.

I've just gotten the athletic shorts on when my cell rings. I reach over and grab it off my nightstand.

Tate.

"Hey, asshole," I say.

"Is that any way to greet your baby brother?" He chuckles.

"It's the only way to greet you."

"How are you doing?"

"Okay."

"Has Ava been there, taking care of you?"

"Yeah. She's here now."

"She stayed over?"

"No, assface. She went home last night and came back early this morning."

"Maybe you should ask her to stay over. Make things easier."

I laugh. Having Speedy stay overnight in my house would make this far from easy. I know it would definitely make something very, very hard. Not that my dick isn't often hard around her as it is.

"No, Tate, I'm not asking her to stay over. She's doing enough for me as it is."

"You could pay her, like a live-in, while you get better."

"I've got a broken foot, not a broken back."

But he's right; I should pay her. It's not right, having her give up her time for me when she should be using that time to find herself a new job.

I've just got to find a way to offer her money for caring for me without insulting her. Because I know for a fact that she'll be insulted when I offer.

"Well, okay. I'm on shift all day till ten."

"You work too many hours."

"I'm a doctor. And a resident at that. Too many hours are part of the job description."

"Just don't kill yourself when you don't need to."

I'm always offering him money to set up his own private practice, but he won't take it.

"I'm fine, Gabe. Look, I'll swing by in the morning before work. I'm not on until lunchtime tomorrow. I'll bring breakfast."

"Sounds good."

"See you then."

I hang up and push my cell into the pocket of my shorts. Grabbing my crutches, I get up and go off to find Speedy.

As soon as I wrangle open my bedroom door, I hear that sound again.

"Baaahhh! Baaahhh!"

I head in the direction of the sound. It's coming from the kitchen.

I walk in the kitchen, and it's empty, but I see the utility room door is open. I can hear the quiet whispers of Speedy's voice.

"Gucci, you have to be quiet."

Gucci? Who the fuck is Gucci?

"I know, baby girl. I'm sorry. I don't want you stuck

in here all day, but I don't have any other choice. I'll figure something out though; don't worry."

I make my way through the kitchen as deftly as I can on crutches. I can see Speedy. She's crouched down, her back to me, still talking away.

It doesn't look like she's on the phone.

"*Baaahhh!*"

"Gucci, please. He'll hear you."

"Is there a fucking sheep in my apartment?"

She nearly jumps out of her skin. Grabbing ahold of whatever is making that noise, she holds it to her chest, keeping her back to me.

"Speedy?"

"*Baaahhh! Baaahhh!*"

"Ava, turn the fuck around and show me what's in your arms."

She turns slowly, a look of guilt and apprehension on her face.

My eyes nearly bug out of my head. "Is that a fucking . . . *goat*?"

"A pygmy goat."

"Why is there a fucking pygmy goat in my apartment?"

"Well, because she's mine. I didn't have anywhere to keep her today, and I needed to come back here to help you. And I know I shouldn't have brought her here, but I didn't have any other choice."

"Why do you have a goat?"

"She's called Gucci."

"Okay." I scratch my head. "I'll rephrase. Why the fuck do you have a goat called Gucci?"

"Because I love Gucci clothes, and it fits her perfectly, don't you think?"

"I don't have a fucking clue!"

She frowns at me. "Don't yell. You'll scare her."

"Oh, I'm sorry. Wouldn't want to scare the goat, now would we?"

"*Baaahhh!*"

Speedy covers the goat's ears. "Stop it, Gabe. She doesn't like loud noises."

"Well, it doesn't have any problem making them."

"She's a she, not an it. And she's called Gucci."

"You're certifiable."

"You're an asshole."

"I thought we'd already established that."

"*Baaahhh! Baaahhh!*"

"Can't you keep that thing quiet?" I frown.

She frowns back at me. "She's not a thing, and you'll hurt her feelings, saying that."

"God forbid I hurt the goat's feelings."

She gives me a dirty look and walks over to her bag. She pulls out a bag of chopped up apples and proceeds to start feeding the goat.

I pull out one of the breakfast stools and rest my ass on it. "Where the hell did you get her from anyway?"

"A farm in Glendale."

"And they just let you take her, knowing you lived in an apartment building?"

"Well, honestly, the guy didn't seem that interested in where I lived. He was more interested in the money I was going to pay for her."

"Asshole."

"What?" she squeaks.

The goat jumps.

"Sorry, Gucci." She puts the goat on the floor and continues intermittently handing apple slices to it.

"I meant, the guy who sold you the goat. Not you. *Naive* is more the word I'd use for you."

"Hey! I am not naive!"

"Look, an apartment is hardly the place for a goat. It needs to be on a fucking farm, or it needs a garden at the very least. They're outdoor animals. Not home-kept pets."

"She's not just a pet! She's my family! And the only family I have around me at the moment! And I didn't know when I got her that she needed a garden! I'm doing my best, okay? I can't do any fucking more than that!"

That's the first time I've heard her say *fucking*. Sounds kind of hot, coming from her sweet mouth. And it is until she does the thing I hate most.

She bursts into tears.

Ah, fuck.

"Jesus. Speedy, I didn't mean to make you cry."

"You didn't." She sniffles.

"Then, why are you crying?"

"Things have just been a bit rough recently. I'm sorry I got upset." She dries her face with her hands. "I'll go figure something out with Gucci, and then I'll come back to take care of you. I just don't know what I'm gonna do . . ."

"Where did she spend yesterday?"

"She was at my apartment."

"So, why isn't she there today?"

She shifts uneasily on her feet.

"Speedy?"

"I don't have an apartment anymore, okay?" Her eyes fill with tears again.

An unfamiliar ache appears in my chest. "What do you mean, you don't have an apartment anymore?"

"I was evicted. It was my last night there. As of this morning, I'm officially homeless. I've been trying to get a new apartment for Gucci and me, but there's nowhere that allows pets."

Fuck. She's lost her job and her apartment.

And I know very well how hard it is to be stuck with nowhere to go.

"Why did you lose your apartment?"

"Well, after Jeremy left, I was feeling lonely and a bit sad. And, one night, I was on YouTube, watching cute animal videos to cheer me up, and I came across this one of pygmy goats. And they were so adorable, and I just felt really happy, watching them.

"So, I Googled pygmy goats for sale, and a website came up. A farm in Glendale. I emailed them to see if they had any, and the guy responded back, saying he had one left. So, I said I'd drive down in the morning to have a look. And, when I saw her, I just fell in love. She was so sweet and friendly. So, I paid the guy and brought her home with me.

"Only I didn't know I wasn't allowed to have a pet in the apartment. And she was being a bit noisy, as she was nervous, I think, from being in a strange place at first. And, when I was at work, she apparently made a lot of noise because some of my neighbors complained to my landlord. He said I either got rid of her or I was out. And, of course, I couldn't get rid of her. So, he gave me a month's notice, and I haven't been able to find another place that allows pets.

"And then I lost my job yesterday, and I hit you with

my car and said I'd take care of you. So, I didn't get a chance to sort anything. But I will."

"You made yourself homeless for a goat."

She frowns. "She's not just a goat, Gabriel. I told you, she's my family."

I don't know if I should admire her loyalty or have her committed for making herself homeless for a goat.

"Where are you planning on sleeping tonight?"

She shifts on her feet, clearly uncomfortable at my question. "Well, my friend Logan said I could crash on his couch until I got myself sorted, but he's not allowed to have pets at his place either, and I don't want to get him into any trouble with his landlord."

"You didn't answer my question, Speedy. Where are you staying tonight?"

She bites her lip, nervously twisting her hands in front of her. "Well, if I can't get a hotel room, I guess we'll be sleeping in my car."

"Where's all your stuff?"

"Why?"

"Answer the damn question."

"Most of it is in storage, and my clothes, shoes, and toiletries along with Gucci's things are in my car."

The goat has things. Of course it does.

"Go get your stuff from your car."

"Why?"

"Because you're staying here until you get things figured out. Oh, and I'm paying you to take care of me until my foot is healed. So, consider yourself hired."

"Gabe . . . you don't have to do that."

"I might be an asshole, but I won't see you homeless.

And I would've been paying for a Big Bertha, so what's the difference? You can take the guest room."

"And what about Gucci? I appreciate the offer, Gabe—really, I do—but we're a package deal."

"The goat can sleep in the utility room. If she wrecks anything, it comes out of your wages."

"She won't wreck anything, I swear. She's a good girl. Aren't you, Gucci?"

The fucking goat looks up at her with adoring eyes.

"Are you sure your building will be okay with it? I don't want to get you in trouble."

"I own this apartment, so I can do what I fucking want in it. And pets are allowed. Well, dogs and cats. Not so sure about goats. But, if they have a problem with it, they can fuck off."

"Thank you so much, Gabe." She rushes over and flings her arms around my neck, nearly knocking me off the stool.

But, man, does she feel so sweet in my arms with her tits pressed up against my chest, the scent of her perfume in my nose.

My cock starts to swell with want.

Well, he can want as much as he likes, but Speedy is now officially off my radar. I don't shit where I eat.

Never fuck anyone who works for me or with me.

I know people think I screw every actress I work with, but it's just not true. And, trust me, it's hard not to screw them at the time. Of course, once I'm done working with them, all bets are off. But I have that rule for a reason. I was once told never to mix business with pleasure; it's too messy. It's the best piece of advice I've ever been given.

Because I don't do messy.

No matter how gorgeous or how much I want inside that someone, I never break my rule.

I feel something nudge my leg. And then again.

I lean back from Speedy and look down. The goat is head-butting my good leg.

This little fucker has some spunk.

I start to laugh.

Speedy steps back, giving me a puzzled look.

"I don't think your goat likes me."

I point down, and Speedy's eyes follow my finger.

Her mouth pops open into an O.

"Gucci! No! Stop that!" She bends down and picks the goat up. "I'm so sorry, Gabe. She's never done anything like that before. Did she hurt you?"

"No." I chuckle.

"She had her horn removed as a baby. It's not as barbaric as it sounds. It's called disbudded. It's not cruel. Did you know that goats with horns can actually kill each other when they fight? And, if kept as pets, like Gucci is, she could hurt me without meaning to."

"Fascinating."

I'm staring at her. Her eyes are red and glazed, her lips puffy, from crying before.

The urge to kiss her is maddening.

I need a subject change and fast. "Ground rules for the goat." I jab a finger in its direction. "No pissing or shitting in the apartment."

"Oh, she won't. She's really good."

"If she needs to go, take her out on the terrace and clean up after, or there's the building's communal garden downstairs."

"Okay. Thank you again, Gabe. We both really

appreciate what you're doing for us. And we won't be any bother. You won't even know we're here, I promise."

I highly doubt that.

Knowing that Speedy's here and that she'll be sleeping a wall away from me is going to make this not-fucking-her thing so much harder.

"I need a drink," I mutter. I start moving away from her, heading for the drinks cabinet.

She's instantly at my side, the damn goat still in her arms. "I'll get it for you. You go sit down in the living room. What do you want?"

I hate that these crutches slow me down so much. It makes escaping near-on impossible.

"Whiskey. Neat."

She stops and puts the goat down on the floor. "Don't you think it's a little early to be drinking?"

I keep moving. "It's five o'clock somewhere."

"But you're here, and it's ten a.m."

I stop and sigh. "I like a drink every now and then, Speedy. And, right now, I'm in pain, and I could do with taking the edge off it. If you've got a problem with it—"

"I haven't," she cuts me off.

I don't even know what I was going to say at the end of that sentence. It's not like I'd kick her out for having an issue with the fact that I want a drink.

"I'm sorry. I wasn't trying to be a bitch. You're right; it's your business. I'll grab that drink for you."

She's backtracking. She's not being herself. Speedy of half an hour ago would have called me a jerk and told me to stick it. But she's in a different position now. She feels vulnerable, and she can't be herself.

I don't like it.

"Speedy." I catch her wrist as she moves past me. "I'm a grouchy asshole most of the time, and apparently, I'm worse when I've got a few broken bones. You don't have to worry that I'll kick you out for voicing your opinion. Oddly, that's one of the things I like about you—when you bitch back at me even if it does drive me nuts ninety-nine percent of the time. So, just don't stop being you because I'm being an asshole. Tell me to shut the fuck up. Okay?"

A smile edges her lips. "You *like* me," she says in a singsong voice.

"Oh, for fuck's sake."

"Gabriel Evans likes me!" she sings, throwing her arms in the air.

And the damn goat starts jumping around her feet.

"Did you hear that, Gucci? He likes *me*!"

"You're so fucking odd," I say. But I'm smiling.

She stops singing and grins. "And you're an asshole."

I laugh, shaking my head, and I start moving toward the living room.

"Gabe?"

"Yeah?"

"I like you, too."

That makes me pause, and something weird happens in my chest, spreading all throughout my body. A tingling sensation.

Maybe I'm having a heart attack. The drinks and smokes have finally caught up to me.

"Now, go sit your grumpy ass down, and I'll bring you that drink."

She walks past me, but it takes me a long moment before I start moving again.

Chapter Nine

Gabe

SPEEDY BROUGHT HER STUFF up from her car, and it required two trips. God knows how she got so much stuff in that miniature car of hers. The alpha male in me was frustrated at not being able to bring her stuff up for her. Then, she disappeared off to the store. You know, 'cause, apparently, we needed more food even though the last trip she'd made could have fed an entire African village, but she didn't have the ingredients she needed for tonight's dinner.

That meant, I was left alone with the goat.

I shut it in the utility room, but all it did was make noise, so I let it out.

I swear to God, the moment I opened the utility room door, she gave me a dirty look, head-butted my good leg, and then proceeded to run around the apartment like a lunatic, looking for Speedy.

It was actually pretty funny. That goat is as crazy as Speedy is.

When the goat realized that she wasn't here, she came down into the living room where I was sitting, watching hockey on TV and enjoying a whiskey and a smoke—without any grief from Speedy—and she plopped herself down onto the rug. She hasn't moved since.

I look over at the goat, who seems to be fast asleep.

She's cute, I guess, for a goat.

But I mean, who the fuck gets a goat for a pet? And calls it Gucci?

Speedy—that's who.

"Honey, I'm home!" Her tinkling voice and laughter ring through the apartment.

It's like I just magicked her back by thinking of her.

I'm surprised at how my body reacts to knowing she's back. My cock twitches, my pulse picks up, and I start to feel warmer.

Gucci the goat hops up from her spot on the rug and starts jumping around. Then, she bolts across the room. I put my cigarette out in the ashtray and finish off my drink.

"Hey, baby girl!" she coos. "You miss Mama? I missed you, too."

The click of her heels on the floor has me turning my head.

I suck in a breath.

Fuck, she's stunning.

Nothing's changed. She's still wearing the same dress as she went out in, but her hair looks windblown, and her cheeks are flushed, her eyes bright. Just how she'd look if I got my hands on her and my cock inside her.

"You were at the store for, like, thirty minutes. How the hell did you miss your goat in that time?"

"I didn't miss you, if that makes it any better." She grins. Then, she wafts her hand in front of her nose. "God, it stinks in here."

She puts the bag of groceries down on the coffee table, and she bends, so I get a spectacular view right down the front of her dress.

Fuck, her tits are gorgeous. I bet her nipples are pink and perky.

My mouth starts to water.

"You really should open a window when you smoke." She walks over to the window where she reaches up and opens it.

And, now, I'm staring at her ass, and my cock is starting to get a chub on.

"And, not to be a pain, but I'd really appreciate it if you didn't smoke around Gucci."

She turns around, catching me staring, so I raise a brow.

"You're asking me not to smoke around the goat?"

"I'm asking you not to give my baby girl lung cancer."

"She's a goat. And can goats even get lung cancer?"

"She breathes, doesn't she? Therefore, she has lungs." She folds her arms over her tits, which pushes them up.

And, of course, my eyes go to them.

How can I not look at them? They're magnificent.

And then my mind starts to imagine just what I'd do with those luscious tits of hers.

I'd start at the base of her neck. I'd lick my way down to them, and then I'd take one in my hand and the other in my mouth. I'd tease her nipple, licking and biting it—"Seriously, Gabe! Will you stop staring at my boobs?"

I blink myself free of their hypnotizing hold. "I'm sorry." A laugh bursts from me. "I don't mean to stare."

"Sure you don't. God, you're such a pig! Do you always stare at women's breasts like you do mine? Because you should really consider not doing it. It's really insulting."

"I'm not trying to insult you. Actually, it's a compliment in an ass-backward kind of way. And, no, I don't always stare at women's tits. I'm not a total asshole. I'm just a tit man, and, Speedy ... you have *the* best rack I've ever seen in my life. Seriously."

"Thanks. I think."

She doesn't look as angry as she did a moment ago, so I think I've managed to smooth things over. But she's right. I really need to stop staring at her tits. If not for my own sanity, then for the sake of my cock because he keeps getting all excited, thinking he's gonna get some action, only to be left disappointed when nothing happens.

Speedy picks up the grocery bag from the coffee table, and I keep my eyes averted from her tits.

"Why'd you let Gucci out of the utility room anyway?" she asks.

"She was making noise, so I let her out, and she quieted down."

"Oh. Sorry. It's probably just because it's a new place, and she's not used to it."

"It's not a problem."

"Okay. Well, I'll just put these groceries in the kitchen, and then I'll take her down to the garden for some fresh air. I'll start dinner when I get back up."

"I'll come with you. I could do with some air." I grab my smokes and put them in my pocket, and then using my crutches, I get up.

"Sure. Great. I'll just be a sec."

She disappears into the kitchen and reappears a few minutes later with a pink diamanté harness and lead in her hand along with what looks to be a pink leopard-print dog coat.

For fuck's sake. That poor goat.

"Are you putting that on the goat?"

"Of course I am." She crouches down and starts putting the collar onto Gucci. "It's a new area for her; she's not familiar with it. And I don't feel comfortable letting her roam free."

"I was talking about the hideous dog coat."

Speedy frowns up at me. "It's a goat coat. I bought it especially for her, and she loves it."

"She tell you that?"

She gives me a look. "She did, as a matter of fact."

"Okay, Dr. Dolittle. But you do realize that we live in LA where it's pretty much hot as fuck all the time."

"It's actually a little chilly out today. I don't want her to catch a cold." She gets to her feet.

"Speedy, the only thing that goat is going to catch is a ribbing from its goat friends."

"God, you're annoying." She shakes her head, irritated, and then spins on her heel.

"Hey, that's my line!" I call to her.

She puts her hand behind her back and flips me off.

I laugh.

I fucking love winding her up. It's become my new favorite pastime.

Smiling to myself, I follow them to the elevator, get inside, and press the button for the ground floor.

Chapter Ten

Ava

I'M FEELING A LITTLE nervous, cooking for Gabe. I
know I've cooked for him already, but that was just
a straightforward soup and some pancakes.

I want to make this nice because I want to thank him
for what he's doing for me and Gucci—hiring me to
take care of him and letting us stay here.

He doesn't have to do that.

Not that I really do that much, apart from getting
him drinks when he wants them and feeding him. Oh,
and helping him out of the bath, which I had to do
again before I started dinner.

And, dear God, it's hard to stop myself from taking
a peek at his cock to see how big it actually is.

I can't exactly give him shit for staring at my boobs and
then go and look at his cock without his permission.

And is it bad of me that I actually kind of like it
when he stares at the girls?

I know it's not very feminist of me, but I like the fact

that he thinks I have great breasts. Not that I'd ever admit that to him.

It's just, he's Gabriel Evans, hottest guy in the world, lusted after by millions, who's probably seen lots of girls' boobs—famous models' and actresses' boobs—and he thinks that I, and I quote, "have the best rack" he's ever seen in his life.

Hell yeah!

But, anyway, I don't really feel like I'm earning my money, and it doesn't sit well with me, so I'm going to ask him if there are more jobs that I can do around the house.

Dinner's almost ready, so I call out from the kitchen to Gabe, "Where do you want to eat dinner? At the table or in the living room?"

"Living room's fine," he calls back. "You need me to do anything?"

"No, I got it."

I serve up the jerk-seasoned pulled pork that I just made into a dish. Then, I turn the heat off the stove and dish out the spicy-jerk prawns with mango into another waiting bowl. I get a tray from the cupboard and put the pulled pork, jerk prawns, tortillas, banana salsa, and coconut dressing that I made earlier on it. I grab the pre-packaged salad from the fridge and empty it into another dish. I put it on the tray, which is looking pretty full.

I'll have to come back for the plates.

I pick up the tray and carry it through to the living room. Gabe is on the sofa, foot up on the footstool, watching TV. Gucci is laid out on the rug, fast asleep, but then her head perks up at the smell of food.

I put the tray on the coffee table.

"I'll just grab the plates, and I'll be back. You want anything to drink?" I grab the two empty beer bottles off the coffee table.

"Do you want wine with dinner?" he asks.

"Sure."

"There are some bottles in the wine cooler. Take your pick."

"Okay." I go back in the kitchen and drop the beer bottles in the recycling bin.

I get another tray and put two plates on it along with some serving cutlery. We don't need any other utensils, as this is finger food. Then, I get two wine glasses and pick out a nice Riesling, which will nicely accompany the food. I remove the cork and then carry everything into the living room.

When I get there, Gabe is sitting on the rug near the coffee table, his leg stretched out on the floor.

"You okay sitting there?" I ask, putting the other tray down.

"Yeah, I'm fine. I thought it'd be easier to sit here, and then I can get to the food."

"I would have made you a plate," I tell him as I kneel on the rug across from him and next to Gucci.

She moves up and rests her head against my leg, so I give her head a scratch.

She *baaahhhs* softly.

And Gabe laughs.

"What?" I ask him.

"Just thinking of when I first heard that noise, and I thought she was a fucking sheep."

"Now, that would have been crazy, if I had a sheep as a pet." I laugh.

"Yeah, about as crazy as having a goat as one."

"Ass." I laugh again and then hand him a plate.

"This looks great. Not to be ignorant, but what is it?"

"That's jerk pulled pork." I point to it. "And that's spicy-jerk prawns with mango." I indicate the other dish. "There's coconut dressing and banana salsa to dress them with."

"You made all of this?"

"Yep."

I pour out two glasses of wine and put one in front of Gabe while he's busy filling up a tortilla with the jerk prawns.

I grab a tortilla and put some pork, salad, and banana salsa in it. Then, I wrap it up and take a bite.

Gabe takes a bite of the taco. His eyes close on a moan.

And my girlie bits come to life in response. My body lights up. And my nipples get embarrassingly hard.

Please don't show through my clothes.

His eyes open, and he takes another bite. The taco is almost gone; his bites are that big.

"Good?" I ask him.

"So fucking good," he groans around a mouthful. He chews and swallows it down. Then, he puts the last of the taco in his mouth. "Fuck, Speedy. My stomach thanks you." He grabs another tortilla and starts loading that up.

My cheeks heat at the compliment. "It's no biggie."

"Maybe not to you since you come from a family of chefs. But, to a guy who lives on takeout, this is amazing. What kind of restaurant do your parents have?" he asks me.

"New American cuisine. It's a bar and restaurant."

"Where is it?"

"It's in New York."

"I'll have to go next time I'm there. What's it called?"

"Simms. You know, our surname. Nothing original. Just let me know when you're going to be there, and I'll make sure you get the best table."

He takes a drink of his wine and then starts in on his taco. "Why didn't you become a chef?"

I put my food down on my plate. "Because I know firsthand how demanding the job is. I saw the hours my parents put into the restaurant—and still do—and, as much as I love cooking, I knew it wasn't for me. I wasn't sure what I wanted to do, to be honest, and after college, I just fell into working in wardrobe. I've always loved clothes, and it's a fun job, so it works for me."

"And your brother? You said he's a lawyer, right?"

"Yeah, a corporate lawyer. It takes him all over the world."

"Where is he at the moment?"

"Tokyo."

"Great city."

"You've been there?"

"A couple of times, promoting movies."

"Ah, right. I'd love to go. The farthest I've ever been is Hawaii on a family holiday when I was a kid." I pick my glass up and take a sip. "So, I know what your brother does. But what do your parents do?"

He doesn't answer, so I glance over at him.

He's frozen still.

"Gabe?"

His eyes flicker back to life. "My parents are gone." He picks his wine up and drains the glass.

"Gone?"

"Dead."

He picks the bottle up and refills his glass to the top.

"God. I'm sorry, Gabe. I didn't know."

"It's fine." He starts drinking again. His glass is half-empty. Then, it's gone.

I pick my own wine up and drink it. I feel terrible. I've made him uncomfortable, bringing up his parents. And we were having such a nice time.

He pours more wine into his glass, but the bottle empties, only partially filling it.

He starts to move.

"Where are you going?" I ask.

"To get another bottle."

"I'll go." I move Gucci's head off my leg, and I'm on my feet, heading for the kitchen.

I get another bottle of the same wine and open it up before taking it back through with me. I pour some more into his glass and then refill my own. I put the bottle on the table before sitting back down.

The tension in the air is awful. It's like a rain cloud on a perfectly nice evening.

"Gabe, I'm sorry. I—"

"Forget it. You didn't know."

I tuck my hair behind my ear. Then, I take a bite of my food. We eat in silence, the sound of the TV giving background noise, but the quiet between us is killing me.

"So . . . I was thinking—"

"Did it hurt?"

And he's back.

I almost laugh with relief. "Jackass."

"Wench."

I look over at him, and the corners of his lips are curled up.

"Anyway," I continue on, "I feel like I'm not really earning the money that you're paying me for taking care of you. All I do is feed you and help you out of the bath."

"And having you do that is worth every penny."

"Perv. And, now that I'm your employee, you do realize, with comments like that, I can sue you for sexual harassment." I lick some sauce off my finger. I don't miss the way his eyes follow the movement or the way they flare.

And I can't deny that I like having that effect on him.

"I was talking about you feeding me, Speedy. Not getting me out of the bath. But good to know where your mind is." He smirks.

My cheeks flame. I quickly pick up my wine and take a big drink to cover it.

"So, I was just wondering if there's anything else I can do around here to help."

"Like what?"

"I don't know. I could clean."

"I have cleaners who come in twice a week."

"What about laundry?"

"They do that as well."

"Oh."

"You could help me run lines if you want? Donna, my PA, usually does it with me, but she's on vacation at the moment."

"That sounds awesome." I light up at the thought. "I don't know how good I'll be. I mean, I did drama in high school and was in some plays, and I was okay, but I haven't done anything since then—"

"Speedy." He holds up a hand, cutting me off. "As long as you can read, you're good."

"I can read," I tell him. "So, when will we start?"

"How's tomorrow sound?"

"Perfect. What's the movie about?"

"It's an espionage thriller."

"Wow. Sounds really good."

"You got that from espionage thriller? Fuck, I must be a better actor than I thought."

"You're such a dick." I laugh, shaking my head.

He cups his hand around his ear. "I have a huge dick? Why, thank you, Speedy. I didn't know you knew. Have you been sneaking peeks when getting me out of the bath?"

"No. Because I can keep control of my eyes, unlike you," I say indignantly, pointing in the direction of the girls.

His eyes meet mine. "So, what you're saying is, if you couldn't keep control of your eyes, you'd sneak a look at my cock?"

"No!"

"Because you don't have to sneak a look. Just say the word, and I'll show you my monster cock anytime."

"You have a monster cock? That sounds terrifying!" I snort. It must be the wine, loosening me up a bit. I always get giddy from vino.

"Monstrous in size but absolutely fucking glorious to look at." He winks. "And a total beast in bed."

I burst out laughing. "You crack me up!"

Yep, I must be tipsy. Not that I've had that much to drink. God, I'm such a cheap date.

"Right back at ya, babe." He chuckles.

Babe.

He called me babe.

I really need to stop with the wine.

We finish dinner, and Gabe polishes off the second bottle of wine.

I'm just stacking the plates on the tray when Gabe starts to get up.

"You okay?" I ask him, as he seems to be struggling a bit.

"Yeah. I've just gone a bit stiff."

I go over to him and offer him my hand. He takes it, and I try to ignore the fireworks that go off in my stomach.

He puts his other hand on the sofa and pushes up as I pull.

He comes upright, but because he's on one leg—and also probably because of the amount of alcohol he's consumed and the fact that I'm not feeling the steadiest after the wine—he tips forward, onto me, grabbing hold of my waist. And I grab his biceps, using every ounce of strength to stop us both from going down.

"Shit, sorry," he says.

"It's fine." I smile up at him.

Then, I'm acutely aware of how close we actually are. My breasts are just brushing his chest.

And we're still touching.

My hands on his arms.

His hands on my waist.

I feel his fingers flex against me.

I suddenly feel hotter. My breaths start to come in shorter.

I see his eyes darken.

Then, they drop to my mouth.

I lick my lips.

He's going to kiss me. Holy shit, he's going to kiss me . . .

Oh.

No, he's not.

He lets me go and is grabbing his crutches, tucking them under his arms.

"Thanks for the save," he says. Then he's moving, hobbling out of the living room.

Okay then. Guess I read that moment wrong.

For the best really.

I sigh.

Gucci comes up alongside me and rubs her head against my leg.

I reach down and pick up the tray with the plates. "Come on, baby girl, let's go do the dishes."

Chapter Eleven

Gabe

I LIED TO SPEEDY BEFORE.

I told her that my parents were dead.

They're not.

It's a lie I've told with ease hundreds of times before. But, for some reason, it's bugging me that I lied to her.

And it shouldn't.

I mean, it's not exactly like I can tell her the truth. About anything from my past.

So then, why am I lying in bed an hour later, wide awake? And, trust me, I'm not the type of guy who lies in bed, analyzing shit. I'm the type of guy who falls asleep as soon as his head hits the fucking pillow.

And it doesn't help, knowing that she's down the hall, all sexy as shit, quite possibly naked—okay, that's wishful thinking on my part. But she's here, staying under my roof, and it isn't making things any easier on the sleeping front.

I sigh and throw my arm over my eyes.

And, now, all I can see in my mind is her. How she was looking at me earlier.

I wanted to kiss her so fucking bad in that moment. She was right there in my arms, and it would've been so easy to take her.

Now, I'm a strong man. I've resisted women before and not lost a minute's sleep over it. But, fuck, it took every ounce of strength to resist her.

And, worse, I know she wanted me to kiss her.

That's not me being arrogant. I just know women. And I know when they want me.

Speedy wanted me to kiss her, no doubt.

I could feel it in the way her body responded to me. The way her pupils dilated when her eyes hit mine. How her nipples hardened, brushing against my chest. The short gasps of her breath. The way her tongue swept her lower lip.

And, now, I'm hard.

Just fucking great.

I curl my hand around my cock, squeezing it through my boxer shorts.

I deserve a fucking medal for stepping away from her in that moment.

Knowing that she would have let me kiss her if I'd made a move only makes it so much harder to stay away from her.

But I don't get involved with people I work with. And I definitely do not fuck people I pay a salary to.

And I never will.

But I can fuck her in my head.

I push my boxer shorts down my ass and take hold of my aching cock.

Squeezing my eyes shut, I let my mind flood with the images of Speedy that I've been trying to ignore all night.

I stroke up my cock, thinking of her bending over earlier, when I could see her tits down her top.

I let that play into fantasy.

I tell her to come to me. She does willingly. She climbs onto my lap. I take her mouth in a rough kiss, tangling my fingers into her hair. Then, I pull her back and yank the front of her dress down, revealing those gorgeous tits of hers.

"Fuck," I groan. My grip on my shaft tightens, and I start jacking it with determined strokes.

I take her tit in my mouth, sucking and biting the nipple, while I slide my hand up her thigh, reaching her pussy. She's not wearing panties. And she's fucking soaked.

My hand is flying up and down my cock. Harder. Faster.

I push a finger inside her, rubbing her clit with my thumb.

She moans my name.

"*Get my cock out,*" *I tell her.*

She quickly unzips me, freeing my dick. Wasting no time, I lift her up and impale her with my cock. She screams.

I start jackhammering her from beneath.

"Fuck."

My hand can't go fast enough.

I need to come.

Her nails dig into my shoulders. "Fuck me harder, Gabe."

"Jesus."

I'm fucking my fist, desperately chasing relief.

My balls tighten up, telling me I'm close.

Her tits bounce as I fuck her. She's so fucking hot.

I grab her head and pull her mouth down onto mine.

My other hand grips my balls as I squeeze my fist tighter around my cock.

Ava. Ava. Fuck.

My cock is buried in her tight pussy, my tongue thrusting deep in her mouth.

"Mine," I tell her.

Pleasure surges down my spine, my muscles contracting, and—*Fuck! My fucking foot!*

And I'm coming in my hand. Pleasure and pain rack my body.

"Fuck," I groan.

My foot is killing me. But, God, it was so worth it.

I take a minute to catch my breath, and then I pull my boxer shorts up and slide out of bed.

Using one crutch, I go to the bathroom and wash my hands.

I need a smoke. I always do after sex or a good jacking off. And my foot is throbbing, so I'll grab a drink to take the edge off the pain.

Still using the one crutch, I hobble toward the kitchen.

When I push the door open, I see the utility room light is on, and the door is ajar.

Weird.

I know Gucci is sleeping in there tonight, but I'm surprised that Speedy left the door open.

I flick the kitchen light on and go over to the utility room. I push the door open wider.

And there, asleep on my floor, with her head on the

goat's fluffy pink fucking bed and the goat curled up against her, is the object of my jacking-off desire.

And she's wearing barely there pajama shorts and a tank top.

My dick instantly goes hard at the sight.

Jesus fucking Christ.

I close my eyes, pinch the bridge of my nose, and count to ten until my dick gets the message and goes down.

Then, I say her name, but she doesn't rouse.

So, I move closer.

"Speedy," I say a little louder.

"Mmhmm?"

"Why are you asleep on the floor?"

"Huh?" She blinks open her eyes and looks up at me.

I stare down at her, amused. "Do you not like the bed I gave you to sleep in?"

"Oh. No. I mean, yes, of course I do." She sits up and rubs her eyes, and the goat is immediately awake. "Gucci wouldn't settle when I tried to put her to bed. So, I came to lie down with her to get her to sleep. She's used to sleeping with me. I must have fallen asleep."

"You let the goat sleep in your bed?"

"Yeah. Of course I do."

I have nothing. So, I say nothing.

And then my eyes make the mistake of going lower, and, Christ al-fucking-mighty, I can see her nipples through her top.

"Well, you can't sleep here. Let's get you to bed."

I put my hand out to her, but she ignores it.

"If I leave her, she'll cry."

"And then she'll go to sleep when she's done crying."

She narrows her eyes at me. "I'm not doing that. That would be cruel."

"No, it would be called the goat doing as it's told."

"Stop being horrible. And she's not called goat; she's called Gucci."

She folds her arms over her tits, and for once, I'm relieved because she's covering those goddamn nipples up.

"Anyway, how does where I sleep affect you?"

My stare darkens. "It doesn't. Sleep there for all I care. But, when you wake up, stiff as fuck, don't come crying to me."

I make it as far as the door before the guilt hits, and I stop and growl out, "For fuck's sake! Fine! Take the goddamn goat in your bedroom with you. But, if it wrecks anything—"

"The money comes out of my wages. I got it. You're the freaking best, Gabe."

And then do you know what she fucking does?

She presses herself up against my back and wraps her slender arms around my stomach, and she mother-fucking hugs me.

Great. Now, I'm gonna have to go jack off again. There's no doubt about it.

"Go on then. Get to bed." My tone is testy, but I'm too wired to care.

"Come on, Gucci," she coos, moving past me and into the kitchen.

And the goat trots on after her.

I shut the utility room light off and move through the kitchen.

She's holding the door open for me.

I shut the kitchen light off, plunging us into darkness.

"You need me to do anything before I hit the hay?"

Suck me off. Show me your tits. Let me fuck you seven ways till Sunday.

"No. I'm good."

I see her smile in the darkness.

"Thanks again, Gabe. I really do appreciate you." Then, she puts her hand on my shoulder, reaches up, and kisses me on the cheek.

Her lips are soft against my rough stubble.

She smells like apples and sex. Really great fucking sex.

"Sleep well," she whispers, withdrawing. Then, she's walking down the hallway, disappearing into her room.

And I'm left with another raging hard-on.

"Jesus Christ," I mutter, dragging a hand through my hair.

I stomp back to my bedroom—well, stomp as best as I can with a broken foot and boner. I drop down onto my bed, tossing my crutch across the room in frustration.

Goddamn hot chick in my house, driving me fucking crazy.

Why did I have to say she could stay here and that I'd pay her for taking care of me?

I could be balls deep in her right now if I'd kept my big fucking mouth shut.

Goddamn it!

I need a drink.

Ah, fuck!

I forgot to get a whiskey because of her sexy ass sleeping on my floor, and I didn't even get to have a smoke.

I swear, she's doing this shit on purpose just to torture me.

I grab the pillow from under my head and cover my face with it.

"For fuck's sake!" I growl into it.

A few days ago, this woman wasn't even on my radar, and now, she's invading my headspace and my home.

I take hold of my throbbing dick and squeeze hard. Speedy is going to be the death of me. I swear it.

Chapter Twelve

Gabe

"*BAAAHHH!*"

"What?"

"*Baaahhh! Baaahhh!*"

I blink open my heavy eyes to see that fucking goat inches from my face, staring at me.

"Jesus fucking Christ. Go away, goat. I'm trying to sleep." I shut my eyes, ignoring it.

"*Baaahhh! Baaahhh! Baaahhh!*"

"For fuck's sake! You shouldn't even be in here. Will you shut—ow!" My hand goes to my nose, my eyes flying open.

She fucking head-butted me!

The damn goat just head-butted me in the face.

"You little bitch," I growl at her.

She rears back and tries to head-butt me again. I stop her with my hand pressed to her, but she won't give up, pushing against my hand.

It'd be funny if I hadn't just been head-butted in the

face. I check my nose with my hand to make sure it's not bleeding while simultaneously keeping the goat away with the other hand.

"Jesus, Gucci, will you knock it off?"

She backs off from my hand, and I think she got the message, but the little bitch hasn't gotten the message at all.

She starts to back away, and I can see it in her eyes.

"Don't you dare." I point at her, warning her, as I sit myself up.

But does she listen?

Nope. The little bastard charges.

"Gucci!"

I try to catch her, but she manages to butt me in the arm.

"Fuck! Little fucker! Speedy! Get your ass in here! Your goat's gone mental!"

Gucci is head-butting any part of my body that she can. I grab hold of her and try to stop her, but she's a strong little fucker.

Moments later, Speedy comes bursting into my room, looking like she just leaped out of bed. "What's going on? What are you doing to Gucci?"

"What am I doing? Stopping your goat from butting the hell out of me—that's what I'm doing! She's gone fucking mental! I woke up to a head-butt in the face, and now, she won't stop butting me!"

"Gucci! Stop," she says in a firm tone.

But she's fighting laughter; I can tell.

At the sound of Speedy's voice, the goat immediately stops fighting me. She wriggles free from me and trots over to Speedy, like nothing just happened.

Psycho goat.

Speedy picks her up. "You shouldn't be in here, baby girl. Now, what have you been doing to Gabe?" She gently taps the goat on the nose with her finger.

"Head-butting me is what it's been doing," I growl. "That goat's as fucking nuts as its owner."

Ignoring me, she says to the goat, "You've got to stop head-butting Gabe, baby girl. He's being really kind, letting us stay here. Now, say you're sorry to him." She turns the goat to face me.

I swear to God, if the goat could give me the middle finger right now, she would.

"I don't think she's sorry," I deadpan.

Speedy puts Gucci down and ushers her out of the room and into the hall, closing the door on her.

"Baaahhh!"

"I'll be out in a second, Gucci."

Silence.

Then, I hear little hooves trotting against the wood floor. She's probably off to destroy something of mine.

Little fucker.

Speedy walks over to the bed and sits down on the edge.

Her hair is all mussed up. Her tan legs are right there, all gorgeous and enticing. She looks sexy as hell.

She's a goddess. The goddess of sexual torture.

And she's still wearing those barely there shorts and tank. And, sweet Christ, I can see her nipples through her top again. More so right now, as they're erect and poking through the fabric. They look so pink and round and inviting.

God, I could just lean forward, take one in my mouth, and suck it through her shirt, making her all wet.

"I'm so sorry about Gucci. I think she's just struggling with the change. I don't know how she got out of my room. I must not have shut the door properly. I'll make sure it doesn't happen again. Are you okay? You said she butted you in the face? Does it hurt? Gabe? Are you listening to me? Gabe?"

"Huh?"

Her hands go to her hips. "I said, are you listening to me?"

"Honestly, no. I can see your nipples through your top, and it's really distracting."

"Oh my God!" she screeches as she clamps her arms over her chest. She jumps to her feet. "You-you crude, rude pervert!"

My eyes follow her up.

God, just look at that tight little body.

"Hey. I'm not the one showing my tits off."

"Jackass!"

"Cocktease."

"I am not a cocktease! You-you're just obsessed with staring at women's breasts!"

"I don't deny that I love women's tits. But, when they're put on display like yours are, what am I supposed to do?"

"Be a gentleman and not look. Or at least tell me that you can see them, so I can go change."

I narrow my eyes. "I did tell you."

"Not before you had a good stare at them! You're just a damn pervert."

"You're the one who has a titty hard-on."

"A titty hard-on? What are you? Twelve? Oh, and you've got drool on your chin by the way." She gives a smug look.

I wipe my hand against my chin, which does in fact have drool on it. But it's not mine; it's that damn fucking goat's. I dry my hand on the duvet.

"That fucking goat," I mutter.

"She's got a name," she bites. "It's Gucci."

"It's a stupid fucking name."

"You're stupid."

"Now who's acting twelve, Nipple Girl?"

Her face is red with anger, her eyes flaring. She's never looked hotter. My dick is as hard as steel under the covers.

"Shut up, Hoppy!" She stamps her foot and then stomps off.

"Is that all you've got?" I call to her back. "Aw, come on, Nipple Girl. Don't go. I was just starting to have some fun."

She half-turns. "You can have fun alone."

She nods in the direction of my cock. I look down, and there's a definite bulge showing under the covers. Seems it wasn't hiding me as well as I thought.

Oh well.

"I'm going to make breakfast," she says in a pissy tone. "Would you like one dose of arsenic in your coffee or two?"

"I'll skip the arsenic, thanks. Just sugar and creamer." I give her a saccharine smile. "Will your nipples be joining us for breakfast?"

Her eyes narrow at me. She looks sexy as fuck.

"I don't know. Is your erection going to join us?" Her face flames the second she hears how that sounded.

I burst out laughing. "Speedy! You dirty little pervert!"

"I-I . . ." she stammers. "Ugh! Fine! Laugh it up, you big jerk!"

She yanks open my door.

"Aw, Speedy! Don't go!"

I can't breathe; I'm laughing so much. Honestly, I can't remember the last time I laughed this hard.

Hard.

And, now, I'm laughing even more.

"Do you want breakfast or not?" she snaps, arms fitted tight over her chest.

I calm my laughter, taking some deep breaths. "Don't worry about breakfast," I say, still a little breathless. "Tate's coming, and he's bringing breakfast with him."

"Fine. You still want coffee?"

"Sure."

She walks out the door.

I call behind her, "Don't forget to put a bra on. Wouldn't want you poking out Tate's eyes with those nipples of yours!"

"Go to hell!" she yells as she stomps down the hall.

I hear her bedroom door slam, and I burst out laughing again.

Chapter Thirteen

Ava

"**U**M, WHAT ARE YOU doing?"

I stop with the spoon midway to my mouth and look up at Gabe.

God, he looks good. The jackass.

He hasn't shaved in days, so he's covered in sexy stubble, and his hair looks like he just ran his fingers through it. He's wearing athletic shorts again, as it's all he can wear with the boot on his leg, and a running vest on top. He's the hottest thing I've ever seen in my life.

Shame he's a jerk.

"I'm eating breakfast."

His brows draw together. "I told you that Tate was bringing breakfast."

I put the spoon back in the cereal bowl. "Yeah, but I thought that was just for you guys."

"He always brings enough food to feed a small army. There'll be plenty for you."

"Oh. Okay. Thank you." I feel really warm at the idea that he's including me in breakfast with his brother.

He removes the crutch from under his arm and leans against the counter. "Where's psycho goat?" he asks, looking around like Gucci's going to jump out and attack him at any minute.

"*Gucci* is out on the terrace."

"Shitting?"

"No. Enjoying the sunshine."

"Talking of sunshine, why are you dressed like it's winter?"

I glance down at my sweater and then back up at him. I narrow my gaze at him. The bastard knows why I'm dressed like this. I wanted to cover up well after Nipplegate.

I'm wearing a padded bra. It makes my boobs look bigger, but at least it keeps the nips from showing. And, just to be doubly sure, I put a knit sweater on. And jean shorts because it is warm out there, so I'm staying cool where I can.

"Just keeping the girls covered. Wouldn't want to have any more showings and give you another reason to be a pervy jackass."

His mouth spreads into a grin. "Aw, Speedy. I was just playing with you. Don't cover up on my account. I wouldn't want you to sweat to death."

"I won't." I sit up and fold my arms over my chest. "I'll be perfectly fine."

"If you say so."

"I do. And here's your coffee." I slide over the cup of coffee I made him, and I pick my own up, cradling it in my hands.

He takes a sip and then puts it down. Using his crutch, he leans over and opens a cupboard where he pulls out a bottle of Scotch.

I watch as he pours a good measure into the coffee. Then, he puts the bottle back into the cupboard and takes another drink of coffee. A gulp this time.

He sees me staring at him.

"You want to make your coffee Irish?" he asks.

"You used Scotch. Wouldn't that make it Scottish?"

His lips press together in a smile. "Someone's snarky this morning."

I raise a disapproving brow. "Don't you think it's a little early to be making coffee anything of the European type?"

His eyes darken, not looking impressed. "If I wanted to be nagged on the regular, I'd get married. I'm not, so I'll make my coffee however the fuck I want." Taking his coffee with him and leaving behind one of his crutches, he heads out of the kitchen.

He's right. I shouldn't be interfering in how he lives his life.

It's not like I have anything to be singing about.

Lost my job, ran over a movie star with my car, homeless. Yeah, I should keep my opinions to myself.

Grabbing the bottle of Scotch, I pick up my coffee and go into the living room. I see Gabe through the window, sitting out on the terrace. He's smoking a cigarette.

Gucci is lying out by the pool. She looks like she's sunbathing. All she needs is a towel and a bathing suit, and she'd be good to go.

I wonder if you can get bathing suits for goats.

I go outside and sit on the lounger next to him.

"Sorry," I say. "I'll keep my opinions to myself from now on."

He doesn't look at me. The only response I get is a nod of his head.

I put my coffee down on the lounger and pour some Scotch into it. I put the Scotch on the floor.

When I look at Gabe, he's watching me with mild amusement.

"I thought it was too early to be making things Scottish."

"Clearly, you're a bad influence. And I figured, if you can't beat him, join him."

His lips lift at the corner. "I'm all for kinky, Speedy, but beating's not my thing. Now, a little light spanking, and I'm your man."

Gabe spanking me? Yes, please.

I laugh, despite myself. "You're incorrigible."

"It's my best feature." He grins. Putting his cup to his lips, he takes a drink.

I do the same. And then I start coughing. "God, that's strong. I think I put too much in."

Gabe laughs.

I like the sound of his laugh. It's raspy and deep. Like it comes from somewhere hidden deep inside him. But I like it most when it's me making him laugh.

I sit back with my coffee and stare out at the view.

It's lovely up here.

And hot.

The sun is beating down, and I can feel myself starting to sweat. This sweater really was not a good idea. Maybe I should change into a T-shirt.

Gabe sighs lightly and leans back on the lounger, staring up at the sky. He takes a drag of his cigarette. I watch him. I see just how dark the skin surrounding his eyes looks. I didn't notice before.

"You look tired," I say gently.

He blows the smoke from his mouth and then turns his head to look at me. "You would, too, if you had been woken up by a head-butt from a goat."

"I didn't mean it as a criticism." I hold my hand up in surrender. "I only mean it as a concerned employee. And I am sorry about Gucci. I'll make sure she stays out of your room."

He takes another sip of coffee. "I didn't sleep well," he tells me.

"No? Why not?"

He stares at me for a long moment. So long that I start to squirm under his penetrating gaze.

Then, he looks away, over at the skyline, and he takes another pull on his cigarette. "My foot was bothering me."

"Gabe . . . I know you said you don't take painkillers, but maybe you should consider it."

"No."

"It would help you sleep."

He quickly sits up. "For fuck's sake, Ava! I said no."

This is only the third time he's called me Ava. But I don't get the warm shivers this time.

Hearing him say my name in anger is the slap I needed. I told myself I'd stop interfering in his life, and here I am, doing it again.

"I don't mean to interfere. My intentions are only ever good. But I am sorry for pushing. I'll do my best to stop sticking my nose in where it's not wanted." I start to chew on my thumbnail.

Leaving his cigarette between his lips, he breathes heavily through his nose and rubs his hand across the back of his neck.

Feeling like I should leave him alone, I pick my coffee up, ready to go.

He takes the cigarette from his mouth. "A good friend of mine . . . he had an injury a while back. Got hooked on painkillers. I saw what he went through. It wasn't pretty. That's why I won't take them." He leans forward and flicks the ash from his cigarette into the ashtray by his lounger.

"Shit. I'm sorry. Is your friend okay now?" I lean over, pick up the ashtray, and place it on the lounger in front of him.

He gives me a grateful smile.

"Yeah, he's fine. But it was hard going there for a while."

"Well, he's lucky that he has you as a friend. But, Gabe, just because your friend got addicted doesn't mean you would. Millions of people take pain medication every day without getting addicted."

"I know." He sighs. "And I have taken pain medication in the past—for headaches, you know." He glances at me.

There's a strange sort of vulnerability in his eyes that I haven't seen before. It makes me want to hold him.

"But I just don't want to risk it. People in my line of business are well-known for their addictions." He gives a sardonic look.

"Sure. I understand. And I'm sorry for pushing the subject."

"It's fine, Speedy."

He gives me a soft smile, and our eyes lock.

My skin starts to tingle under the weight of his stare. The breeze blows, kicking up my hair. And I watch as his eyes change from dark brown to almost black. An ache starts to form between my legs. My breasts suddenly feel heavy.

And I somehow seem to be closer to Gabe. Like my body moved without informing my brain.

"Gabriel," I softly say his name.

And those dark eyes rage like fire.

"Gabe! I'm here! Where the fuck are you?"

I jerk back from Gabe at the sound of the male voice.

"On the terrace," Gabe calls to him, seeming unfazed.

Tate appears through the door, wearing a white T-shirt, dark blue shorts, sneakers, and Ray-Bans over his eyes. He looks really different from the last time I saw him when he was wearing his white doctor coat and scrubs.

"Hey, Ava. Good to see you again." He smiles at me. "How's the patient?" He jerks his head at Gabe.

"Frustrating. Annoying. Bitchy. Aside from that, he's fine." I give a light, teasing smile even though, inside, I feel anything but light. I feel like I'm about to climb out of my skin.

"Funny. Speedy's a comedian nowadays," Gabe says dryly.

"Are you joining us for breakfast?" Tate asks me, holding up a brown bag with the name of some deli on it. "I brought pastries and muffins."

"Sounds delicious. Sure, I'll join you, if you don't mind?"

"Course I don't. I'll just grab us some plates."

"I'll get them," I say, getting up. "Would you like a coffee?" I ask Tate as I move past him.

"Coffee would be great."

"Gabe? Refill?"

"Sure." He drains his coffee and hands me the cup.

"Scottish?" I ask him.

He smiles. I feel that smile everywhere.

"American's fine."

I grab the bottle of Scotch from the floor and take it back inside with me.

I rinse my and Gabe's cups out and get a fresh one for Tate. I pour out three coffees and put them on a tray with creamer and sugar, as I'm not sure how Tate takes his coffee. I get three small plates, some cutlery, and napkins and put them on the tray as well.

When I go back outside, they are sitting at the seating area. Gucci is sitting on Tate's lap. Well, she's laid out on him, and he's rubbing her belly.

"You've met Gucci." I smile. "I think she likes you."

My little hussy is rubbing herself all over the doctor.

Seems us Simms women have a thing for the Evans men.

"Yeah, it's just me she hates," Gabe mutters.

"She does not hate you," I tell Gabe as I take the seat next to him.

"I'm just really fucking loveable." Tate smirks.

"That's why you haven't gotten laid in two months."

Tate's eyes briefly flick to me. I avert my eyes and make Gabe's coffee.

"It's called being busy with work, brother. And it's not like you're getting any at the moment, so don't be giving me shit."

They're talking about sex. I start to get hot again. And it's not just because of this fucking sweater.

I hand Gabe his coffee.

"The only reason I'm not getting some is because of this fucking thing on my leg," Gabe says to him.

And, now, I'm thinking about sex. With Gabe.

Good God.

"Tate, do you take creamer and sugar?" My voice is high-pitched. I clear my throat.

Gabe chuckles lightly next to me.

"Just creamer," Tate tells me.

I make Tate's coffee and hand it over.

I pick my black coffee up and take a sip when Gabe says, "Talking of sex, Speedy showed me her nipples this morning."

I almost choke, and coffee sprays from my mouth.

I slap a hand over my mouth, and my head whips around to Gabe. My eyes are as wide as saucers.

The bastard is grinning.

I grab a napkin and start to dry my mouth, hand, and then the table. "God, I'm so sorry, Tate."

"You didn't get the food. It's fine." He smiles, but I can tell he's dying to laugh.

Gucci hasn't moved an inch from her spot on Tate's lap.

I turn back to Gabe, who's still wearing a winning smile that I want to wipe from his gorgeous face.

"I can't believe you just said that."

"Me? What did I say?"

I open my mouth to say it, but then I realize, that's exactly what the big jerk wants. He wants me to say *nipple* in front of Tate.

The perverse asshole.

"There's something seriously wrong with you." I shake my head and turn back to Tate. "Was he dropped on his head as a baby?"

Tate laughs. "Quite possibly."

"Well, I think you should get him tested. I'm pretty sure he has mental problems."

"Speedy?" Gabe's voice prickles the back of my neck.

I slowly turn to look at him. My eyes are like lasers burning a hole in his skull. "What?"

He dips a nod at my chest. "You've got coffee on your sweater. You might want to change it." Then, he smiles big as he picks up a muffin and takes a big bite.

I want to kill him. Dead.

I hope he chokes on that muffin.

Gah!

I need to move out of his apartment, and the sooner, the better. Before the hot bastard drives me insane.

Chapter Fourteen

Ava

I'VE BEEN LIVING HERE for three days so far, and it's been pretty much more of the same.

Gabe seems to be getting crankier as the days go on. Honestly, I think he needs to get out. He must be going stir-crazy. I know I am. I'm used to going out to work every day, so working and living in the same place is driving me nuts.

I keep making excuses to go out just to get some air and sun on my skin. I've been to the store about a hundred times already.

Gabe's in his office at the moment. He said something about calling his manager.

I'm on the terrace with Gucci, and I've drunk three cups of coffee already. I'm starting to get a caffeine twitch.

Gucci loves it out here. She seems to be a sun queen. I am worried about her spending so much time in the sun though. It can't be good for her skin. I hope goats can't get skin cancer.

God, it's warm today. I gaze at the swimming pool. I haven't been in yet.

Maybe I'll go in today. Once Gabe's done with his call, I'll see what he needs me to do, and if nothing, then I'm getting my bathing suit out and taking a dip.

I hear the buzzer go on the internal intercom.

Knowing Gabe's busy and not the fastest on his feet at the moment—well, foot—I get up to go into the living room and pick up the phone.

"Hello?"

"Hey, Miss Ava." It's Harry. "The cleaners are here."

"Oh. Do you know if they are scheduled to come today?"

"Every Monday and Friday," Harry tells me.

"Oh, right. Well, send them on up. Thanks, Harry."

I replace the receiver and then look around the place. It's pretty tidy. I've been keeping on top of it, but I still walk around, tidying things up before the cleaners arrive. I move the sports magazine that Gabe left on the sofa to the top of a neat pile on the coffee table. I take his empty coffee cup into the kitchen and put it in the dishwasher.

I've just shut the dishwasher door when I hear activity in the foyer.

I head through the apartment to introduce myself.

There are two women. One older, one younger. And they both look surprised to see me.

"Hi," I say, lifting my hand in a wave. "I'm Ava."

The older woman smiles warmly. "Nice to meet you, Ava. I'm Barb, and this is Sadie." She points to the younger woman.

Looking at her, I'm pegging her to be around my age, maybe a little younger.

She doesn't smile. Just regards me with narrow eyes.

She's a really pretty girl. Brown hair tied up into a messy bun. Taller than me. Slender figure. Clear, fresh skin.

The way she's staring at me is starting to make me feel uncomfortable.

Maybe she thinks I'm with Gabe. And maybe she likes Gabe.

Can't blame the girl. I mean, who doesn't like him? Dude is hot as hell. And he's a movie star to boot. Just a shame about his crude mouth and disgusting smoking habit.

"Gabe's just in the office," I tell them, moving my eyes back to Barb. "I'm not his girlfriend or anything. Just a friend. He broke his foot. I'm here, taking care of him, until he's healed."

"Oh no," Barb says. "How'd he do that?"

"Oh, I did it. I hit him with my car."

Barb's eyes widen, and I hear Sadie snigger.

"No, I mean, I ran over his foot with my car by accident. Total accident."

Jesus Christ, Ava.

"Oh, well, so long as he's okay," Barb says kindly.

"He's fine. Absolutely fine. Only two bones broken, first and second metatarsals. He'll be back to new in six to eight weeks."

Jesus, I'm sweating.

"Right. Well"—I clap my hands together—"I guess . . . I'll leave you to it."

I turn on my heel and go to the terrace where Gucci is still lying in the same place as I left her.

"Come on, baby girl." I scoop her up into my arms, and she snuggles in close.

I walk quickly through the living room where Sadie and Barb have started cleaning, and I head to the office.

The door is closed, so I tap on it and push it open.

Gabe is staring at his computer screen. And he's wearing his glasses.

Good God, he looks sexy. Really sexy. Like a hot, nerdy whiz kid who's really a superhero by night.

A superhero who gives amazing orgasms to women. Well, me.

Ha! Keep dreaming, Simms.

He moves his eyes to me.

I clear my throat. "The cleaners are here," I tell him.

"Right . . ."

I move into the room and shut the door behind me. I take a seat in the chair in the corner.

"You staying?" He raises a brow.

"I feel weird out there with the cleaners here."

His lips lift. "Why?"

"I don't know." I shrug.

"Okay." His eyes go back to his computer screen.

"I like your glasses. They suit you."

His response is a nod.

I scratch Gucci's head, and she lets out a soft, *"Baaahhh."*

"Whatcha doing?" I ask him.

"Working."

"Oh. What on?"

He looks back to me. "Work."

I stretch my legs out and look at my bare feet. My toenails could do with a fresh coat of varnish on them. The red I painted on is starting to chip. Maybe I'll do that once the cleaners are gone.

"How long will they be here for?" I ask Gabe.

"The cleaners? A few hours or so."

I lean my head back on the headrest and stare up at the ceiling.

I'm so bored.

I really need to get out today.

I look over at Gabe, who's squinting at his screen. "Do you want to go out today?"

He sighs and leans back in his desk chair. "Where do you want to go, Speedy?"

"I don't know. Anywhere. We could just go out and get some fresh air."

"You're not going to let me work until we go out, are you?"

I smile wide.

"Fine. But I'm bringing work with me. I need to start learning this script."

"Can I help?"

"Yes, Speedy, you can help."

"Cool. So, where shall we go?"

"I have just the place."

"Can Gucci come?"

He sighs. "Yes, Speedy, the goat can come."

Chapter Fifteen

Ava

I PULL GABE'S CAR TO a stop on a roadside outside a field in Beverly Glen.

"This is where you want to go?"

"Mmhmm."

"A field?"

"Yep."

"Well, I guess Gucci will like it here. But can I ask, why have we come to a field?"

I was thinking he meant like a café or something when he said he had somewhere for us to go.

Gabe opens his car door and puts the messenger bag that he brought with him over his head, so the strap is across his chest. Then, using his crutches, he gets out of the car.

I lean over into the backseat, unfasten Gucci's car harness from the seat belt, and bring her into the front with me. I clip her lead to the harness and carry her out of the car.

I go stand next to Gabe. "Okay, so what do we do now?"

"Come with me."

He starts moving, so I put Gucci down to the ground, and holding her lead, I follow Gabe across the grass.

"Wow," I say when he comes to a stop on the other side of the field.

Now, I see why he likes to come here. There's a clear view of Stone Canyon Reservoir.

"What a view."

"Yep."

"Do you come here often?"

"Is that your pick-up line, Speedy? Because, if it is, it's no wonder you're single."

"Jerk."

I nudge him with my elbow, and he chuckles.

"And, to answer your question, I come here as often as I can."

"I can see why you like it. It's really peaceful."

"Peace isn't something I get a lot of in my line of work. And there aren't many places I can go without someone recognizing me. Here, I can come and sit out in the open air, and no one bothers me."

"Who owns this field?" I ask him, looking around.

"I do."

I stop and look up at him. He's staring down at me.

"You own a field?"

"It's not just a field, Speedy; it's land. Land that I plan to build a house on."

"Ah. How long have you owned it?"

He laughs softly. "Eight years."

"Eight years?" I look at him, dumbfounded. "So, this

might be a stupid question ... but why haven't you built a house?"

He lifts a shoulder, his eyes briefly meeting mine. "I've been busy working for the last eight years, and I'm not sure exactly what type of house I want to build here. I bought it because it was a great deal at the time for what I was getting. I just haven't gotten around to doing anything with it."

"Except coming here to admire the view."

"Except that."

"Well, if it were me, I'd build a huge ranch-style house with a paddock for Gucci and a swimming pool."

"The pool for the goat or you?"

"Both of us." I grin.

He shifts on his crutches, a slight grimace appearing on his face.

"You okay?"

"Yeah, standing just gets uncomfortable."

I look around, but there's nowhere to sit, except the grass. "What do you want to do?"

"There's a fold-up chair and blanket in the trunk of my car. Would you mind grabbing them? Then, we can sit up here, and you can run lines with me."

I jog over to the car, Gucci trotting alongside me, and I get the chair and blanket out of the trunk.

I grab my bag from the backseat, as I've got a couple of bottles of water and Gucci's water bottle, built-in tray, and some cut-up vegetables in a sandwich bag ready for her.

I head back over to Gabe and set the chair up. He sits in it, putting his crutches on the ground. I hook Gucci's lead to the chair and extend it, so she's got plenty of space to roam around. Then, I lay the blanket out in front of Gabe and sit down on it, tucking my legs under me.

He removes the bag and pulls out what I think are a couple of scripts.

He hands one to me.

Yep, it's a script.

On the front, it reads, *Insanity Calling by Jonah Pickle and Catarina Wiseman, Second Draft.*

"*Insanity Calling*. That's a cool name for a movie," I muse.

"Yeah. It's a really great script," he tells me.

"When do you start filming?"

"Couple of months' time."

"So, your foot will be healed in time. That's good news. Where will you be filming?"

"Mostly in the studio. Some on location in New York."

"The asshole studio that fired me?" I playfully narrow my eyes.

"Yep. That asshole studio."

He's quiet a moment, and then he says, "I can talk to someone, get you your job back. Or get you a job on this movie."

"No, it's fine. But thank you. I appreciate the offer." I open to the first page of the script. "So, who's in this movie with you?"

"Desmond Hooper."

"Ooh, I love him."

"Right?" He grins.

Desmond Hooper is old-school Hollywood. He's done so many films, ranging from Westerns to comedies to love stories. He's a veteran in the movie business and twice an Oscar winner.

"Who else is in it? Who's playing your love interest?" There's always a love interest.

"She's not been cast yet."

That's not unusual for a studio to not have the full cast, even at this point.

"They did have Harriett Jenkins at one point, but . . ." He trails off, scratching his chin. He still hasn't shaved, and he's getting the definite signs of a beard growing.

"But what?"

"Nothing."

"You can't say that to someone like me!" I sit up on my haunches. "That's like dangling a cigarette in front of you and not letting you smoke it."

"Talking of cigarette." He pulls a pack out of his shorts pocket and lights one up.

I watch him suck on the cigarette and blow the smoke out into the air.

"Gabe."

"Ava."

Containing my shiver, I press my hands to my hips and tip my head to the side.

"Fine." He sighs. "We fucked a few times, and she got a little . . . hung up on me."

I ignore the stab of jealousy I feel at knowing he had sex with Harriett Jenkins—the beautiful once-child star, now full-on bona fide movie star.

"She went *Fatal Attraction* on you?"

"She didn't boil any bunnies on my stove, but it did get a little weird for a time. She was turning up at my apartment at all hours of the night. Went bitch crazy on some chick I was talking to in a club. Scratched my car. When I woke up in the middle of the night to find her in my bed, I had it."

My mouth pops open. "She was in your bed? How did she get in your apartment? The only way I know up there is via the elevator."

"There's a service elevator in the back—that other door in the kitchen."

"Oh. I thought that was just a cupboard."

"No." He laughs.

"So, how did she get in?"

"She bribed one of the building staff and got the elevator key from them. I was so close to calling the cops, but I didn't want the press attention. So, I kicked her ass out and called my lawyer. He threatened her people with a restraining order, knowing they wouldn't want that to get out in the press. It would be killer for her golden-girl image. So, they checked her into rehab for 'exhaustion.'" He air-quotes. "I haven't heard from her since. That was three years ago.

"But no way am I working with her. So, I told the studio that I didn't want to work with her for personal reasons, and I was happy to pull out. But they wanted me for the role, so she was taken out of the picture."

"Oh, well, I'm glad for you. And any future bunnies that might have been boiled in your name."

"It goes without saying, this is just between you and me."

I make the locking motion over my lips and pretend to throw away the key.

"You know, I usually have my staff sign an NDA," he says in a thoughtful tone.

"I can sign one if you'd like."

His eyes soften on me. "No. You're good. I trust you."

That warms me all over.

I glance over at my Gucci, who's walking around, sniffing the grass.

"You don't think Harriett will go weird if she finds out I'm staying with you?"

"Gucci's safe, Speedy. She won't come back. It's been a long time now. She's probably off stalking some other poor bastard."

"Sucks that you had to go through that."

He shrugs. "It was more annoying than anything."

"If I had someone stalk me like that, I'd shit my pants."

"Literally?"

"Yeah. And I'd probably piss myself, too."

He laughs.

I can't believe I'm talking about shit and piss with Gabe.

I'm so weird.

"So, anyway"—I look down at the script—"you want to get started on this?"

"Sure." He pulls his glasses from his bag and puts them on.

My girl parts shimmy in response. I have to squeeze my thighs together to relieve the ache.

"So, which part are we working on?"

"Go to page five. You read the part of Estelle. I'm Henry."

"Is Estelle Henry's love interest in the movie?"

His eyes connect with mine. The darkening of them makes my mouth dry and my stomach quiver.

"Yeah. She's the one he wants to fuck. Badly."

For a moment, I wonder if he's actually talking about him and me.

"Do they . . . have sex? In the movie?" I can't believe I actually asked that.

"Yes."

Our eyes are still locked. I run my tongue over my dry lips.

Gabe's eyes follow the movement.

I swallow. "Is there . . . dialogue? In the sex scene."

"Yeah. Henry's a talker during sex. A really dirty talker."

Holy crap.

"And . . . will you need me to help you run those lines?"

His eyes come up to mine. It feels like an age before he speaks, but when he does, it's worth the wait. "Definitely."

Sweet mother of Jesus, my panties are soaked.

I drag my eyes from his, feeling like I can't breathe. My body is on fire, and the only thing it wants . . . needs to soothe itself is him.

God, I want him. I've never wanted a man more.

"Ava . . ."

Jesus, when he says my name, I want to die.

"Gucci's off her lead."

"What?" I snap to attention to see she's wandered off over to the other side of the field. "Shit!"

I jump to my feet and start running over to her. When I call her name, her head comes up from the flowers she was sniffing. She starts jumping around with excitement.

"Come here, baby girl."

I crouch down, and she comes trotting over into my arms. Thank God she didn't run away from me.

Always to me. Bless her heart.

I walk back over to Gabe.

"Okay?" he asks.

"Yeah, I'm not sure how she got free." I put her down and refit the lead to the harness, making sure it's secure.

As I stand, Gabe's hand touches mine and lingers there. "Ava."

I look down at him, and words fail me. He's so beautiful, and the way he's looking at me reignites my body back to life.

"Look, I—"

Something catches my eye, and I look up. "Gabe," I cut him off.

Not that I want to cut him off because I really want to hear what he was going to say, but there's a guy waving at me from the other side of the field, near Gabe's car.

"There's a guy near your car, and he's waving at me."

After talking about stalkers, I'm feeling a little creeped out by a random stranger waving at us. What if he's recognized Gabe? At this distance though, that wouldn't be possible, would it?

Gabe turns his head to look. "Oh, it's the pizza delivery guy."

I look down at him, surprised. "Pizza delivery guy? You ordered pizza? When?"

"When you went to the car to get the blanket and chair." He digs in the pocket of his shorts and pulls out a fifty-dollar bill. "I ordered a couple. One plain and a meat feast. You mind going over to pay him?" He holds out the bill.

"Uh, yeah, sure." I take the money and walk over to the delivery guy.

When I return with the pizzas, Gabe digs in straight-away. Before I know it, we're eating pizza and running lines, and I never do ask him what he was going to say before.

Chapter Sixteen

Gabe

S PEEDY'S BEEN LIVING HERE for two weeks now, and I can honestly say, it's the most fun I've had in ages.

She's crazy but in a totally great way. She never stops talking, but now, instead of finding it annoying, I like it. Hearing her ramble on is soothing in an odd kind of way.

I've never met a woman like her before. She's totally comfortable with who she is. She doesn't care that she talks too much. Or that she's quirky. She's not constantly worrying about how she looks or fixing her hair and makeup all the time.

She's sweet and kind, and the way she loves that goat . . . I swear, that thing is lucky as fuck.

And the goat's even growing on me. I'm not sure what's happening to me, but I think I'm going soft.

Not that I'd ever admit that to Speedy—or the goat.

I like having them here, which isn't something I thought I would ever say about anyone—ever.

I spend nearly every minute of the day with Speedy, and I never get bored of her company. Not once.

I can't even spend this much time around Tate without wanting to strangle him.

I've always been the kind of guy who needs his own space, but with her ... I don't want to be away from her for longer than necessary.

And the urge to sink my cock deep into her body is stronger than ever. The more I get to know her, the more I want her.

I swear, it's taking a lion's strength not to grab her and kiss the hell out of her.

It's all I think about. Kissing her, tasting her, licking every inch of her skin, watching her come apart in my arms.

In my head, I've fucked her in a hundred different ways on every surface of my apartment.

If only I could fuck her for real.

But she's my employee. And I just can't do it.

Aside from feeding me amazing food—I swear, I'm going to have to hit the gym so hard when this boot comes off—and taking care of me—helping me out of the bath, and she gave me a shave the other day with an electric, as there was no way I was letting her near me with a wet razor—she's been running lines with me every day.

But I keep avoiding the sex scene in the script. Because, honestly, I don't know if I'll be able to distinguish fact from fiction if we do read that scene together. And I've never had that problem before, but with her ... it'll be a problem. Thank God my PA, Donna, is back from vacation, which means I can get her to run those lines with me when I need her to.

I'm so pent-up with wanting Speedy. I know, if I get anywhere close to acting out a sex scene with her, even with words, I'll blow like a fucking pressure cooker.

And I don't like feeling out of control. The way she makes me feel, it's confusing and not something I'm used to.

I'm always in control. Even in the past, when people might have thought I wasn't, I was.

I've never jerked off as much as I have been with Speedy living under my roof. First thing in the morning. Then, another around lunchtime after watching her sexy ass strut around the apartment all morning. Then, once more right when I'm lying in bed, thinking about her sleeping just down the hall.

And, if it's a day when she's been in the pool . . . well, I have to add an extra jerk in because those tits in a bikini . . . holy fuck. I've never seen anything like them. It's like they have a life of their own, and their sole purpose is to taunt me.

The instant I see her in her bikini, water dripping from her skin and those perky tits with the nipples saluting me from the confines of the fabric, my cock stands to full attention, raring to go.

I jerk off so much that I'm getting chafing burns. And I haven't had those since I was a teenager after I discovered online porn.

And, yes, I'm using lube. That's how hard I'm going at it.

The worse thing is, I can jack off till the cows come home, but it's not going to fix anything.

I still want to fuck her.

So, I either fuck Speedy or fuck someone else.

And I can't have sex with her because I pay her a wage.

And the thought of having sex with someone else just doesn't appeal to me anymore, which is odd in itself. Because that's never happened to me before.

It's either Speedy or no one.

"Hey." She appears in my doorway to check on me before bed, like she has every night since she's been here.

"Hey." I smile.

She's standing there, her hair up in one of those messy buns with loose strands falling around her face, which is free of makeup, as she's ready for bed. She's wearing that damn tank and tiny shorts set that she likes to torture me with. She's got a bra on though, so no nipples show for me tonight.

"Whatcha watching?" She nods in the direction of the TV.

"*The Godfather*." It's showing on Netflix, and it'd be rude not to watch it. Not that I've been paying much attention since it started, as my mind has been fixated on that gorgeous creature standing in my doorway.

"Is it good?"

"You've never seen it?"

She shakes her head.

"How is that even possible?" I stare at her, wide-eyed.

"I don't know. I've just never gotten around to watching it."

"One of the greatest films of all time, and you've never seen it. And you work in the movie industry."

"Did work."

"You work for me. I'm an actor. You still work in the

movie industry." Like I need to remind myself that she works for me.

"Fine, fine." She steps a little further into my room. "It's not that I don't like gangster movies; they're just not at the top of my list."

"Don't tell me; chick flicks are your favorite."

She huffs at me. "Stereotype much? Actually, I love horror movies and comedies. And haven't you starred in a bunch of chick flicks? Pot, kettle, black."

"Touché." I grin. "So, horror movies, huh?"

"Yeah. Like the old-school Freddy Krueger, Jason, *Hellraiser* movies. I love them."

Just when I think I have her all figured out, she throws me a curveball, and it makes me just want her all the more.

"You're weird. You know that, right?"

"Oh, yeah, I totally know." She smiles.

"Well, weirdo, come and sit your ass down." I pat the space on the bed next to me. "And let me educate you in the greatness that is the *Godfather* movies."

Her lips lift at the corners, and then she pads across the room. Coming around to the other side of the bed, she climbs up and sits back against the headboard, her legs stretched out in front of her.

Okay, so maybe inviting her onto my bed wasn't the best idea. Because, now, I've got the scent of apples filling my nose, and those smooth, silky bare legs are right in my line of sight.

Torture, sheer torture.

I need a distraction.

"Where's Gucci?" I ask.

"She's just in the kitchen, having a late-night snack."

Only her goat would be having a late-night snack. "You wanna get her?"

She turns her head and looks at me. There's a warmth in her eyes that makes me feel weightless for a moment. "You sure?"

"At least, if she's in here, then I can keep an eye on her."

She smiles, like she's onto me, and then calls for Gucci.

The goat appears seconds later, running straight into my bedroom and up onto the bed. She flops down at Speedy's feet, laying her head on them.

I stare down at the goat. "Um, Speedy?"

"Do you want me to move her off the bed?"

"No, she's fine," I say. I'm clearly going soft in my old age. "And I don't even know why I'm asking this because I'll probably get a stupid answer in response . . . but what the fuck is Gucci wearing?"

She sits up, beaming. "Oh, pajamas. I found them on Amazon. Aren't they just the cutest?"

"No. She looks fucking ridiculous." I zero in on them. "Are those . . . strawberries on them?"

"And little pink flowers. I thought they were super cute, and she seems to love them."

"You do actually realize that she's a fucking goat. She has a built-in coat. Therefore, she doesn't need pajamas to sleep in."

Her eyes narrow at me. "So? I don't need pajamas to sleep in, but I still wear them."

And, now, I'm imagining her without her pajamas on. Naked Speedy.

And . . . now, my cock's decided to join the party.

Great. Just fucking great.

I sigh.

She flops back onto her pillows. "God, you're so grouchy at times."

"Yeah, and you're fucking ridiculous."

I turn my head to her, my face unable to keep the smile off it.

She returns that smile with one that I feel is like her dainty hand curling around my hard cock.

"You putting this movie back to the beginning, so I can watch from the start?" she asks in a soft voice.

And, because I love tormenting myself with her presence, I put the movie back to the beginning and press play. I reach over and turn my bedside lamp off because movies are always better in the dark.

Yeah, you keep telling yourself that, Evans.

Then, I settle back on my pillows to watch one of the best movies ever made with the object of my desire lying right next to me.

Chapter Seventeen

Gabe

I WAKE TO THE smell of apples and a warm body curled up against mine.

Speedy.

My arm is around her, her head on my shoulder, her arm resting on my stomach, her leg slung over my left one. Her steady, even breaths tell me she's sleeping.

I'm guessing she wouldn't be lying on me like this if she were awake.

The TV is still on, but the movie has long since finished. Gucci is asleep at the bottom of the bed. I have no clue what time it is. But I don't want to move in case I wake Speedy up.

I'm not ready to let her go just yet.

We must have fallen asleep while watching the film. Fuck knows how we ended up lying together in this position, but fuck if I'm not happy about it.

Having her in my arms with her body draped over mine like this ... it's the sweetest kind of hell.

And it's a hell I'd happily spend an obscene amount of time in.

Who knew holding a woman like this, without being inside her, could feel so good?

I've always gotten off and then got off with every woman I've slept with, no matter the circumstance.

No cuddling. And definitely no attachments.

Speedy is the first woman I've actually slept with without screwing first.

I glance down at her face.

Her eyes are closed, lashes brushing her cheekbones.

Fuck, she's pretty. Perfect. Beautiful.

I can't stop looking at her.

And, right now, I don't have to. I can freely stare at her without fear of being caught.

Her rosy lips are full and plump, like she's just been kissed. And she should be kissed, all the time, by me.

Freckles that I've never noticed before dust the bridge of her pert little nose. A tiny mole is near the corner of her right eye. A small scar on her chin looks like a chicken-pox mark.

My fingers itch to touch her. To see if her skin is as soft as it looks.

But I can't. I shouldn't.

But just one little touch can't hurt, right?

I lift a hand to her face and brush the tips of my fingers over her cheek and to her forehead. I brush the stray strands of hair off her face. Then, I move the backs of my fingers down her other cheek to her jaw where I trace my fingertips along it, stopping near her mouth. My thumb hovers dangerously close.

I can feel her warm breath on my skin.

I wonder how she tastes.

Fuck, I want to know so badly.

My mouth is dry with longing. Constant longing. And wanting her.

It's driving me insane.

Look how bad it's gotten. Like a total creeper, I'm touching up her face while she sleeps.

I withdraw my hand and force myself to look away. I take a deep breath.

"Gabe."

The word is so quietly spoken, I think I imagined it.

Until I look back to her and see her eyes are open.

And filled with need. They mirror my own.

God, I want her.

Her hand comes up and caresses my cheek.

"Ava." Her name comes out like a warning. A warning I don't mean.

She traces her fingertip across my lips, leaving a path of fire in her touch.

I cup her cheek and press my forehead to hers as I try to control my feelings.

"Kiss me," she whispers.

Those two words.

Two fucking words.

And I'm undone.

My mouth crashes onto hers, and she immediately opens for me on a gentle moan that I feel all the way down to my cock.

My tongue sweeps inside her mouth.

Just one taste. And that's it. I'll stop after one taste of her.

I pull the tie from her hair, and my fingers slip inside

the silky strands. I angle her head, so I can kiss her deeper.

Her hand is on my chest, sliding up, moving over the T-shirt I really wish I weren't wearing right now and around to the back of my neck. Her leg shifts up mine.

With my other hand, I grab the back of her thigh and move her leg higher. I can feel the heat from her pussy against my thigh, through her clothes and mine.

I want to lick her, taste her, and hear her screaming my name.

I lick her mouth like I want to do to her pussy.

I'm burning. I'm an inferno. I'm out of control.

And I'm never out of control.

But, fuck, she feels good. Too good.

My tongue is plundering her mouth. My hand is moving higher up her thigh, and those soft whimpers that she makes with each climb of my hand are just fueling me on.

I don't know how to stop. If I can stop.

My cock is like granite in my shorts.

I want to fuck her. I want to do everything to her.

She moves closer, pushing herself against me. My hand leaves her thigh and glides up her waist.

She whimpers when my fingers graze the underside of her tit. Blood roars in my ears.

I cup her tit in my hand, skimming my thumb over her nipple.

She groans and presses her pussy against my thigh, trying to find friction.

I want her tits in my mouth. I want to lick and bite her nipples. Drive her as crazy as she's been driving me these past couple of weeks.

Her hand moves down my chest. When she reaches the waistband of my shorts, I shudder and kiss her harder.

I want to feel her small hand around my cock.

But, if she touches me, I'll fuck her. I'm sure of it. I won't be able to stop once that line has been crossed. Because, for some reason, I have zero fucking control around her.

I need my control back.

Using gargantuan strength, I catch hold of her hand before it can slip around my dick, and I slow down our kiss to a stop.

Her eyes open, rejection and hurt lining them.

The last thing I want to do is hurt her. I can't hurt her. I won't hurt her.

I bring her hand to my mouth and kiss it.

"We can't . . . my foot," I say.

"Oh. Would it hurt if we . . ." She leaves the words hanging.

I nod in response.

It's not a total lie. It does hurt every time I come when I jack off to thoughts of her, and it would probably hurt even more if I fucked her, but it would be more than worth the pain.

That's not why I stopped.

I stopped because I can't fuck someone I pay a salary to. I just can't.

But, because I'm a masochist and I just can't help myself, I kiss her one more time.

Just one more taste.

I softly kiss her. Loving the moan that hums from her mouth.

Then, I force myself to stop.

I pull back and wrap my arms around her. She snuggles into me, her head resting on my chest.

I press a kiss to her forehead. "Night, Speedy," I whisper over her skin.

"Night, Hoppy."

I smile at her use of that stupid nickname, and then I stare up at the ceiling, knowing I won't get a second of sleep for the rest of the night.

Not after that. Not with her lying in my arms. And definitely not with me hating on myself for being so fucking weak.

A rule I've stuck to for close to a decade, broken, because I'm so desperate for this woman.

Well, at least I didn't fuck her. So, I guess I have that.

But I have to stay away from her from now on.

Says the man who still has her in his arms.

Tonight. I'll have tonight, and then tomorrow, things will go back to how they were.

She takes care of me while I'm stuck with this fucking thing on my leg, and I pay her a wage for doing so.

I'll go back to jacking off to thoughts of her. I'm definitely going to need to jerk off after this. The chafing on my dick will be immense.

But there will be absolutely no more touching and definitely no more kissing while she works for me.

End of.

Chapter Eighteen

Ava

I WAKE TO FIND Gucci lying asleep where Gabe was last night.

I glance at the clock to see it's nine thirty. It's not like me to sleep this late.

Sleeping with Gabe must have done it. I've never been so comfortable as I was last night. Helps that his bed is the most comfortable bed ever, but it was him. Being with him. In his arms.

And, holy crap, we kissed!

The memory slams into me, and a big goofy grin appears on my mouth.

I bury my face into the pillow, and I get a strong whiff of Gabe.

When I woke up last night to the feel of his hand touching my face, I thought I was dreaming. Until I opened my eyes and looked at him.

And then I asked him to kiss me. I can't believe I was so bold!

But then he did, and oh my God . . .

It was everything and more than I'd thought it would be.

And I've thought a lot about Gabe kissing me. Especially since I've been living here with him. Well, I've thought about more than just kissing.

Let's just say, my fingers have been busy in bed since I moved in here.

Gabe is an incredible kisser. I've never been kissed so thoroughly and with so much passion as he kissed me.

I've never felt more wanted.

Not even by Jeremy.

Jeremy is nothing compared to Gabe.

They're not even comparable.

Gabe is amazing. A jerk at times, but that's part of the charm. I like everything about him, including his assholish ways.

Actually, I more than like him. And I want him so very badly.

I was gutted that he stopped us last night before we could go any further, but I understood completely. The last thing I want to do is cause his foot any more damage than I already have.

I can wait to sleep with him.

If he wants to, that is.

But, going by the boner he was sporting last night while kissing me, then I'd say he wants to.

Pushing the covers back, I climb out of his bed. Gucci lifts her head.

"Come on, girl. Toilet time."

She jumps off Gabe's bed and follows me out into the living room.

Gabe's out on the terrace.

My heart jumps at the sight of him, sitting on a chair, smoking a cigarette.

Gucci trots on ahead of me, out onto the terrace.

Gabe turns his head at the sound of her. Then, he glances up at me when I walk out onto the terrace. But he barely looks at me before he moves his eyes away and takes another drag of his cigarette.

But what I did see on his face makes my stomach feel hollow.

He regrets kissing me last night.

My eyes move, and I see a glass filled with clear liquid on the table. I'd like to think it's water, but something tells me it's not.

"Morning," I say, my voice sounding rough.

I walk over to the railing and rest my arms against it, looking out at Hollywood.

I hear his glass clink against the glass tabletop as he picks it up, but he doesn't say anything.

Even though I feel a little sick inside, I force myself to turn around and face him.

I notice now that his hair is damp, and he's dressed smarter than he has been for the last couple of weeks. He's been wearing athletic shorts, as they're all he can get on over the boot, but today, he's wearing black cargo shorts and a white short-sleeved shirt.

He must have bathed without my help. And he had to have taken the boot off to get the shorts on and then put it back on. Couldn't have been easy for him to manage alone. Clearly, he didn't want me helping him.

I rest my back against the railing. I see Gucci is sitting by the pool, her head tilted to the side, watching me.

I look back to Gabe, who definitely does not want to

look at me. "Have you eaten?" I ask him. "I can make breakfast—"

"I'm fine." Another drag of his cigarette. A tap to get the ash in the tray. Another drink of his liquor.

"Okay. Well, I was going to make coffee. Would you like—"

"I said, I'm fine." His eyes snap up to mine.

Well, at least he's looking at me now, but honestly, I wish he weren't.

His eyes look hard and cold. A complete contrast to how he was looking at me in the dark of his room last night.

A chill coats my skin even though it's warm. I rub my hands over my arms.

He looks away, drains his glass, and puts out his cigarette. Getting his crutches, he gets to his feet. "I have a few meetings today, so I'll be out for most of the day."

He never said anything yesterday about having meetings today.

A little voice whispers in my head, *He wants to get away from you.*

"Oh. Right. Do you need me to drive you?"

"No. I arranged for a driver to take me." He starts to head for the door to go back inside.

"What should I do today then?"

He stops moving, the line of his shoulders taut. "Do whatever the fuck you want, Ava. You don't have to check with me. I'm not your boyfriend."

And there it is.

"But you are my boss." I force my voice to sound stronger than I feel.

The silence that follows is intense and painful.

"Then, as your boss, I'm telling you to take the fucking day off," he bites out.

Then, he's gone, and I'm left standing here.

I go over to the table and pick the glass up.

Vodka.

I grab the ashtray and take that and the glass inside where I wash them out. I feed Gucci.

Then, I stand here, in his apartment, feeling hurt and a little lost, not really sure what to do with myself.

Chapter Nineteen

Ava

AFTER FEELING SORRY FOR myself for a few minutes, I got mad with the big jerk and decided to do what he'd said to do. So, I took the day off.

Gucci and I went to a dog park and had fun. A lot of people were interested in her, so I got to chatting with a few of them, which was nice, and it took my mind off of Gabe the asshole.

After I dropped Gucci back at the apartment and fed her a lunch of hay and carrots, I went shopping alone.

Solo shopping always helps to perk me up.

I bought some new pajamas and sunglasses. And a pair of Choos that I couldn't afford. Also, I bought Gucci a new coat and a water bowl.

When I was done, I stopped and had sushi.

I didn't really feel that hungry, but I thought I'd better eat.

When I finally came back to the apartment, I was

expecting to encounter Gabe. But there was just Gucci waiting for me.

So, I let her out onto the terrace, cleaned up after her, and then made her dinner. Then, I got started on dinner for Gabe and me. Even though I wasn't hungry, I figured he would be.

Turned out I was wrong, because he didn't come home for dinner.

I broke down and texted him at nine to check if he was okay. But he never replied.

And, now, it's ten thirty, and he's not back. He's been out all day.

Even though I'm still mad at him, I am getting kind of worried.

I know he's a grown man, but he's also on crutches, and getting around for him isn't the easiest.

I'm not really sure what to do.

I'm sitting on the sofa with Gucci when there's a commotion of voices and laughter in the hallway.

Picking up Gucci, I get to my feet just as Gabe comes hobbling into the living room, minus his crutches, with about ten people accompanying him. And one of those people is beautiful and tall and blonde, and he has his arm around her.

Just like he had it around me last night.

Pain and jealousy shoot up my spine.

"Speedy." His voice slurs a little, and there's a smirk on his face, but nothing's cheery about the way he's looking at me.

His eyes are cold and empty. Like he's telling me with his stare that he doesn't care about me or what happened between us last night.

And it really fucking hurts.

"Is that a goat?" the woman propping him up says.

I ignore her.

"Where are your crutches?" I ask him.

He shrugs. "I lost them."

"You lost them? How the hell do you lose a pair of crutches?"

"I don't know, *Mom*. I just did."

The blonde laughs. Gabe slips out from under her arm and walks—well, staggers closer to me. He reeks of liquor and cigarettes.

"Now, be a good little employee, and get my guests some drinks." He taps me on my nose with his fingertip and moves past me.

Um, what the fuck just happened?

I turn, my eyes following him. "What the hell was that?"

He stops and looks back to me. His eyes are almost black.

His friends have all scattered around the living room, some going out onto the terrace.

"I said, get my guests some drinks. You work here, right?"

"Last I knew, I was here to care for you, not be a waitress for your friends."

His face darkens. "Fine. I'll get their fucking drinks." He hobbles away, in the direction of the kitchen.

I go to my room and put Gucci safely in there, and then I go into the kitchen to find him pouring drinks.

"Where have you been?" My tone is snippy.

"Out," he answers without looking at me.

"I got that. But all day? I thought you just had a few

meetings, and then you'd be home. I was worried. I texted you."

His eyes lift to mine. "My phone died."

I try to control my temper and soften my voice, but it doesn't work. "And you couldn't borrow a phone to let me know you were okay? You must've known I would worry."

"No. I didn't know. Because you're not my fucking wife!" he roars.

The force of his anger takes me back a step.

Tears hit the backs of my eyes, but I refuse to cry. "I know I'm not."

"So, stop fucking acting like you are!"

"I'm not!" I yell back, my hands curling into fists at my sides. "I'm just trying to be a good friend."

His hard eyes burn into mine. "But that's just it. We're not friends, Ava. You work for me. End of story."

Well, if that isn't a slap in the face. My face stings with the pain from his words.

"Okay." I wrap my arms around my chest. "I understand."

"You understand what?"

"That you're a heartless fucking bastard!" I spin on my heel and start to walk away.

He laughs harshly. "I never once claimed to have a heart. And do you talk to all your bosses that way, Speedy? Maybe that's why you got fired from your last job."

That has me stopping and turning back to him. Undiluted rage is burning in my veins. "My last boss would never have treated me the way you just did."

Some unnamed emotion flickers across his face. "I don't have to put up with this shit," he bites.

I laugh. There's no humor in it. "That makes two of us. And you don't have to worry about putting up with me anymore. Because I quit." I stare him hard in the eyes. "Clearly, you don't need me to take care of you anymore. You look like you're doing just fine. So, I'll be out of your hair in the morning." I don't give him a chance to say anything in response. I storm out of the kitchen and to my room, and I slam the door shut. I fall back against it, breathing hard.

Fucking asshole!

Tears fill my eyes. But I won't cry. I won't fucking cry.

I press the palms of my hands to my eyes, stopping the tears from coming, and I take cleansing deep breaths.

I feel Gucci nudge her head against my leg. I move my hands from my eyes, and she's staring at me.

"I made us homeless again," I tell her. "I'm sorry, baby girl. But I'll figure something out. I always do."

"Baaahhh."

I like to think she's telling me it's okay, but then she nudges my leg again and trots to the door, giving it a butt with her head, and I know she needs to go outside.

"Ah, right now, Gucci?" The last thing I want to do at this moment in time is go out there.

"Baaahhh."

"Crap," I mutter. "Okay."

I grab a hoodie, the elevator key, and my cell. I slide my feet into my flip-flops. Then, I pick Gucci up and leave my room.

I'm going to have to walk through the living room.

I take a deep breath. Holding my head up high, I quickly start walking through the living room.

The music is playing. A couple of women are dancing together.

I don't want to seek Gabe out, but my eyes do.

And they immediately lock with his.

He's sitting on the sofa with that blonde plastered up against his side. She's leaning in close, speaking in his ear.

Jealousy explodes in my chest, spreading the agony out to fill my whole body. Breathing through the hurt, I force my feet to move faster, so I'm almost breaking into a jog.

When I reach the elevator, I jab the button a few times. "Come on, come on," I mutter, tapping my foot, desperate for it to hurry up and arrive.

It pings its arrival, and I step inside the safety of the elevator.

"Ava."

My eyes find Gabe hobbling toward the elevator.

I jab the button for the ground floor. I don't want to talk to him, no matter how childish that might be. I just want to get away from him right now.

"Where are you going?" he says, his voice demanding.

But the doors close on his words, and the lift starts to descend.

I exhale and hug Gucci tight to my chest, burying my face in her soft fur.

When I reach the ground floor, the lobby is empty. The security guard must have just stepped away from his desk.

I walk out of the lobby, heading for the back of the building, and out into the communal garden.

Once outside, I put Gucci down on the grass, and I go take a seat on one of the benches.

I get my phone out and bring up Candy Crush to play while I wait for her to do her business. I'm not exactly in any rush to go back upstairs.

But something makes me change my mind, and I shut Candy Crush down and open up Google.

Then, I type in Gabe's name in the Search bar and hit Enter.

The screen fills with links and stories. I go to Recent News.

At the top is *Radar Online*. Always the first with a story.

I click on the link, and the headline says something about Gabe appearing to have a broken leg.

Broken foot, dipshits.

They need to do better with their so-called journalism. And then it goes on to say how he's been hitting up the bars all day.

So much for his meetings.

There are pictures of him from earlier. In one picture, he's in a booth with a bunch of people I don't recognize, and next to him is a pretty brunette, his arm around her.

Someone's been busy tonight.

Fury rains down on me.

I just can't believe him! The fucking asshole!

He was out partying with other women while I was feeling crappy all day, sitting and worrying about him when he hadn't come home, thinking something had happened to him.

Going out and getting drunk isn't the smartest thing to do when you've got a broken foot, but obviously, he doesn't care.

So, why the hell should I?

Because you have feelings for him.

Ugh! I hate that I like him. The big fucking jerk.

It's clear that he doesn't give two shits about me. He's up there with another woman, doing God knows what with her right now.

The thought of him with her makes me feel physically sick.

At least I know he won't be having sex with her because of his foot. That's the reason he wouldn't sleep with me.

Or maybe he was just saying that. Maybe he just doesn't want you, my insecurities scream at me.

This morning, he acted like last night never happened, and then he went out partying and brought people back to his apartment. And he's currently cozied up on the sofa with that blonde.

So, yeah, clearly, it's me he doesn't want.

Well, fine.

But, when I do go back up there, if he's in his bedroom with that woman, then I'm going.

I'll pack my stuff and leave tonight. Because there is no way that I'm sleeping in that apartment while he fucks someone else in his bedroom.

He might not care about me, but I do have feelings for him, and I'm not putting myself through that.

I shove my cell in my pocket and look over at Gucci. She's running around, jumping in and out of the bushes, looking happy.

Well, at least one of us is happy.

I let out a long, sad sigh and stare up at the sky, trying not to think about what's going on up in Gabe's apartment right at this moment. Or what he might be doing with the blonde. If he's touching her like he touched me last night.

Instead, I force myself to think about what I'm going to do tomorrow when I'm once again homeless and jobless.

Chapter Twenty

Gabe

I'M AN ASSHOLE.

A complete and utter fucking asshole.

I've hurt Speedy. The one person who didn't deserve to be hurt by me. The one person I didn't want to hurt, but I went and did it anyway. And I did it fucking spectacularly.

I saw the hurt in her eyes, and I put it there. It almost brought me to my knees.

I could barely look at her this morning, knowing I was going to hurt her.

And I know she thinks I've been fooling around with that blonde tonight, but I haven't.

I couldn't even if I wanted to. And I don't.

I just want Speedy.

She's been on my mind all day. I can't think of anything but her. How she tasted. How she looked in my bed. How she felt against me.

Knowing all these things makes me want her so much more.

I had to get out of the apartment today. I couldn't be around her. So, I lied and said I had meetings.

I didn't.

I called up some drinking buddies, and I was out all day.

But I knew I had to come home at some point, but being here, alone with her, just wasn't an option. I knew what would happen the second I saw her.

I wouldn't be able to stop myself.

So, I invited everyone back here. And I acted like the fucking bastard that I am.

But, now, she's gone, and I don't know where she is.

I'm worried. It's late. I don't want her and Gucci out alone.

I tried calling her, and it went to voice mail. I texted her, asking her to come back home, but she's ignored it.

Guess this is a taste of my own medicine for ignoring her text earlier and making her worry.

I cleared the apartment of everyone right after she left.

I want to go look for her, but I'm stuck because of my goddamn foot. I can't fucking drive.

And her car keys are still here on the coffee table, and so are mine, so she's out there, walking around.

I'm going to call the driver back and have him drive me around until I find her.

I've just pressed call on his number when I hear the elevator ping its arrival.

I hang up the phone and move toward the elevator.

She comes in with Gucci in her arms. Her eyes look red, like she's been crying.

You did that, asshole.

"Where have you been?" My words come out sharper than intended.

She puts Gucci down and walks past me without a word.

"Ava, I asked, where the fuck have you been?"

She whirls around, her eyes narrowed. "What business is it of yours?"

"You live in my place. That makes it my business."

She laughs. "Fuck off, Gabriel. I was going to go in the morning, but screw this shit. I'm going now."

An emotion I don't recognize grips my chest.

"Don't be fucking stupid."

"You're stupid! And a gigantic asshole! And I'm out of here." She moves quickly through the apartment.

I'm not as fast as she is because of this damn boot, but I catch up to her in the hallway. I grab hold of her wrist, and she whirls around on me. Her eyes are wide and fired up, her cheeks flushed.

She's never looked hotter than she does in this moment.

"What are you doing?"

I don't answer. I push her up against the wall and kiss her. Hard.

She doesn't resist me either. She opens up for me straightaway, kissing me back just as forcefully as I'm kissing her.

It's hungry and wet and deep and easily the hottest fucking kiss I've ever had.

She's sexy as hell. I can't get enough of her.

Then, without warning, her hands that were caressing my chest a second ago are now pushing me away.

She stares at me, breathing heavily, her lips swollen from our bruising kiss. "You don't just get to kiss me and hold me all night and then treat me like garbage the next day and bring other women home and do God knows what with them and then kiss me when they're gone, Gabriel! It doesn't work that way!"

"You're right. And I'm sorry. I'm sorry that I acted like a complete asshole this morning and tonight." I take her face in my hands, unable to not touch her. "But, I swear to you, the only woman I've touched today is you. The only woman I've touched in weeks is you."

Her anger seems to calm a bit with my admission, but she's still pissed off, and she has a right to be.

"Why were you an asshole today?" Her tone is filled with annoyance, but there's a vulnerability there, too, that makes my chest ache.

I sigh, lowering my eyes for a moment before looking back at her. "I just ... I have a rule. I never sleep with people I work with or who work for me. And I'd never broken that rule until last night."

"Oh."

"It's not an excuse, but it threw me for a loop that a rule I'd worked to follow for a long time, I broke so easily with you. It made me realize just how deeply you were under my skin. I didn't feel in control. And, when I don't feel in control, I'm an asshole."

Warmth fills her eyes. "You're forgiven." Her words are soft, but they lift the weight I was carrying around all day off my shoulders.

"So ... you broke your rule for me." She bites her lower lip.

"Clearly, I have no self-control when it comes to you, as I just broke my rule again." I press my thumb against her mouth, pulling her lip free from her teeth.

A light flickers in her eyes. "No, you didn't. I don't work for you. I quit, remember?"

Yes, she fucking did.

A smile spreads across my face. "I guess that changes things."

"I guess it—"

My mouth is back on hers before she's even finished that sentence.

This kiss is different from our first and second. It's less hurried. Maybe it's because we both know that, this time, this kiss will end up with me inside her.

Guess the third time is a charm.

She tugs at my shirt and starts unbuttoning it.

I stop kissing her to grab the back of my shirt, and I pull it over my head and toss it to the floor. Then, I take hold of her hoodie and remove it. Then, her tank top is next, leaving her in just her bra.

Black and lacy.

Thank the fucking Lord in heaven.

I cup her tits, my thumbs grazing over her nipples.

She whimpers, her hips seeking me out.

I push my good leg between her thighs as I bring my head down, pressing one hand on the wall for support, and I suck her nipple through her bra.

"Gabe."

The sound of her moaning my name is the best fucking sound I've ever heard. She's grinding her pussy against my leg. I can feel the heat of it through our clothes.

I need her horizontal and naked.

If I didn't have this fucking thing on my leg, I'd be on my knees right now, tasting her pussy.

My hands go to her ass, and I pick her up.

"What are you doing? Put me down. You'll hurt your leg."

"Hush. I've carried bags that weighed more than you."

"But you didn't have a broken foot then."

"Speedy?"

"Yeah."

"Be quiet, and let me do my thing."

"Your thing?"

"Yeah. I'm the guy. And I can carry my girl to my bed and fuck her, broken foot or not."

She bites down on a smile and then leans in close to my lips. "Okay, Gabe, do your thing."

Then, she kisses me, her lips moving down my jaw and my neck, as I walk us into my bedroom.

I drop her down on the bed, and she lands with a soft oomph.

I take her flip-flop from her foot. Seems she lost one in transit. Then, I reach over and take hold of her yoga pants, pulling them down her legs.

Black lacy panties to match the bra.

"Fuck, you're hot. I jacked off to thoughts of you every fucking chance I had, and nothing I pictured was as good as what I'm looking at right now."

I reach a finger out and drag it down the front of her pussy.

She's soaked.

"You want me, Ava?" I put my finger in my mouth and suck.

Her eyes are wide and following my every move. Her taste hits my tongue.

"You taste so good," I hum. "Even better than I imagined."

Her lips are parted, her breaths coming in short.

I meet her eyes. "You didn't answer my question, Ava."

She lifts her chin. The spark of defiance in her eyes zip-lines excitement straight to my cock.

"Yes, I want you. As much as you want me."

I follow her stare to my dick, which is currently trying to break free from my shorts.

And I want him out of them and in her hands and her mouth and her pussy, but first things first.

I get up on the bed and lie on my back, and then I pull her over to straddle me.

"Take off your bra. I want to see your tits."

She reaches back, unclips her bra, and pulls it off.

If there's a God in heaven, I'm thanking him right now.

She has the greatest pair of tits I have ever seen in my life. Ever. And I've seen a lot of tits.

They are full and pert with rosy-pink nipples that are just the perfect size for those perfect-as-fuck tits.

"You have no fucking idea how long I've waited to see these babies."

"I have a pretty good idea." She laughs softly.

I cup them with my hands.

"Baby, if I died now, I would die a happy man."

She laughs again. Then, I sit up and take one of those luscious tits in my mouth, and she stops laughing.

"Gabe," she gasps my name, her hands gripping my hair.

She's pressed up against my cock, her pussy rubbing against me, making me impossibly harder.

I feel like I'm about to explode. Or implode. Or both.

I move to the other tit and lavish it with the attention it deserves.

Her hands move to my shoulders, gripping, and she starts riding my cock through the barrier of our clothes.

Heat blazes under my skin wherever she touches me. I can't get enough of her.

Pressing one last kiss to each of my girls, I flop back onto my pillows. Then, I pat her on the ass. "Come up here, baby. Sit on my face. I want to taste you."

She bites her lip and then gets to her feet. Standing over me, she pulls her panties down her legs, stepping out of them.

She's completely bare.

Fuck yeah.

"Get that pussy here. Now." I beckon with my finger.

She walks up the bed and lowers to her knees on either side of my head. And I don't waste any time. I grab hold of her hips and pull her down, straight onto my mouth.

She groans, falling forward, holding on to the headboard.

I lick a path down her clit to her pussy, and I plunge my tongue inside.

A desperate, feral noise falls from her mouth.

I slide my hands to her ass. I'm itching to slip a finger between her ass cheeks and into her ass. I want to be inside every part of her. But it's our first time together, and I don't know where she stands on anal play. I don't want to fuck this up, so I keep my hands where they are, and I focus on fucking her pussy with my tongue.

Then, I move upward, and I start to work on her clit. Licking and sucking on it, teasing it with light grazes of my teeth.

She's whimpering and chanting my name. Her hands come off the headboard and cup her breasts, her fingers playing with her nipples.

God, she's so fucking hot.

I tip my face back and stare up at her. "I want you to fuck my face, Ava. Go wild."

Then, I plunge my tongue straight back inside her.

She cries out. Her hips move, riding my face, taking what she wants. It's such a fucking turn-on.

It's less than a minute before I feel her movements get frantic, her muscles tightening around my tongue, and I know she's close.

She screams my name and bears down on my face, coming hard.

I keep licking her until her body is shaking. Then, I lift her off my face and move her backward, placing her on my body, straddling me.

Her head is on my chest. I wipe my mouth with the back of my hand.

"You okay?" I press my lips to her hair.

She lifts her head. Lust blazes in her eyes. She brings her mouth to mine and kisses me.

"I want you inside me," she whispers.

"Unbuckle my shorts," I tell her.

She moves quickly down my body. She unbuckles the belt on my shorts, undoes the button, and pulls down the zipper.

She glances back at the boot on my leg. "How are we going to do this?" she asks.

We either take the boot off—and ain't no one got time for that right now—or I fuck her with my shorts on.

Shorts, it is.

"You're gonna have to ride me, baby. Pull my shorts to my knees, and then hop up onto my cock."

I slap her ass, and she laughs, shaking her head.

"Sure thang, sugar."

She shifts to the side, pulling my shorts and boxers to my knees, and I lift my ass to make it easier.

"Oh my," she says, looking at my cock.

Damn straight, baby.

"I told you he was big."

Her eyes meet mine, glowing with desire. "And you weren't kidding."

"Babe, I never joke when it comes to my cock." I reach over to my nightstand and grab a condom out of the drawer. "Now, suit me up, so I can fuck you good."

She takes the condom from me and rips it open with her teeth. It's such a turn-on.

"Fuck, you're hot," I tell her.

She smiles and raises a knowing brow, and then she rolls the condom on my cock.

"Come here, Ava." I beckon to her with my finger.

She moves over my body, bringing her face to mine. I cup her cheeks, staring up at her.

I can't remember ever wanting a woman more than I want her.

"I love it when you call me Ava," she says softly, sounding almost vulnerable.

Funny thing, that's just how I feel every moment I'm with her. Vulnerable.

I take her mouth with mine and kiss her deeply. Exactly how I'm going to fuck her.

"Put me inside you," I say against her lips. "I want to feel you."

She moves back and rises up onto her knees. She looks like a fucking goddess.

She takes my cock in her hand and lines it up with the only place I want to be right now.

She rubs the head against her slippery entrance. And then she slides down on my cock, taking all of me inside.

"Fuck," I groan, my eyes rolling back in my head. "You feel fucking amazing."

She's so tight and hot and snug.

I look at her. She looks as overwhelmed as I feel.

"So do you. I've never ..." She squeezes her eyes shut. "You're so deep, Gabe."

"It's because my cock is so big."

She laughs softly, her eyes opening back up. "And modest."

"Just honest." I grin.

Then, I nudge my hips up, pushing me in even further.

"Oh, fuck," she whimpers.

"Ride my dick, Ava. Show me what you've got."

A look of determination flashes through her eyes. Excitement vibrates through my body. By saying that, I knew I would piss her off, which in turn would set her off.

She rises up, almost bringing me out to the tip. Then, she slams back down on my cock.

"Fuck yeah, that's it, baby. Ride me hard."

And ride me hard, she does.

She fucks me with wild abandon. Her pussy squeezes my dick. Her magnificent tits bounce with every move she makes.

My hands grip her hips.

God, she's fucking incredible. I've never felt anything like her before.

I let go of her hips and tug on her nipples.

"Oh God, Gabe," she moans, her head tipping forward.

She bears down on my cock, circling her hips, getting the friction she needs on her clit.

I drop a hand to her pussy and flick her clit with my finger. She cries out and starts bucking on my dick.

Hell yeah.

I slap her ass with my other hand. Once. Twice.

I pinch her clit.

She fucks me harder.

Skin slapping skin.

The sweetest sound in the world.

And, as good as her riding me is, I like to be in control. If I didn't have a broken foot right now, I'd be fucking her all over this bed.

But this is all I can do, so it'll have to do for now.

Reaching up, I grab a fistful of her hair and pull her down to my mouth. I run my tongue over her lips, across her cheek, until I reach her ear. "My turn," I tell her.

I bring her mouth back to mine, and I start to fuck her from underneath.

I'm plundering her mouth with my tongue, my hand on the back of her head. My other hand is spanned over her ass, holding her in place, as I piston my hips up and down, fucking her hard and wild. Her tits are crushed to my chest, sweat slicking between us, as I fuck like there's no tomorrow.

"Oh God," she cries against my lips. "I'm close."

"That's it, Ava. Come for me, baby."

She starts chanting my name, and it's never sounded sweeter, hearing her say it with so much want and need.

Her body is trembling.

I'm burning all over. Every inch of my body is on fire, desperate for release. My balls have tightened up, ready to explode.

I feel her body stiffen against me, and then she screams, a slew of, "Fuck," and, "Oh God," and, "Gabe," flying out of her mouth.

A shock of pleasure shoots down my spine. My muscles tighten. Seconds later, I'm right there with her. Coming so fucking hard that I suffer temporary blindness.

My foot ignites with pain.

But I don't care because I feel fucking awesome.

Her body sags onto mine. I wrap my arms around her.

She tilts her face up and presses a kiss to my jaw. I turn my face to her and capture her swollen lips with mine, tenderly kissing her. A complete contrast to the way I just fucked her.

"Mmm," she murmurs. "That was amazing."

"It was better than amazing. It was out of this world. It was astro-fucking-nomical."

She laughs softly. I hold her closer.

"We should clean up."

"Not yet," I tell her. "We'll clean up in a minute."

I'm feeling lazy, but the truth is, I'm not ready to let her go just yet. And this isn't like me. Normally, the instant I come, I can't wait to get out of bed and get my pants back on.

Wanting to stay inside her and hold her in my arms like this is a completely new experience for me, and I want to savor it. I want to savor her.

And, when she doesn't pull away, instead letting out a sound of contentment, snuggling deeper into me, it lights up the dark parts inside me.

It's then when I realize just how truly fucked I am.

Because I like Ava. Quite possibly too much.

And she's far too good for someone as fucked up as me.

But, right now, the selfish part of me doesn't care. The selfish part of me wants to take every good thing she gives me, and I want to give her every good thing back in return.

I want to make her happy.

I just don't know if, or for how long, I'm capable of doing so before I wreck things and end up hurting her—again.

Chapter Twenty-One

Ava

I WAKE, AND I'M alone. Gabe's side of the bed is empty. I have a flashback to yesterday morning, and my stomach sinks.

What if he regrets having sex with me?

It's still dark out. I check the clock, and it says one a.m.

I sit up and slide my legs out of bed. Gucci lifts her head from the chair she's sleeping on.

"Go back to sleep, baby," I tell her.

She lays her head back down. I get to my feet and pull my panties on, and then I get one of Gabe's T-shirts from his chest of drawers. I pull it on and go to find him.

He's out on the terrace, smoking. His chest is bare, and he's still wearing the shorts from last night.

"Hi." I linger in the doorway.

"Hey." A smile lightens his face, and a weight lifts off my chest.

I pad over to him. He reaches out and takes my hand, pulling me down onto the sun lounger with him.

He drops his good leg to the floor, so I can sit between his legs.

His free arm wraps around my waist. I slide my hand over his, and he links our fingers.

I rest my head back on his chest. I can feel his heart beating against my back.

The smell of his cigarette smoke surrounds us, but it doesn't bother me like it used to. In fact, I'm growing to like the smell. Because it's him.

"You couldn't sleep?" I ask him.

"No." He takes a pull on his cigarette and blows the smoke away from me.

"Are you . . . having regrets? About . . . us?"

"No." His hand comes to my chin, and he tips my head back, so I'm looking at him. "No regrets at all. I just needed a smoke. I always need a smoke after great sex."

"Great sex?"

His eyes twinkle back at me in the dark. "Astro-fucking-nomical sex."

"Better." I laugh softly, and I rest my head back on his chest, running my fingers over the soft hairs there.

"You . . . don't have any regrets, do you?" His voice is surprisingly tentative.

I tip my face up to look at him again. "No."

I didn't realize his expression was tense until I see it relax with my answer.

I run my fingers over his cheek. "I could never regret last night, Gabe. I've wanted you for a long time."

He takes hold of my hand and kisses the palm. "Me, too. But not as long as you've wanted me 'cause you've wanted in my pants ever since you saw me in my first movie, right?"

"Jackass."

I lightly slap his chest, and he chuckles.

"Just kiddin'." He kisses the top of my head.

He's not wrong though. I have wanted him since I first saw him onscreen.

But he's nothing like I thought he would be.

He's even better.

But then I worry he thinks I want him because he's famous.

"I'm not just here because—"

"I know, Speedy."

I look at him. "I just don't want you to think I'm here because you're famous. I'm here for this." I tap my finger on his forehead. "And this." I draw a heart with my finger on his chest. "And, of course, this." I grin as I slide my hand down and cup his cock between his legs.

"Who could blame you? It is massive." He smirks and takes a pull on his cigarette. "And, just so you know, Speedy, I only want you for your big tits and tight pussy."

"Jerk." I narrow my eyes at him, my lips fighting a smile.

"And your smart, argumentative, nonstop-talking mouth." He covers my lips with his, softly kissing me, making my stomach flip. "And just . . . you. I kinda like you. A lot."

My heart beats double time in my chest.

"Good. 'Cause I kinda like you a lot, too."

I snuggle back into him, my insides glowing with joy as I enjoy the warmth of his hard body. And the gentle sounds of the city below. The burn of his cigarette each time he takes a drag. The way he exhales the smoke.

"We do need to think about how this is going to work though." His voice cuts through the silence.

"How what's going to work?"

He takes one last pull on his cigarette and then stubs it out. "You and me. And the fact that I won't fuck you while you work for me."

I sit up and turn in his lap, straddling him. His hands grip my hips.

"Okay. But I don't work for you anymore, remember?"

He frowns. "I won't have you jobless just so I can fuck you."

"Isn't that my decision to make?"

"No. It's our decision to make."

Our.

I like the sound of that.

"Well, I don't know about you, but I want this— whatever's happening between us—to keep happening. So, if that means I can no longer work for you, then that's the way it has to be."

"What will you do for money?"

"I'll be fine. I have some savings that I can use until I get another job."

He rubs his forehead, looking frustrated. "I don't want you using your savings, Speedy."

"It's fine."

"No, it's not." He tips his head back, eyes going to the sky, and sighs. "It's just . . . I can't fuck you while you're my employee. But I don't know how not to fuck you." He looks at me, eyes filled with turmoil. "I want you all the fucking time."

A shiver runs down my spine. "And I want you, too. So, I'll find another job and move out of your place."

"No fucking way." His head snaps back down.

"You're not sleeping in your shitty car just so we can keep screwing."

"My car is not shitty. And I wasn't suggesting sleeping in my car. I'll find another place to live."

"And how are you going to do that with no job?"

"I don't know." I sigh. "But I'll figure it out. It's my problem to fix, Gabe."

The look that flickers over his face tells me he doesn't agree with that statement. "I'm fucking you, so that makes you mine. And any problem of yours is mine to fix."

"Is that so?"

"Yeah. And, while we're at it, while we're sleeping together, you're not fucking anyone else. Got it?"

Ha! Like I'm so interested in sleeping with anyone else.

"Goes both ways," I tell him.

He laughs dryly. "Yeah, like I want to fuck anyone else. We're in this position because the only person I want to be inside of is you."

Holy shivers.

"Well, that's sorted then."

"That might be sorted, but your job problem isn't."

"Gabe"—I sigh—"it'll be fine."

"I want you to work for me again."

Now, I'm the one frowning. "No."

"Look, just listen . . . I want you to work for me. But I won't pay you a salary. I'll just pay you an hourly rate. So, you work for me during the day, and we keep our hands off each other during that time, purely platonic. Boss and employee. And then, when you clock off at night . . ."

"I get off the clock and onto your cock."

Laughter bursts from him. "That's one way of putting it. So, what do you think?"

I tap my finger to my lips. "Will that work for you though? Because, even when you're not paying me, technically, you'll still be my boss."

"I can live with that. So long as we're screwing off the clock."

I smile. "Okay then. I accept your proposition to have sex off the clock."

He grins seductively. "And you keep living here."

"Yes."

"And sleeping in my bed."

"Yes, Gabe." I lean in and press my lips to his, silencing him.

His fingers slide into my hair, his mouth humming a sound of appreciation.

The kiss quickly deepens into something more.

"I want you," he says against my mouth.

"You already have me."

And he does. He has all of me.

"You look good in my shirt," he murmurs. "But I prefer you out of it."

His hands find the hem of his T-shirt, and he pulls it over my head.

"No bra. I like." He runs his finger between my cleavage. "New house rule: No bras will be worn in the apartment."

"That go for working hours?"

His eyes meet mine, a dirty glint in them. "Definitely."

"You sure? I know how easily you get distracted by my girls."

"Um, I think you'll find they're mine now." He cups

my breasts in his hands and lazily rubs his thumbs over my nipples.

Lust bolts straight to my clit.

"Yours?"

"Yep. I licked them, so they're mine."

I laugh loudly. "I don't think it actually works like that."

He lifts a brow. "I think you'll find that it does. And possession is nine-tenths of the law." He provocatively gives them a squeeze. "So, yep, they're definitely mine. And I'm going to name them."

"Okay, Master of My Boobs, what are you going to call them?"

He stares at my breasts and then pushes them together. "Pinky and Perky."

Another shot of laughter flies from my mouth. "Pinky and Perky? God, you're odd and a little bit crazy."

He grins up at me. "Just crazy about my girls." Then, he presses his face into my boobs and starts to motorboat them.

"Get off!" I squeal, grabbing at his head, trying to pull him off.

But then he captures one of my nipples in his mouth and gives it a hard suck.

"Oh God." I melt against him. My fingers slide into his hair.

He lavishes attention on both my breasts. His hands grip my ass, and one of his fingers slides under my panties, teasing at my hole.

"I need you to fuck me," I gasp.

The next thing I know, I'm moving, and Gabe is carrying me over to the railing. I don't even argue about his leg. I just want him.

He puts me to my feet and turns me around. I take hold of the railing. His hands grab my hips, and he yanks my ass back, so I'm bent over.

"Can anyone see us up here?" I ask him.

"Do you care?"

I stare back at him. His eyes are dark and inviting. I shake my head.

He pulls my panties down. I kick them off and widen my stance, ready for him.

He groans. "You look so fucking sexy, Ava. Like a goddess." He slaps my ass, making me moan. "*My* goddess."

His.

I definitely like the sound of that.

I hear the zipper on his shorts pull down.

Excitement slides through me.

"Are you on birth control?" he asks, his voice raspy with desire.

"Yes."

"I can go inside and get a condom, or I can fuck you like this. It's your call. Just know that I'm clean. I always suit up."

I glance back at him. "Always?"

His stare fixes on mine. His eyes are as dark as the night surrounding us. "Always," he reaffirms.

"So, why do you want to go bare with me?"

The question seems to surprise him. Or maybe it's not the question that surprises him, but the fact that he's just realized that he asked to do something with me that he's never done before.

"I don't know," he says honestly, his voice sounding raw. "All I do know is that I want you like I've never wanted anyone in my life. And I want to feel you. All of you."

His words touch me everywhere.

"Am I getting the condom?"

"No."

Possession flashes in his eyes. His expression is taut with need.

He grabs hold of my hips with both hands and slams his cock inside me.

I cry out at the wanted invasion.

"Fuck," he groans, stilling. "You feel incredible." His hand slides up my spine, and he gathers my hair up and winds it around his hand.

He presses a kiss to my back and then tugs my hair. "Hold on tight 'cause I'm gonna fuck you hard."

Biting my lip, I stare over my shoulder at him.

He looks beautiful. Stunning.

And he's all mine.

Every rough, gorgeous, dirty part of him.

"I like hard. So, give me everything you've got."

His nostrils flare. "Fuck, you're gorgeous."

His fingers on my hip bite into my skin. He tightens his hold on my hair, and then he starts to fuck me like I've never been fucked before.

Hard and raw and maddening.

And I never want it to end.

Any of it.

Chapter Twenty-Two

Gabe

LIFE IS GOOD. ACTUALLY, it's fucking great.

Things with Speedy are going really well. For the past three weeks, we've stuck to our rule. We keep our hands to ourselves during the day, and at night, we fuck like rabbits on Viagra.

I'm surprised I've managed not to fuck her in the daylight hours because she's so damn sexy. But the wait until she's off the clock is like the best kind of foreplay.

I can't get enough of her. And it's not just the sex. It's her. She's smart and funny—no one has ever made me laugh like she does—and she's just so fucking gorgeous. I love spending time with her. She's like no woman I've ever known before.

She sleeps in my bed every night, and of course, with her comes Gucci, who has set up a permanent sleeping residence on the chair in my bedroom.

But I don't care. The goat has surprisingly started to

grow on me. And, to have Speedy, I'll take anything. Even a head-butting goat.

Speedy just got back from having an early dinner with her friend Logan. He's gay. And, yes, I checked. Not that I don't trust her. I just don't trust other guys. I mean, look at her; she's fucking beautiful.

She brought back take-out dessert. My favorite, raspberry cheesecake, because my girlfriend is awesome like that.

Hold the fuck up.

Girlfriend?

Is she?

We fuck. She spends every night in my bed. We live together.

So, yeah, I guess I'd say she's my girlfriend.

Well, fuck me sideways. I have a girlfriend.

Not that we've actually put a verbal label on this thing between us, but she must know that she's my girl.

And, right at this moment, my girl is in the kitchen, making me pizza for dinner.

Homemade pizza and cheesecake for dessert. A beer in my hand and the Lakers game about to start soon.

I'm the luckiest bastard on the planet.

Life isn't just great. It's fucking amazing.

My cell starts to ring, so I grab it from the coffee table.

It's my buddy Julian. Julian's one of my closest friends. I don't have many, mainly because I don't trust people. Just Julian and Vaughn.

Aside from Tate, Julian's one of the best people I know. But I'd never tell the fucker that. His ego's big enough as it is.

"Hey, asshole. Long time no speak," I answer.

"Aw, you missed me?"

"Like a hole in the head."

He chuckles. "So, I'm back in town. Heard you broke your foot, you clumsy fuck. How'd you manage that?"

"Long story." I smile, thinking of what brought Speedy and me together.

"Well, I saw that the Lakers are playing tonight. Figured you'd be watching."

"Of course."

"I'm gonna come round with pizza, and we can catch up over the game."

"If it's to talk about the dicks you sucked while you were in Vancouver, I'd rather not hear about it."

Julian's gay. But he's in the closet, so to say. His closest friends know he's gay but not the rest of the world. He's an actor on a hit TV show, and the studio wants him in the closet.

He laughs again. "Spoilsport. Fine, no dirt on the dicks I sucked while I was away. But, FYI, it was a lot."

"For fuck's sake!" I sigh.

He laughs louder. "I'll be round in twenty."

"Fine. But don't worry about bringing pizza. Speedy's in the kitchen, making homemade pizza."

Silence.

"Who the fuck is Speedy?"

"Ava. She's living here. Taking care of me."

"You have a woman living with you?"

"That's another long story."

"And it's definitely one I want to hear. I'll be there in ten."

I laugh and hang up my cell. I get to my feet and hobble to the kitchen.

God, I can't wait to get this fucking boot off. One more week to go, Tate said, and then I'm back to normal.

I walk into the kitchen, and she's standing there, wearing an apron and rolling out pizza dough. She looks like a domestic goddess. And I want to fuck her right now. I wonder if we could slip in a quickie before Julian arrives.

"Hey, babe." I move toward her.

She looks up at me and smiles.

Every time she smiles at me, it feels like a punch to the chest. And it's a punch I want to receive.

"My buddy Julian just called. He's back in town. He's gonna come over in ten to watch the game."

"You want me to make extra pizza for him?"

"That'd be great."

"Anything he doesn't like?"

I pause. "I don't have a fucking clue. But he definitely likes meat."

I laugh, and she looks at me funny.

"Never mind."

I don't share Julian's sexual preferences with anyone. If he wants someone to know, then he'll tell them himself.

"Okay, so I'll make a meat feast and a barbeque chicken and garlic bread."

"You're amazing. I ever tell you that?" I move behind her, slide my arms around her waist, and press a kiss to her neck.

"Nope. I don't think you ever have."

I hear the smile in her voice as she starts to spread tomato puree on the pizza dough.

"You're amazing and sexy, and I want you all the damn time." I slip my hand up her skirt and into her panties. I run my finger between her folds and slide it inside her.

"Gabe." She drops the spoon that she was spreading the puree with. "I thought your friend was coming?"

"He is. But I want you to come first."

"Where's Gucci?"

I still my hand. "Um, why?"

"Because I don't want her watching as you finger me in the kitchen."

"Speedy, she's a fucking goat. I'm pretty sure she doesn't know what day of the week it is."

She tilts her head back, looking up at me. "Yes, she does. She's smart. And I don't want her seeing us going at it."

I give her a look. "She sleeps in my bedroom with us every night while we fuck."

"Yeah, but she's asleep then."

"Babe, a deaf person couldn't sleep through our screwing. You're not exactly quiet. And Gucci's out on the terrace, sunbathing, so stop talking and let me make you come."

I start fucking her with my finger, my palm pressing against her clit. And she closes her eyes on a soft moan, her back falling against my chest.

With my other hand, I pull her top down. She's wearing a bra, which is annoying. I'm going to have to remind her of the no-bra rule but not right now. Right this second, I have more important things to do.

I shove her bra out of the way and start to tease her nipple between my thumb and finger.

She moans a hot, breathy sound. Her legs are trembling. My dick is rock hard against her back.

I fucking love the sounds she makes when she's turned on. The way she says my name with a mindless need.

I push another finger inside her, thrusting them in and out.

"God, Gabe."

"That's it, baby. Come on my hand. I wanna hear you scream my name."

I suck her earlobe into my mouth, and her hips jerk against my hand, seeking more pressure.

I press my palm to her pussy, rubbing it hard against her clit.

"Gabe . . . please . . . I need . . ."

I pinch her nipple, and it sets her off like a rocket.

She screams my name, her pussy grinding against my hand, while she rides out her orgasm.

Making her come satisfies me in a way nothing ever has before. I don't care if I don't come—well, of course I care, but I care more about getting her off.

She goes slack in my arms. I put my arm around her waist, holding her up.

She turns her dazed eyes to me.

I love that just-came look in them that's there because of me.

Mine.

Her mouth reaches up and softly kisses me.

I'm crazy about her.

The buzzer goes on the intercom, telling me that security is calling. Meaning Julian's here.

Jesus, that was quick. What did the fucker do? Run here?

"It'll be Julian," I tell her.

I carefully pull my fingers from inside her and remove my hand from her panties. She pulls her bra and top back up, and I smooth her skirt down.

"He got here quick."

"No kidding."

"You might want to get rid of that before you let Julian up." She grins down at my visible erection. She goes over to the sink, pumps some soap onto her hands, and turns on the tap. "And you might want to wash your hands."

"No need." I run my tongue up the palm of my hand, licking her come from it, and then I slip the fingers that were inside her into my mouth, sucking her from them.

I chuckle at the scandalous look on her face.

"Delicious." I grin.

Then, I rearrange my dick in my pants and leave the kitchen to let Julian up while I think of every non-sexy thing I can to get my hard-on to go down.

Chapter Twenty-Three

Gabe

"**S**o, you ran over his foot with your car?" Julian laughs.

"Yeah." Speedy winces, a small smile on her lips.

"And broke his foot?"

"Yep."

"Her car is huge." I size out with my hands.

"What car do you have?" Julian looks at Speedy.

She glances at me, a smile creeping onto her face.

Don't you fucking dare, babe.

"A tank."

Julian looks at me and then back at Speedy, and then he bursts out laughing. "God, she must like you if she's willing to lie for you!"

"Vaughn, the fucking asshole." I narrow my eyes.

"Of course he called me to tell me you got your foot broken by a tiny car!"

"They might look small, but they weigh a fucking ton!"

Julian is belly-laughing, and Speedy joins in with him.

"Bastards." I frown. "The pair of you are total bastards."

"Aw, babe. We're just teasing." Speedy leans over and plants a kiss on my cheek.

I see Julian's brows go up in question.

I haven't told him that Speedy and I are sleeping together. Well, dating. That she's my girlfriend. Not that I've told her that. I mean, asked her.

Fuck. Am I back in high school?

When he arrived, I introduced them, and Julian remembered her from that time we all met in the club—you know, the meeting I pretended to forget—which made me feel like a total shit when I saw how happy it made her that Julian had remembered her. And that was it. They were off gossiping together like a pair of long-lost friends.

Turns out, Speedy is a big fan of his show. Her friend Logan got her into it.

Good thing Julian likes dick, or I might be getting jealous with how well they're getting along.

The pizza is gone, and the game has finished, but I hardly got to watch it because Speedy and Julian were too busy talking. But, honestly, I didn't even mind, which is weird because I hate it when I watch a game and it gets interrupted.

What is this woman doing to me?

"So, you two are dating?" Julian says to us both.

Speedy looks at me, a question in her eyes.

I keep my eyes on her. "Yeah, we are."

The smile that lifts her lips lights up my insides. And my dick instantly wants to party with her pussy.

Saying those words out loud has just made this thing I have with her even more real. And I like it. A fuck of a lot.

I turn to Julian. "Speedy is my girlfriend."

And I sound like a teenage boy.

The grin on Julian's face tells me I'm going to get the ribbing of my life because of that comment. But you know what? I don't give a fuck.

See what she's doing to me? Turning me into one of those guys who goes brainless over his girl.

"You do realize that you've got your hands full with him, right?" Julian says to her.

"Oh, yeah, totally." She giggles.

"Hey! I'm an easy guy to get along with."

She snorts.

I look at her. "What?"

"Nothing." She shakes her head, smiling innocently. "Right, boys, as much fun as this night has been, this girl is tired, so I'm gonna hit the hay." She squeezes my thigh with her hand and then softly kisses my lips. "Night, babe," she whispers.

My dick instantly perks up.

Not yet, big fella.

"It was really nice to meet you, Julian."

She gets up and goes over to him. He gets to his feet and kisses her on the cheek.

"Thanks for the pizza."

"Anytime." She waves him off. "Hope to see you again soon."

"You definitely will." He smiles.

"Come on, Gucci."

She pats her thigh, and Gucci looks up from her spot by Julian's feet, not seeming to want to move.

"I'll bring her through when I come to bed."

"Oh, okay." She smiles.

"Night, babe." I watch her leave the room, her gorgeous ass swaying in her skirt as she walks. My cock begs to get up and follow her.

"So ... she's your *girlfriend*," Julian says in a sing-song voice.

I flip him off, and he laughs.

"Smoke?" I say, suddenly needing a cigarette.

"Sure."

Julian never used to smoke. He only started up a few years ago when he was getting clean from his addiction. Yeah, Julian's the friend who was addicted to painkillers. It's not uncommon for addicts to replace one addiction with another. Lesser of the two evils. They'll both kill you in the end. It'll just take the smokes longer to send you to the grave, and you won't lose everything because of them.

We head out onto the terrace, and Gucci follows.

I take a seat on one of the chairs at the table and pass Julian a cigarette. I light my own up and then hand him the lighter.

Gucci parks her butt next to Julian's chair.

"I can't believe you have a fucking goat living in your apartment." Julian chuckles, reaching down to scratch Gucci on the head.

"I know. But she comes with Speedy. They're a package, so what can I do?"

"I like her."

"Speedy or the goat?"

"Well, Gucci's cute. But I meant Ava."

"Yeah. She's great." I smile and then take a drag of my cigarette.

"And she makes great fucking pizza."

"Ain't that the truth."

We're silent a moment, and then he says, "You look real happy, Gabe."

"Don't I always?"

"Nah, you're a moody fucker, and you know it. But, now, you seem ... I don't know ... different. Lighter. Less tense."

He's right; I am. And it's because of Speedy.

"She's good for you, Gabe."

"Yeah, I guess she is." I smile.

"It's about time you found someone to love your sorry ass."

And that knocks me back in my chair.

"Whoa! What? Love? Calm yourself the fuck down. We're just dating. Well, fucking. I mean, we haven't actually even been out on a date."

Shit. I haven't even taken her out on a date. What kind of boyfriend am I? The clueless-shit kind obviously.

He raises a brow. "A minute ago, she was your girl-friend. And, not to point out the obvious, but you do have her living in your house."

"She is my girlfriend. And she only lives here because of circumstances," I protest. "With my broken foot, I've needed help, and she needs a place to stay."

"You still need help?"

"Well ... no, not anymore, as I can take it off to bathe now. But she hasn't found a place to stay yet. She can't find anywhere in her price range that takes pets."

"Mmhmm."

"What's that supposed to mean?"

"Nothing." He's watching me with an amused look on his face. "I just think Gabe doth protest too much."

"Don't fucking quote Shakespeare to me, you douche. And I don't love Speedy. Sure, I love *fucking* her. She's hot as fuck. She's funny and smart, and she cooks amazing food. I like having her around. *Like*," I emphasize. "I *like* her. Not love."

"I never said you did. I said, it's good that you have someone to love you. But, now, I'm thinking that you do love her."

I flip him off, and he laughs.

Why is this bothering me so much?

I don't care what he thinks. I know I'm not in love with Speedy, and she's not in love with me.

We're just having fun.

Right?

Right.

Julian stubs his cigarette out and gets to his feet. "I'm gonna head off. I've got an early start in the morning."

"You going back to Vancouver?"

"Day after tomorrow. Got a meeting with the studio heads first thing. I'll catch you before I head back to Vancouver though."

"Sure thing."

I stub my cigarette out and go to get up to see him out, but he pats me on the shoulder.

"Don't get up. I'll see myself out."

"Okay. Later, man."

He gives Gucci a stroke and then leaves.

I light up another cigarette and stare out at the night sky and the city moving below me.

I can't believe Julian thinks I'm in love with Speedy.

I've never loved a woman in my life, and I don't intend to change that.

The only person I've ever loved in my life is Tate. Well, I loved my parents once, but that died a long time ago.

But do I love Speedy? No. No way.

I like her, sure. But not love.

Fucking Julian, winding me up.

I finish my cigarette and make sure that Gucci has done her pissing and shitting for the night. Then, I take her inside with me.

She follows me to my bedroom. I push the door open, and Gucci runs in and jumps on her chair.

Speedy is asleep. The lamp is on, and her Kindle is facedown on her chest. She must have fallen asleep while reading.

She looks beautiful.

My heart starts to beat faster.

But I don't love her.

I'm just in *like* with her.

I go over, pick the Kindle up, and put it on the nightstand. Then, I turn the lamp off and go into the bathroom to take a piss and brush my teeth.

When I'm done, I climb in bed. Speedy rolls toward me in her sleep, her arm sliding over my waist, and it makes me smile.

"Speedy?"

"Mmhmm?"

"You awake?"

"Mmhmm."

I scoot down the bed, so my face is closer to hers.

"I need to tell you something."

One of her eyes pops open.

"I lied to you. The day you ran me over, I said I didn't remember you from the club. I lied. I did remember you."

She opens her other eye. "Why did you lie?"

"Because I'm a jackass."

"Yeah, I think we've already established that."

She's silent a moment.

"You mad at me?"

"No, of course not. I just . . ." She exhales. "You don't have to say you remembered me to make me feel better. I know Julian remembered me, but—"

"You were wearing a red dress that showed off your gorgeous legs. Your lips were painted red to match. I remember thinking how much I'd like to see that red lipstick smeared all over my cock. Your hair was down and curled. And you were the most beautiful girl in the room."

The expression that my words put on her face makes me feel like a fucking king.

"So, why didn't you hit on me that night?" she asks softly.

"Because you had a boyfriend."

"I told you that?" She screws her face up.

"Yeah, you did."

"It must have been to remind myself that you were off-limits because I wanted you so bad that night."

"I wanted you, too, Speedy. And I wanted you when you ran over my foot even though I wanted to strangle you."

She laughs the sweetest sound.

"And I want you now. I always want you."

"Me, too," she whispers.

She moves in closer, hugging me. I wrap my arms around her and press a kiss to her hair.

"Thank you for telling me. I'm glad that you were honest with me. I don't want any secrets between us."

I roughly swallow down.

There are secrets. Things I can't tell her.

Things that, if she knew, she'd never look at me the same again. And she sure as hell wouldn't want me anymore.

Chapter Twenty-Four

Gabe

"OH GOD, YEAH." I open my eyes to the sight of Speedy's head bobbing up and down, my cock in her mouth.

She looks up at me and smiles. Her lips are painted red, and that red is smeared all over my cock.

Fuck, she's amazing.

"Thank God you finally woke up," she says. "I was starting to feel like a creeper."

"Babe, feel free to wake me up with your lips wrapped around my cock whenever you want. And this"—I reach down and rub my thumb over the corner of her mouth, smearing the lipstick onto her skin—"I like a lot."

She smiles shyly. "You said last night, about the first time we met, that you wanted my red lipstick on your cock, so I thought I'd make it a reality for you."

Something squeezes my chest.

But it's definitely not love.

Nope, no way.

"You're the best girlfriend ever. Now, put my cock back in your mouth, and deep-throat me just how I like."

"Bossy," she murmurs.

"And you love it."

Love. There I go with that fucking word again.

Her eyes meet mine. "Yeah, I do."

I grab a handful of her hair and move her back down to my cock. "So, show me how much you like my bossy ways with that sexy mouth of yours."

Like. See? I do know how to use that word.

She licks the tip of my cock, and it sends a thrill shooting up my spine. Then, she starts kissing up and down my cock, teasing.

"Speedy . . ." I warn. "Don't tease me. Give me what I want."

"And what do you want?" She grins and runs her tongue up the length of my cock.

"Suck it. Now."

She opens up her mouth, and I push her head down onto my cock, sliding in between those sexy red lips.

"Fuck yeah," I groan.

Her hand goes to cup my balls, rolling them, as she relaxes her throat and moves further onto my cock, taking over two-thirds of it in.

And I'm big, so it's a lot of cock for her to take.

She's fucking incredible. She deep-throats like a champ.

Knowing where her limit is, after doing this a good few times now, I start to fuck her mouth, my hands holding either side of her head.

"Shit, that's good, baby. So fucking good."

She wraps her fingers around the base of my cock, gripping it just like I love, and continues teasing my balls.

Again with that fucking word love!

But, Jesus, fuck, this is good. Too good.

I could yell out right now that I loved her, and I don't think I'd give a shit. Especially not while she's working my dick over like a porn star.

Dots start to dance in front of my eyes. I close them, my hips jacking up and down, as I fuck her mouth.

"You're so fucking hot and dirty, and you suck me so good, Ava."

Heat licks up my spine, and my quad muscles start to tighten.

Fuck, I'm close. I don't normally come this quick from a blow job, but when she puts her mouth around my cock, I shoot like a teenage boy.

She pulls off my cock, needing a breather, and she starts jacking me with her hand. Then, she's back on my cock, taking me in deep again, and I let her do her thing.

She sucks hard, fingers squeezing the base of my cock.

"Fuck yeah, keep doing that. Shit, yeah, that's good." I press my head back into the pillow.

She runs her fingernail over that sensitive part of skin right at the base of my cock at the same time as she takes my cock all the way in. I blow like a rocket, coming in her mouth.

And I keep coming.

And coming.

And she takes it all. Finishing me off with a kiss on the tip of my cock.

I lift my heavy arm over my eyes.

"You okay?" She giggles.

I move my arm. "Come here."

She climbs on top of me, and I wrap my arms around her.

"That was astro-fucking-nomical." I kiss her forehead.

She giggles. "I figured I owed you after last night, in the kitchen."

"Babe, you didn't owe me anything. I love making you come."

Like! For fuck's sake, Evans! You like *making her come.*

"I know. I just wanted to make you feel good."

"Well, you definitely did that."

"I bet I look like a clown right now."

I tip her face up to me. She's got red lipstick smeared around her mouth.

I kiss her. "You look gorgeous."

"I look a mess."

She goes to get up, but I stop her.

"Where are you going?"

"To wipe this lipstick off."

"No, you're not."

She raises a brow. "I'm not?"

"Nope. You're staying right here, and I'm going to kiss that lipstick off your face while my cock kisses your pussy."

"Huh?"

"That was code for, I'm going to fuck you."

"I got that. I'm just surprised you think you can go again. You literally just came, Gabe."

I shake my head, disappointed. "You doubt me, Speedy? I'm a little insulted. We've been fucking for three weeks now, and you still haven't figured out that I'm a machine in bed. Clearly, I've not been doing my job properly."

"Oh, you've been doing your job just fine. It's just impossible, Gabe. No one can get hard again that quick after just coming, let alone come again so soon. No matter how good they are in bed."

My eyes narrow at her. Then, I pull her down to the bed and roll on top of her. "Challenge accepted," I say.

Then, I cover her mouth with mine and get to work.

Chapter Twenty-Five

Ava

"OKAY, FINE. I WAS wrong," I pant, breathless.

"I'm sorry, what?" He cups his ear, like he didn't hear me, when the smug bastard heard exactly what I just said.

"I said, I was wrong. You clearly are superhuman when it comes to sex."

"Damn right I am, baby. And, wait, I need to get my camera, so I can have it on film—you admitting that you're wrong."

I give him the middle finger, and he bursts out laughing. A full-on belly laugh, and it's one of the best sounds I've ever heard.

And I can't help but laugh, too.

He reaches over, cupping my face, and brings my mouth to his. He softly kisses me. "You rock in the sack, too, Speedy. I've never had it as good as I do with you."

When I hear that, my stomach flips over, but I play it cool. "Well, that's 'cause I'm the best. And, if you put

the best and the best together, you're going to get spectacular sex."

"Mind-blowing."

"Astro-fucking-nomical."

"Amen to that, baby."

He puts his fist up to me, and I bump it with my own.
I glance at the clock. "I should get up."

He pulls me into his arms and kisses me again. "Not
yet."

"I really need to get showered and ready. My boss
is a bit of a tyrant. I'm already on the clock, and he'll
go apeshit if he knows he's paying me to have sex on
the job."

He freezes cold. I've never seen anything like it.

And I instantly know I said the wrong thing.

"Gabe?"

He pulls away, and then he's getting out of bed. He
puts on his athletic shorts and gets a T-shirt from the
drawer. He drags it on over his head, his movements
rough and jerky.

I say his name again, getting to my knees. I hold the
sheet around me.

He doesn't answer.

"Gabe!"

He stops and slowly turns to face me.

"What's going on?"

"You wanted to get up. I'm getting up."

"You're acting weird."

"Maybe I just don't want to lie around in bed with
you all fucking day. I've got shit to do."

"You were just asking me to stay in bed with you, so
don't give me that crap. Just tell me what's wrong. Is it

something I said? The joke I made about you paying me for sex?"

His face hardens to stone. "I'm just done, Ava."

"What?" My heart starts to pound in my chest.

"Are you deaf? I said, I'm done." He turns and walks to the door.

"Done with what, Gabe?"

"You," he says without turning around.

Then, he walks out, slamming the door behind him.

Fighting tears, I scramble out of bed and throw some clothes on. Then, I'm flying out of his bedroom, straight after him.

I find him in the living room, sitting on the sofa. A lit cigarette in his hand.

I stand at the end of the sofa, staring down at him. "What the hell was that?"

"Go away, Ava."

"No, I won't fucking go away. I want to know what just happened back there. Because I'm confused. One minute, we were fine, and then I made a joke—which, granted, wasn't my finest joke—but the next thing I know, everything has gone to shit. So, you're gonna have to explain this to me because I'm in the dark here."

His head turns, and he levels a dark look at me. "I don't have to explain shit to you."

"Yes, you do."

"No, I don't! I fucking told you, I can't do this anymore. End of."

"No, it's not end of just because you say so! There are two of us in this, Gabe! Not just you."

He stubs his cigarette out and stands up. "But that's just it. It is just me in this. Because you and I are just fucking, Ava. I might have said we're dating, but we're not. I fuck you because I can, and I tell you we're dating to keep you happy. And, now, I'm done fucking you, so you can go." He throws an arm in the direction of the door.

Pain ricochets through my chest, like he just shot me. But I hold myself together.

"You're a fucking asshole, Gabriel! And you're so full of shit that it's pouring out of your ears! Say what you want, but I know you're lying."

"No, you're just fucking deluded."

"Fuck you. The only one deluded around here is you. And I know this has to do with me saying something about you paying me for sex. Because I saw your reaction the second I said it. I know you're sensitive about it. I just don't know why. But I know this"—I jerk a hand between us—"has something to do with you not wanting to pay me a salary while we're sleeping together. So, you can try to tell me it's not that and that you're done with me, but I know it's all bullshit. And, if you give a shit about me, you'll tell me the truth. And if you don't . . . then I guess we really are done." I spin on my heel and walk away.

My heart is beating out of my chest, my pulse thrumming in my ears.

"Ava."

I stop at the sound of my name, but I don't turn around.

He sighs loudly. "Jesus. Okay! You're fucking right! It is about that. About me being sensitive about the money-and-sex thing. I was being an asshole when I said I was done. I don't want you to go."

I turn around, but I fold my arms over my chest. I don't want him to think I've forgiven him yet. "And?"

"And what?"

"Why are you so sensitive about the money-and-sex thing?"

He looks away.

"Gabe, you don't have to tell me anything. I wish you would trust me enough to want to, but you don't have to."

His eyes snap back to mine. "It's not about not trusting you. I trust you more than I've ever trusted anyone."

"Then, what is it?"

His eyes go to the floor. His hands on his hips, he heaves out another sigh. "I don't want to change the way you look at me."

I drop my arms and take a step toward him. "Nothing could change the way I look at you."

He lets out a laugh, but it's hollow and humorless. "That's an easy statement to make when you don't know everything."

"So, tell me."

He shakes his head, like he's having an internal battle with himself.

"Gabe . . ."

"I used to sleep with women for money."

"What?"

"And my parents are in prison for drug trafficking, racketeering, and murder."

Chapter Twenty-Six

Ava

"I'M SORRY, WHAT?" REELING from what he just said, I reach out for something to hold on to, but there's nothing but air.

"Ava, do you need to sit down?"

"Uh, yeah. I think so."

I walk over to the sofa on wobbly legs and sit down on the edge, fingers gripping it.

Gabe stays standing by the window. The light frames him, making him look incandescent. And beautiful. So very beautiful.

He's not looking at me. His dark eyes are on the floor.

His words keep echoing around in my head.

"I used to sleep with women for money."

"And my parents are in prison for drug trafficking, racketeering, and murder."

I thought his parents were dead. Apparently not.

He's not saying anything. I think he's waiting for me to speak.

Honestly, I don't know what to say.

But I go with the latter, as that seems more important. "So, your parents aren't dead. They're in prison," I say in a quiet voice.

"Yes." His voice is rough.

"Both of them?"

"Yes."

"How? Why?"

"It's a long story."

"I've got all the time in the world."

His eyes finally meet mine. Emotions are running riot in them. It makes me ache for him.

He looks away from me. "My dad is originally from Italy. He was born into the Russo crime family."

He glances at me, a question in his eyes, and I shake my head, not familiar with their name.

"My grandfather was the head of the family, my dad his eldest son. And my grandfather built up a business relationship with a Jewish mob boss who pretty much ran Las Vegas. My grandfather sent my dad out to Vegas to secure the deal with the Jews, and he was to head up the running of it.

"My dad met my mother, who was the niece of the Jewish mob boss. She worked in one of his casinos. They got married. I was born a few years later. Tate, five years after that. Together, they ran several casinos. Or so I thought. The casinos were a front for the money laundering and drugs they were filtering through the casinos."

He comes and sits down on the sofa chair beside me. I shift to face him.

"I knew they weren't squeaky clean. I knew my dad's

family history. I knew they did some dodgy dealings. Kids would say stuff about them to me at school. The police came calling at home a few times. But, honestly, I didn't know the true extent of it. I didn't know they were mixed up in drugs or . . . that they'd killed people.

"I was seventeen when the house was raided, and my parents were arrested. It was the middle of the night. Tate and I were dragged from our beds, put into the back of a police car, and driven to a boys' home run by social services. We weren't told anything. We only knew what we read in the newspapers in the following days. They wouldn't let us see our parents. Tate was devastated. Then, I heard that my mom and dad were being charged with racketeering and the murder of several people. I knew that Tate and I were never going home. At seventeen, about to turn eighteen in six months' time, I was smart enough to know that I'd stay in the boys' home, and with Tate being twelve, they would try to rehome him.

"I'd just lost my parents. I wasn't going to lose Tate as well. So, we left. My parents' assets had been frozen by the government, but I had some savings in my account. So, I withdrew everything I had, and I bought two bus tickets to Los Angeles. I thought the idea of living near the beach sounded good. So, we rode the bus here, and I decided to change our surname to Evans in case anyone came looking for us."

"So, your real name is Gabriel Russo?"

"Yes."

"Why Evans?" I ask him.

"The bus driver had on a name badge that said Evans."

"That simple."

"Yeah, Speedy, that simple." He grabs his smokes from the table and lights one up. He takes a drag and exhales the smoke.

"I managed to find us a studio to rent, using the rest of my savings. And I got a job waiting tables. I got Tate enrolled in school. But the one job wasn't bringing in enough money, so I got another. In the end, I was working three jobs.

"There was a guy I waited tables with. The night he quit, he told me all about how he'd scored this job being an escort, and he was making a shit-ton of money doing it. So much that he didn't need that job anymore. He said I should give it a try. He gave me a card with the number of the place he'd started working for. So, I gave them a call. What could it hurt, right? And, if taking some women out for dates or whatever would give me more money to give Tate a better life, then it was all for the better.

"So, I went in for an interview. Told the woman I was twenty-one. I looked it. But she laughed and said I had to show her ID. So, I told her I was eighteen. She said she had no problem with that. That her clients liked younger men. Said they would love me. She hired me on the spot. But said there were rules. Under no circumstances was I to have sex with a client. I told her that wasn't something I was looking to do. So, she sent me off to HR, which was basically an overweight middle-aged woman behind a desk, smoking a cigarette. She took my photo for the database. I was given a form to fill out. Then, it was done. I was signed up with the agency and told they'd call me soon. I left, and they called three days later with a job for me.

"A woman needed a date to her friend's wedding. It was her first time using an escort. And my first job, so it worked well, as we were both nervous. I picked her up in a cab, took her to the party. We danced and drank. Had fun. When the night was over, I dropped her back home, and she thanked me for a great evening. Easy. Then, a few more jobs started to roll in, and I was getting more and more popular.

"Then, one night, I was out with this woman. She was in her forties. But really good-looking, you know. She oozed class, and the jewelry she wore could have fed Tate and me for the rest of our lives. She started telling me how her husband didn't pay her any attention. She was sure he was screwing his secretary. She mentioned how lonely she was. Then, she reached over and slid her hand up my leg. She stared me square in the eye and said she'd pay me a lot of money to make her feel good about herself.

"I knew it was against the agency's rules, but I was young, and I thought, *Hey, here's a beautiful woman offering to pay me to fuck her when I would have fucked her for free.*

"So, I said yes. And, the next thing I knew, we were going to a hotel. Then, we were in the room, and we were fucking. And, when it was over, she kissed me on the mouth, thanked me for a great time, and told me she'd be telling all her friends about me. Then, she left a thousand bucks on the nightstand.

"A thousand bucks." He laughs, but it's a sad sound. "I was eighteen years old with a thirteen-year-old brother depending on me for everything. So, I took the money with a smile on my face. The next morning, I took Tate out for a huge breakfast and took him shopping for new clothes."

"Does Tate know—"

"No." His eyes snap to mine. "And he never will. Understand?"

"Of course." I swallow. "You can trust me, Gabe."

He holds my stare. "I wouldn't be telling you all of this if I didn't think I could."

Knowing that warms the ache I feel for him in my chest, but it doesn't soothe it completely.

"Anyway, a few days later, she called me, asking to see me again. So, I said yes. Why wouldn't I? It was easy money. After I fucked her in her hotel room, she told me she had some friends who wanted to spend time with me, too."

It's hard not to wince when he talks about having sex with those women. His voice sounds empty of emotion. Honestly, it makes me want to bawl my fucking eyes out.

"I kept escorting with the agency for a while," he tells me. "But, soon enough, I was too busy to take jobs they had to offer, as my own clientele had grown fast. I quit with the agency and became a full-time hooker. Screwing rich women for money.

"And, for a long time, it was easy. Fun even. Fucking hot women for money—what's not to like about that, right?"

He laughs, but it's hollow, and my heart hurts at the sound.

"I moved Tate and me out of the tiny studio we had been renting and into a two-bedroom apartment. I got a car. I put money aside for Tate's college tuition fund.

Life was good. Or so I thought. After a while, it started to not feel good anymore. It just felt empty. Soulless. There was nothing fun about it anymore. I just started to feel dirty. Even spending the money felt dirty. And I guess, somewhere along the way, I'd fooled myself into thinking that these women actually cared for me." He makes a self-deprecating noise. "That was stupid as fuck because, of course, they didn't care about me. I was just a monetary means to a great fucking orgasm.

"I was ready to get out of the business. But I didn't have any qualifications. I was good at fucking and nothing else. Then, as fate had it, I got a new client. She was a first-timer. Her husband had been having an affair with a younger woman, and he'd left her. Her friends had told her she needed to get back on the horse. One of her friends was a client of mine and had said she should get in touch.

"So, we arranged to meet in a hotel room. When I got there, I could tell off the bat that she wasn't ready. So, we talked instead. And I found myself opening up to her. Told her I was tired of doing what I was doing. I told her about Tate. How I needed the money for him. She had a kid the same age. Then, she told me that she was a producer for a network. They had a part on a show they were auditioning for, and she said I had the exact right look for the character. Asked if I had any acting experience, which I didn't. She gave me the name and number of an acting coach. Told me to get some lessons and that she'd set me up with an audition for the show.

"And she was good on her word. Called me up the following week with a date and time for an audition.

So, I went to the audition. I'd never been so fucking nervous in my life. I threw up in the restroom beforehand. And then I went in and auditioned.

"The next day, I got a call. I'd gotten the part. I couldn't fucking believe it. It wasn't big money, less than I earned hooking, but it was a regular part on a fucking television show. So, I called up my clients and told them I was out of the game. The hit on the money was hard for a while, but then I auditioned for some film roles, did some small parts, and then landed a lead role in my first movie. And that was it." He gestures his hands around his apartment.

"When I first hit the big time and my popularity was rising, I was nervous that maybe the escort agency would come out and say something to the press or one of the women I used to sleep with might, but then I figured the agency wouldn't want the press, and those women wouldn't want to admit to paying for sex. They definitely wouldn't want it to be public knowledge. Some of these women were married. And the others had high-powered jobs. None of them would want it getting out. They all had as much to lose as I did. So, I knew I was safe.

"And, when it came to my parents, I definitely didn't want that getting out, so I had my lawyer take them NDAs to sign, saying they'd never talk about me and Tate to the press. I couldn't have the fact that my parents were in prison for racketeering and murder in the papers. And I didn't want it fucking up Tate's life either. They'd screwed things up enough for the both of us already. I had us back on track, and I wasn't going to risk them fucking it up when they saw my face on TV."

"Did they sign the NDAs?"

He rubs his hand over his jaw, sadness filling his eyes. "Surprisingly, yes. Maybe they thought they owed us for fucking up our lives. I don't know. I'm just glad they did."

"God, Gabe. I don't know what to say."

"Don't worry. I just dropped a mother lode in your lap. And it's not a story you hear every day. You probably need some time to digest it." He gets up. "You want a drink? Brandy's always good for shock."

I stare up at him. "I'm not in shock, Gabe."

I reach up and take hold of his hand, and he lets me.

"Yes, it's a lot to digest. But I'm just so sorry that things were so hard for you back then."

His eyes narrow at me, hard and black. "I don't want your fucking pity, Ava."

I get to my feet, standing in front of him. "You don't have it. I don't pity you. But I am allowed to feel sorry for what you went through with your parents. And, honestly, I don't think prostitution is a great way to earn money, but I don't think it's horrific if done in the right circumstances and for the right reasons. And yours was. How could anyone think that what you did to keep you and your brother together was a terrible thing? If they did, then they'd be fucking idiots. I'm just sorry that it made you feel bad toward the end, and I'm so glad that lady gave you an opportunity to get out and change your life."

He's staring at me. There's a multitude of emotions in his eyes. But I'm not sure where his head is.

"It doesn't change how you see me?" His words are almost a whisper.

"Only that I see all of you now. And it makes you even more amazing in my eyes."

He looks confused. Like he can't make sense of the words I said. "And you still want to be with me, even after knowing that I used to fuck women for money?"

"Can't say I like to hear about you fucking other women in general, so let's not say that anymore." I step closer to him. "But, yes, Gabe, I still want to be with you. Nothing in this world could make me not want to be with you. Apart from if you cheated on me. Because then I would have to chop your dick off, and that wouldn't be good 'cause I'd have to go to jail. Or you stole money from me, which would be weird 'cause it's not exactly like you need it. Or if you—"

"Ava."

"Stop rambling, I know. I don't mean to. I just—"

"I love you."

"What?"

He steps into my body and takes my face in his hands. "I love you. I'm in love with you or what-the-fuck-ever you want to call it. I'm in *it* with you."

He loves me.

Tears well in my eyes. And my heart is going crazy in my chest right now. "I love you, too. You know that, right?"

A smile edges his lips. "I do now."

Then, he kisses me so hard and passionately that it knocks the breath from my lungs.

He presses his forehead to mine. "How did I get so lucky to find you?"

"I ran you over with my car."

"And being with you is worth the broken foot, Speedy."

"I think that's the sweetest thing you've ever said to me."

He tips his head back, staring into my eyes. "And me just telling you that I'm in love with you wasn't?"

"Of course it was. I meant, that's the second sweetest thing you've ever said to me."

He pulls me into his arms. "Nice save."

"I thought so."

He chuckles softly and holds me even tighter. And I don't ever want him to let go.

Chapter Twenty-Seven

Ava

IT'S EIGHT THIRTY A.M., and I've just climbed back into Gabe's bed after letting Gucci out onto the terrace to do her morning business. I'm snuggled into his warm body when the intercom starts to ring.

"It's probably the cleaners." Gabe sighs. "I'll go let them in."

"No, it's fine. I'll go. I move faster than you do anyway."

"Not for much longer." He swats my ass as I get out of bed.

I speed walk out of his bedroom, jog over to the intercom, and pick the receiver up. "Good morning, Harry."

"Good morning, Miss Ava. The cleaners are here."

"Let them up, please."

I hang up the receiver and go back into the bedroom.

"It is the cleaners," I say, but I'm talking to myself, as the bed's empty. I hear water running in the bathroom.

When I go in the bathroom, he's at the sink, brushing his teeth, with the faucet going.

"Is it the cleaners?" he asks in between brushing.

"Yep."

"Cool. Well, get your ass ready because I'm taking you out."

"You are?"

He spits and rinses his brush under the faucet. "Yep. We're going out for breakfast."

"Like a date?"

"Yes, Speedy, like a date."

"You've never taken me on a date before."

He comes close and slides his arms around my waist. I press my hands to his bare chest and gaze up at him.

"I'm well aware of that fact. Hence, I'm taking you out for our first date today. To rectify me being a bad boyfriend."

"You're not a bad boyfriend."

"I am. But I'm working on being a better one for you."

"No need. You're perfect as you are."

"Even when I'm being an ass?"

I slide my hands to his butt and give his cheeks a squeeze. "Even then."

He smiles and leans down to give me a minty kiss. *Yummy.*

"Can I have pancakes on our breakfast date?" I ask him.

"You can have whatever you want."

He gives me one more kiss and then goes and turns the shower on.

I brush my teeth while he takes off the boot and his boxer shorts, and then he climbs under the spray.

I finish brushing and put my toothbrush back. "I'm going to get a shower," I tell him.

"Get in here with me."

"No way." I laugh. "I get in there with you, and I know what'll happen. And I am definitely not having sex with you while the cleaners are here."

He laughs and pokes his head around the shower screen. "Come on, baby. Get in the shower with me."

"No."

"I've got something for you. It's about nine inches, and it loves your pussy a whole lot." He palms his cock, knowing I can see through the glass.

"You're a deviant."

He grins seductively at me.

My clit throbs.

"I'm going!"

I bolt out the door to the sound of his laughter.

I walk out of Gabe's bedroom and straight into Sadie.

"Oh, hey, I was looking for you," she says.

And those are the most words she's said to me since I first met her.

"You were?"

"Yeah. My boss has implemented this new form we have to get signed by each job that we do. It's just to prove that we've been here and done the work."

"Oh, right. Do you need me to get Gabe to sign it? 'Cause he's in the shower at the minute."

"No. It'll be fine if you do it, as you live here." She smiles and holds out a pen and a sheet of paper to me.

It's the first time she's ever smiled at me as well.

I take the pen and paper from her.

My eyes drift over it. The cleaning company logo is at the top.

"Just print and sign your name and date it at the bottom." She points to the dotted line.

I scribble my name down. And then I sign and date it. I hand the pen and paper back to her.

She folds up the paper and puts it along with the pen in the pocket of her dustcoat.

"Thanks," she says. Then, she turns and walks off.

I head into my bedroom to get showered and ready for my breakfast date with Gabe.

I'm ready for breakfast. My hair is down and straight. Makeup light. And I'm wearing my Zara paisley-print maxi dress and jeweled white flip-flops.

I look good for our first official date.

And he loves me.

I just need to keep reminding myself of that because it's so amazing.

I grab my bag and head for my bedroom door.

"Come on, Gucci."

She jumps down from her spot on the bed. She kept me company while I got ready. I hate to leave her behind, but I can't take her to a restaurant with us. I'll leave her in the kitchen with her favorite food—sliced apples and pears.

Gabe is sitting in the living room when I appear. He puts out the cigarette he was smoking and lets out a low whistle that makes me smile from ear to ear.

"You look gorgeous."

"Right back at ya, handsome."

He's wearing a pair of navy-blue cargo shorts and a light-blue button-up shirt.

"You ready?"

"I just need to feed Gucci, and I'm good to go."

"She's coming with us," he says.

"Oh. I didn't think I'd be able to take her to a food place."

"We can take her where we're going."

"Okay. I'll just grab her harness and lead."

I grab her stuff from the kitchen, go back to the living room, and put them on her.

"Ready?" he asks.

"Yep. I'll just grab your car keys."

"No need. I've got a car waiting downstairs."

"Oh. Well, okay. Lead the way then."

He takes hold of my free hand, and he leads me and Gucci into the elevator.

A town car is waiting for us outside his building. The driver is standing by the car. He opens the door for us.

I get in first with Gucci, and then Gabe slides in next to me.

I fasten the seat belt through her harness and put my seat belt on. She climbs into my lap, and I stroke her head.

"So, where are we going?" I ask Gabe.

"Not far." He smiles.

Twenty minutes later, in Beverly Glen, we pull up outside his field—or his piece of land, as I should probably call it.

"What are we doing here?" I ask him.

"Having breakfast."

The driver opens the door, and Gabe takes his seat

belt off and climbs out. I take my seat belt off and unclip Gucci. With her in my arms, I take the hand that Gabe offers to me.

"I'll call you when I need you," Gabe tells the driver.

Keeping hold of my hand, Gabe walks us across the field. We veer off a little to the left where there's a big old oak tree. And underneath the oak tree, laid out, is a huge dark blue picnic blanket with a light-blue wooden block in the middle, like a makeshift table. On the table are plates and cutlery. Flowers in a small vase. Candles. Champagne glasses and a bottle of champagne in a wine bucket. And beside it is one of those old-fashioned wicker picnic baskets.

I turn to him, smiling from ear to ear. "You did this?"

"I paid for someone to do this, but, yeah. You like?"

"I love." I reach up on my toes and kiss him. "It's so romantic. I didn't know you had it in you."

"Neither did I."

We sit on the blanket. Gucci sits next to me. Poor Gabe doesn't look the most comfortable with his booted leg stretched out.

"Are you okay?" I ask.

"I'm fine. Just can't wait to get this fucking thing off."

"Not long now."

"No. And then I can fuck my girl with all four working limbs."

A thrill shoots through me at the thought.

"I've been more than satisfied with what you can do with three working limbs, so I can't wait to see what you can do with four."

"You won't be able to walk straight for a week," he says, the words a sexy growl.

I take him at his word because I know he means it. And I can't freaking wait.

He opens the champagne with a pop that makes Gucci jump, so I stroke her to soothe her. Gabe pours the champagne into two glasses.

I pick mine up and hold it out. "Toast?"

"To us." He taps his glass against mine.

"And to my bad driving that brought us together."

"So, you finally admit that you're a shitty driver."

"I admit nothing." I grin and take a sip of my champagne. The bubbles go straight to my head.

Gabe opens up the picnic basket. "I hope you're hungry 'cause there's a fuckload of food in here."

"I'm starving," I tell him.

"I got some food for Gucci, too." He pulls out a Tupperware container and pulls the lid off. "Chopped apples, pears, grapes, and strawberries. That okay for her?"

The fact that he brought food for her warms my insides.

"That's more than okay." I beam at him.

"What?" His brows push together as he hands her container of food over to me.

"You love her."

"Who?"

"Gucci. She's grown on you. Go on, you can admit it. I won't tell anyone."

"Fine," he huffs. "I *like* her. But I don't fucking love her. She's a goat, for fuck's sake."

I'll take that. It's the best I'm going to get from him.

"I love you," I tell him.

His eyes meet mine. "Love you, too. Now, feed your damn goat, so we can eat."

I blow him a kiss and put Gucci's food out for her while Gabe serves up our breakfast.

Waffles, pancakes, and fresh fruit. Fresh bread rolls and a selection of cheeses.

This man knows the way to my heart.

When I'm stuffed to the brim and I can't fit in another thing, I move over to Gabe's side and lie down, resting my head on his good leg. Gucci is wandering nearby, sniffing some flowers.

"I love it here," I tell him, looking up at him.

He brushes my hair off my forehead. "I've been in touch with an architect."

"You have?"

He nods. "I told him what I'm looking for here. He came to scope it out the other day. Said he's going to draw some plans up and come back to me with them next week."

"Wow. That's exciting. You're finally going to build your home."

"Yeah." He runs his fingers through the strands of my hair as he stares out at the stunning view of the reservoir.

"Well, I'm super happy for you. What did you tell him you wanted?"

His eyes come down to mine. "A ranch-style house. With a paddock. And a swimming pool."

That's what I said I'd put here if I were building a house.

"You stealing my ideas?" I tease.

"No. Just kinda hoping, if I build your dream house, it will give you a reason to stay."

My mouth dries, and my heart starts to hammer in my chest.

Is he saying what I think he's saying? No, surely not.

I sit up and turn to face him. "You could build a shack, and I'd stay. I'm here for you, Gabe. Nothing else."

His fingers trace a line along my jaw. "Speedy, I want to build you a house because I want you to live in it with me."

Oh.

Wow.

"I know that it might seem soon, but we've been living together from the start. Before I was even in love with you. Living with you, spending all that time with you, is what made me fall in love with you. So, why wait? Don't look for an apartment. Stay with me at my apartment. Live with me permanently. And, when the house is built, move there with me. You and Gucci."

"Gabe, I . . ." I'm struggling for words for the first time in my life.

"Don't think about it. Just say yes."

I stare at him, thinking this is crazy but knowing it feels right.

I press my hands to his face and kiss his mouth hard.

"Yes," I whisper against his lips. "Yes, you beautiful, crazy man. Of course I'll live with you."

Chapter Twenty-Eight

Gabe

WE'RE ON THE WAY to the hospital, so I can finally have this fucking boot taken off. I can't believe it's been six weeks since Speedy literally crashed into my life.

And, now, I'm in love with her, and she loves me back. And we're going to build a future together.

It's nuts but amazing. I've never been happier than I am with her now.

No one gets me like she does. No one makes me laugh harder or turns me on like she does.

She knows the worst things about me, and she still loves me.

She's incredible. And I'm the luckiest guy in the world.

With a smile on my face, I roll my window down and light up a cigarette. Then, I reach across the console and take hold of her hand.

She glances at me and smiles, and my insides light up.

I'm like a lovesick puppy over her, and I don't care.

She's mine, and I'm never letting her go.

She drops me off at the front of the hospital and insists I go inside while she parks the car.

Instead of going upstairs, I grab some coffees and wait for her.

Her face brightens when she sees me. "I thought I told you to go upstairs."

I hand her the black coffee and kiss her mouth. "Since when do I ever listen to you?"

"True dat."

Chuckling, I catch hold of her hand, and we ride the elevator up to the X-ray department.

Tate said he'd meet us there, as he wants to run an X-ray after he's taken the boot off just to make sure everything's okay. But I'm sure it is because my foot feels fine. I just want this fucking thing off for good.

Tate is waiting for us in reception when we get there.

"Hey, brother." I hug him. In a manly way, of course.

"Hey, Ava." Tate kisses her on the cheek.

My brother is fully up to speed on the status of my and Speedy's relationship.

When I told him we were together, his response was, "About time."

I don't know whether that was meant in reference to the time it took Speedy and me to get together, which wasn't that long, or that I finally got myself a girlfriend.

And that's not as pathetic as it sounds. I could have had a girlfriend anytime I wanted. I just never did.

Not until Speedy.

"Right. Come on then. Let's go take this boot off and make sure you're all healed."

"I'll wait here," Speedy says. Taking a seat in the reception area, she picks up a magazine from the table.

"Won't be long, babe." I kiss her.

"Oh, here. Don't forget your other shoe." She pulls it from her bag.

I brought my other shoe with me, so I won't have to walk around with one bare foot and look like a cunt.

I take the shoe, grab another kiss, and then head to the X-ray department with Tate.

Forty-five minutes, and I'm boot-free and all healed. *About fucking time.*

Tate walks back with me to reception. "So, things are going well with you and Ava."

"Really well. I've asked her to live with me permanently."

"Wow. That's great, Gabe. I'm really happy for you. You, more than anyone, deserve to be happy. I hope Ava knows how lucky she is to have you."

"She knows. I make sure to remind her every day." I grin.

He stops me with a hand on my arm before we reach the reception area. "Look, I know I don't say this often enough, but I am grateful for everything you did for me after Mom and Dad—"

"Tate, you don't have to thank me for anything. I'm your big brother. It's my job to take care of you. There isn't a single thing that I wouldn't do for you. I've always got your back."

"Goes both ways, you know that?"

"I know. Now, stop with the sappy shit 'cause my girl is waiting out there for me, and I intend to take her home and fuck her good and proper now that I have my leg back."

Tate's cell goes off. He checks it. "I have to go. I'm needed upstairs. I'll call you later."

"Later."

I leave Tate, and Speedy's right where I left her.

"Well, look at you." She gets to her feet, smiling and looking sexy as fuck.

"No more boot, baby. You know what that means?"

"That you're driving the car home?"

I chuckle and grab hold of her hand. "Half right. Yes, I'm driving my car home, and as soon as we get there, I'm fucking you up against the living room wall. How does that sound?"

"Let's go."

It's a race for who can get to the car faster. It feels good to drive my car again. But I have us back home in record time.

I'm on her the second the elevator doors close, pinning her to the wall and thrusting my tongue into her mouth.

We reach my apartment. The elevator doors open, and we stumble out, still kissing.

She drops her bag to the floor and kicks off her shoes.

I kick mine off, ignoring the slight pain in my foot.

She grabs my T-shirt and yanks it up. I break our kiss to grab the back of my shirt and pull it over my head, tossing it to the floor.

Her mouth immediately goes to my chest, and she starts kissing her way down, lowering to her knees.

She unzips my shorts and pulls them down along with my boxers. I kick them aside.

She presses a kiss to the tip of my cock.

I reach down and take her chin in my hand. "Don't tease me, Ava. I'm a man close to the edge."

Lust sparks in those gorgeous eyes of hers. She takes my cock in her mouth, and my head drops back, thudding against the wall.

This feels way too fucking good, and if she keeps at it, I'll be coming way too soon.

I run my hand through her hair, and gripping the strands, I ease her head back off my cock. She releases me with a wet pop that has desire bolting down my spine.

"My turn," I tell her.

Then, I grab her arm and pull her to her feet. I turn us around, and I push her back against the wall.

"You're still dressed."

"I am."

I grab the front of her button-up dress and rip it open. She gasps. The buttons ping across the marble floor. I push the tattered dress off her shoulders. Next goes her bra. Then, her panties.

"Much better." I run my eyes up and down her body. The curve of her hips. The softness of her belly. Her tits . . . those fucking gorgeous tits that belong entirely to me. As does her pussy.

All of her belongs to me.

And I'm hers completely. She owns me.

Something possessive and primal rips through me.

I slam my mouth down onto hers. Her arms wrap around my neck. I grab her ass and hike her legs up around my waist.

"I was going to lick your pussy, but I can't fucking wait. I need to fuck you now."

"Yes. Do it. Fuck me."

I thrust up inside her. She screams out my name. I start to fuck her with the maddening intensity that I feel for her.

I pump every feeling I have for her into her with my cock, trying to show her how I feel with my body. I can tell her a thousand times that I love her, but it just doesn't feel like enough. It's not a big enough word to express how much I want and need and desire her.

"Gabe. Gabe. Gabe," she chants my name.

"You feel me inside you? How deep I am?"

"Yes. Yes!"

"This is it, baby. Just you and me. Forever."

"Forever. Yes, Gabe. God, yes," her breathless voice whispers over my skin.

Her small hands slide up into my hair, tugging on it. My mouth drops to her neck, and I kiss and lick at her skin.

"Bite me," she moans. "Mark me. Please."

Her words are like gasoline on a match. Desire rages through my blood. It roars in my ears.

I sink my teeth into the delicate skin at the base of her neck and suck hard.

Her heels dig into my ass, pushing her pussy even closer to me. Her hands drop to my back, and she rakes her nails into my skin.

"Fuck yeah." I pump in and out of her. "That feels so fucking good."

She drags her nails up and down my back, and I take her mouth in a desperate kiss.

We're all teeth and tongues and total fucking need.

"Are you close? 'Cause I can't hold off much longer. It's too fucking good."

"I'm nearly there. Just keep doing . . . God, yeah, just keep doing that."

Knowing just what will set her off, I hold her up under her ass with one hand while the other pinches her nipple hard.

She screams. Her muscles clamp down on my cock as she starts to come, setting off my own orgasm.

I pour everything I have inside her. It shakes me to the core.

My legs are trembling, my heart pounding.

Her head drops to my shoulder.

"Jesus," I utter.

"Yeah." She lifts her head from my shoulder and tenderly kisses my jaw.

I turn my head in and capture her lips with mine.

She hums a sweet sound and wraps her arms around my neck.

"Love you," she murmurs.

"Love you, too."

I give her one final kiss and then push off the wall. I carry her to the bathroom to clean up.

I deposit her on the counter and run the faucet, wetting a cloth under it. I wring it out and then wipe between her legs.

I clean myself up, and still naked, I pick her back up and walk us to the living room.

"We not dressing?" she asks.

"No point. I'll only be getting you naked again soon."

I put her down on the sofa, and she stretches her

gorgeous body out on it. I walk over to the window and open it.

I grab my smokes off the coffee table and light up.

"Baaahhh!"

"Shit! Gucci's still in the kitchen." Speedy bolts up. "I can't believe I forgot to let her out. That's your fault, distracting me with hot wall sex."

"Good to know I have that effect on you. You stay there. I'll let her out."

I head to the kitchen and push the door open. The moment I do, Gucci head-butts me in my leg and then bolts off to the living room to find Speedy.

"You're welcome," I call after the little brat.

I go back into the living room, and Ava's on her phone, a blanket wrapped around her.

"No, that's fine. I can make that day. Sure, yeah. That's great. Thank you so much." She hangs her phone up, a big smile on her face.

"Good news?"

"I got a job!"

"No way! That's amazing, babe." I drop my cigarette in the ashtray and go over and hug her. "Where's the job?"

"Here in LA. At a theater downtown. They need a new wardrobe mistress. Their last one just upped and quit on them. So, they need me to start pretty much straightaway."

"That's fucking great. I'm happy for you." I reach over and grab my cigarette. Then, I sit back and take a drag.

"I'm happy for me, too." She snuggles into my body.

"So, when do you start?"

"They want me to go in on Monday."

"So, I've got two more days with you."

She tips her head back and looks up at me. "You've got forever with me, if you still want me?"

I lean my head down and kiss her lips. "I'll always want you."

"Good." She plants another kiss on me. Then, she moves her head and tucks it under my chin.

I take another drag of my cigarette and watch the smoke curl up into the air.

"What a great day," she murmurs. "You got your boot off, and I got a new job."

"We should go out. Celebrate."

She sits up and turns to me. "Yeah?"

"Yeah." I smile. "Go get dressed 'cause I'm taking you out dancing."

Chapter Twenty-Nine

Ava

M Y HAIR IS UP in a sleek ponytail with some strands framing my face. My makeup is neutral, my lips red. I'm wearing a Victoria Beckham dress that I snagged from the last film I worked on. It's a calf-length fifties-style dress with a rosebud pattern, cinched waist, and asymmetrical high neckline. I've red heels on my feet.

I spray my favorite perfume on, and I'm ready to go.

I look at my reflection in the mirror.

My cheeks are flush. I look happy.

That's because I am.

I'm going out dancing with the man I love, and I've just gotten a new job. There's a lot to be happy about right now.

I smooth my hands down the front of my dress. Grab my clutch and head out of my room to Gabe. Gucci trots along behind me.

When I walk into the living room, my heart nearly trips over itself.

Gabe is standing at the window, his back to me. He's wearing a gunmetal-gray suit. His hands are pushed into the pockets of the pants.

"Hey." I smile.

But he doesn't reply. Doesn't move. Doesn't turn around.

"Gabe?" I step closer, my heels clicking against the floor, suddenly loud in the silence.

"Why?" That one word, whispered with a serious intensity, confuses me but sends a warning signal to my brain that something's definitely not right.

"Why what? What's wrong, Gabe?" I take another step closer, putting my clutch down on the arm of the sofa.

Finally, he turns. And I wish he hadn't. His face is like stone.

My brow furrows. "What's happened?"

His hands drop from his pockets. He balls them at his sides. "Why did you do it, Ava?"

"Do what? You're going to have to help me out here because I have no clue what you're talking about."

"Don't play fucking stupid!" he roars, surprising the hell out of me. "I know, Ava. I fucking know. Just tell me why you did it."

I frown. "Don't yell at me like that, Gabriel. And I honestly don't know what the hell you're talking about. What did I supposedly do?"

"You know exactly what you did. You sold me out. You fucking sold me out, Ava."

"I'm sorry, what?"

"Gil called me." Gil is Gabriel's manager. "Bradford Digby's fucking lawyers called Gil to notify him that a story on me is going live on Digby's trashy fucking news site in an hour."

"What?"

"Don't play dumb. It doesn't suit you. Did they not tell you that it'd be going live so soon? What were you going to do? Just up and disappear before I found out it was you?"

"Jesus, Gabe!" I tug on my ponytail, frustrated. "I honestly don't have a clue what you're talking about. I didn't sell any story to anyone. I haven't spoken to anyone. I don't know what's going on here, but it doesn't have anything to do with me."

He advances across the room so quickly, it forces me back a step.

He looms over me, face taut with anger. "You recorded our conversation. When I told you about my parents being in prison, about me fucking women for money, you got it all on tape, and then you sold it to Bradford fucking Digby!"

"No!" I gasp. "No, I didn't!"

"Liar," he hisses. Then, he laughs an empty sound. "Well, you sure got lucky with that conversation. I bet you couldn't believe your fucking luck. No wonder you were pushing me to be honest with you. I bet you weren't expecting what came out of my mouth though. It was probably as close to winning the lottery for you, hearing all that. Did you record all our conversations? Or just that one?"

My hands ball into fists at my sides. "I've never recorded any of our conversations."

"Liar."

"I'm not lying!"

"Just fucking stop, Ava. The lawyers sent Gil the interview that you signed off on and a copy of the recording of our conversation."

He pulls his cell from his pocket and presses the screen. A second later, the room is filled with the sound of Gabe's and my voices.

"I used to sleep with women for money."

"What?"

"And my parents are in prison for drug trafficking, racketeering, and murder."

He presses stop on the recording.

"Gabe . . . I don't know how our conversation was recorded, but it wasn't me."

He swipes the screen on his phone and turns it to me. "It's all there, in black and white, Ava. Every single thing I told you. As quoted by you."

I grab the phone from him and scan the words in front of me. I catch sight of my name.

> *. . . details from the woman who knows him best. His live-in lover, Ava Simms.*

"No," I gasp, my eyes flying to Gabe. "No, I didn't do this. This wasn't me, I swear." My heart is pounding in my chest, my mind reeling with confusion.

"Stop fucking lying to me!" he yells.

"I'm not lying! It wasn't me! Someone else recorded our conversation because it wasn't me."

His eyes fix on me, cold and hard. "Swipe the screen."

"Why?"

"Swipe the fucking screen!"

I do as he said, and there's a document.

"You probably recognize that. It's the contract you signed with Digby, giving him exclusive rights."

"I didn't sign any contract! You have to believe me!"

He laughs hollowly. "And I suppose that isn't your name and signature at the bottom either."

I zoom in on the bottom of the document, and there, in black ink, is my name and signature. It's mine. I recognize it as mine.

"No." I'm shaking my head. "Gabe, I didn't sign this. I would never betray you like that. I swear to you."

He snatches his phone from my hand and turns his back on me.

"Gabe." I step up to him and place my hand on his back.

He jerks away, like I burned him. In his mind, I have. He thinks I've betrayed him.

"Don't fucking touch me." His voice is so chilling that I shiver. "Don't ever fucking touch me again." He turns to look at me, and his eyes look right through me. "I just hope the money was worth it."

"What money? Gabe, I swear on my entire family, I swear on Gucci's life, I didn't do this."

He steadily stares back at me. "I don't believe you."

It's like a blow to the stomach. I fold my arms over the ache his words just put there.

"How much did you get? How much was I worth, Ava? If you'd told me you needed the money, I would have given it to you. You wouldn't even have had to fuck me. I'd have given it to you for free."

"I didn't get any money from anyone! Jesus, Gabe! Listen to me! I have a thousand bucks to my name. Here, I'll show you." I grab my cell from my clutch. I pull my online banking up and thrust my phone at him, showing him the screen.

He barely looks at it. "It means nothing. People can have more than one bank account."

"But I don't have another bank account! I have one! I didn't do this, Gabe. You have to believe me."

He stares at me. Black eyes devoid of anything but anger.

"I can't believe this is happening." I drop my phone to the sofa and press my hand to my shaking head.

Tears push at my eyes. My lips tremble. I bite down to stop from crying.

"Gabe, I didn't do this. You know me," I implore, my voice shaking with the force of the emotions running through me.

"I thought I did. Clearly, I was wrong."

"Please . . . I didn't do this. I know my name is quoted on that story and that my signature is at the bottom of that document, but I'm telling you"—I press my hand to my chest—"it wasn't me. I didn't tell any journalist anything. I haven't told anyone about what you told me. And I never would. You have to believe me."

I look at him, begging him to believe me.

It feels like forever before he speaks, "I don't have to do a fucking thing."

I suck in a sharp breath. "You really think I'm capable of this? That I could do this to you?"

"Yes."

A word has never cut me more. I feel like I've been sliced open and left to bleed out.

A tear runs down my face. I brush it away with the back of my hand.

I want to beg him to listen, but my dignity won't allow it. So, I take a fortifying breath before I speak again, "Then, I guess there's nothing more left to say."

"No, there isn't. Only that I want you out of my home and out of my life."

With my heart in tatters, shredded at my feet, I turn and run back to my room. As soon as I'm inside, a sob breaks from my mouth. I press my hand to my mouth to catch it. Tears run down my face as I grab my hand-bag and shove a few items of clothes into it. I'll have to come back for the rest. I just need to get out of here now. I grab my car keys off the dresser, and I go back through to the living room.

Gabe's still there, back to me, staring out the window again.

I pick my cell up from the sofa and scoop Gucci up in my arms. She presses her face into my neck, comforting me, like she understands what's going on. Her comfort makes me hurt so much more.

"I just . . . I can't believe this is happening." My quiet words echo around the room.

Gabe slowly turns to me.

I watch him with pleading eyes. "I didn't do what you think I did. You're making a mistake."

His mouth tightens. Eyes darken. "The only mistake I've ever made was trusting you."

I thought he couldn't cut me more. I was wrong.

I close my eyes against the pain. Tears run from the corners of them.

He says my name.

I open my eyes to him.

"I don't *ever* want to see you again. Understand?"

I nod my head because it's all I can do. Words have failed me.

And, using every ounce of strength I have, I turn and leave his apartment for good.

Chapter Thirty

Ava

CLIMB IN MY car and put Gucci on the passenger seat. I throw my bag into the footwell.

For a moment, I just sit here, hands on my steering wheel, staring out the window in disbelief.

I can't believe what just happened.

Tears run down my face and onto my lips. I wipe them away with my hands.

"*Baaahhh.*"

I glance over at Gucci. "I know, baby. I just . . . I don't know what's happening. I'm as confused as you are."

I pick her up and set her in my lap, hugging her to me. I bury my face in her soft fur. Tears start to soak her coat.

"Sorry, baby girl." I dry her fur with my hand and wipe my eyes dry.

I don't know what to do. I could call my brother, but he's in Japan at the moment, and I don't want to bother him. And I know, if I call Mom and Dad, they'll want me to come home to New York. Stupidly, I don't want to leave here. Because Gabe's here.

I know; I'm a fucking idiot.

But he's alone, and he's hurting.

He might hate me and think I've done an awful thing. I might be angry and hurt as hell that he thinks I could have done that to him, but I love him, and I don't want him to be alone when this story hits the press.

I think about calling Tate because I know Gabe won't, but I don't know his cell number. I don't want to call the hospital.

Then, it hits me.

There is one person I can call.

I lean over and grab my cell from my bag. I take a deep breath, steadying my breathing, and press her number.

"Hey, stranger."

"Hey, Charly."

Charly is a good friend of mine. I've known her for years. I've not spoken to her in a few months, but this is how we've always been. And I know I can call her whenever I need help.

"I know it's been a while since I last called, but I really need your help."

"Sure. What's up?"

"Are you in LA at the moment?"

"No, I'm in Oregon."

Charly lives there with her boyfriend, Vaughn West, who's a famous movie star, and he also happens to be a close friend of Gabe's. That's the reason I've called her. I know Gabe has just been a world-class asshole to me and has hurt me like no one has before, but I also know he's hurting over the fact that the whole world will soon know about his past, and I don't want him to be alone when that happens. I know it's killing him that this will be getting out.

"Oh. Okay. Just . . . could you do me a favor?"

"Sure. Anything."

"Could you have Vaughn call Gabe?"

"Gabe? As in, Gabe Evans?"

"Yes."

"Okay. But why are you asking me to get Vaughn to call Gabe? I didn't think you guys knew each other well. Or at all."

I take a deep breath. "We didn't. But we do now. It's a long story. I just really need Vaughn to call Gabe."

She picks up on the urgency of my tone. "What's going on, Ava?"

An unexpected sob bursts from me. I press my hand to my mouth.

"Shit, Ava. What's going on?"

"Just Gabe and I were together, and now, we're not because he thinks I did something that I didn't. And, now, something's about to be made public and it's going to really hurt him and I don't want him to be alone and I would have called his brother, but I don't know his number, and I know Vaughn is a good friend and I thought he could call him—"

"Okay, babe. I'll get Vaughn to call Gabe. But, first, I need you to take a deep breath and tell me everything from the start."

So, I do. I tell her everything—from the moment I hit Gabe with my car to what just happened in his apartment. The only things I leave out are the details of Gabe's past. It might be public knowledge soon, but I made a promise that I wouldn't ever tell a soul, and I'm keeping that promise even if Gabe thinks I didn't.

"Jesus, Ava. I don't know what to say. I just—"

"It's fine, Charly."

"No, it's not fine. He blames you for this when you haven't done anything wrong."

My heart swells because she believes me at my word, which is more than Gabe did.

"And the first thing you do is call me, so I can have Vaughn check on him. Guy doesn't know how lucky he is."

"He's hurting."

"He's an asshole. I'm sorry, Ava, but he is."

No, he's in pain. He thinks I've betrayed him.

But I don't want her to think I'm making excuses for him, so I say nothing.

"Will you just have Vaughn call him, please?"

"He's calling him now."

"Oh. Good. That's great. Thank you."

There's a brief pause, and then Charly says, "So, what are you going to do now?"

I let out a sigh. "I don't know."

"Do you have anywhere to stay?"

I look around my car and at Gucci, who's climbed back onto the passenger seat while I've been talking to Charly.

"Well, I can try to get a hotel room, but I don't know of any hotels that'll take Gucci."

"Who the hell is Gucci?"

"She's my pygmy goat."

"You have a pygmy goat? When—actually, never mind. What about Logan? Can you go to his place?"

"He got a job in Maine. Went there a few days ago. But I'll be fine, honestly. Don't worry about me."

"Yeah, of course I'm not going to worry." I can practically see her rolling her eyes at me. "Look, I'm gonna call the hotel where Vaughn and I stay when we're in LA. I'll get you a room there."

"What about Gucci?"

"They'll take you and Gucci, or they'll lose business they don't want to lose."

Her confidence makes me smile.

"It's really kind of you to offer to do this, Charly, but my bank account won't stretch to the kind of hotels that you and Vaughn stay in. I'll just try and get a motel. And, if not, I'll sleep in my car."

"The hell you will. I'm calling the hotel now, and I'm paying—"

"Charly, no."

"Ava, I'm not taking no for an answer. I'm booking a room for you and your goat. And then I'm catching a flight to LA first thing."

"You don't have to do that."

"I know I don't. But I want to. You're my friend, babe. And I know, if this were reversed, you'd do the exact same for me."

"Of course I would. In a heartbeat."

"So, it's settled then. I'll text you with the hotel details in a few minutes. Call me if there are any problems when you check in. And I'll see you in the morning."

A tear rolls from my eye and down my cheek. "Thanks, Charly. I've missed you."

"Missed you, too, babe. I'll see you tomorrow, bright and early."

"See you then."

I hang the phone up and hold it to my chest. Then, I rest my head back on the headrest and stare up at the roof of my car, praying that Gabe is okay up there, in his apartment, alone.

Chapter Thirty-One

Gabe

I PICK UP THE bottle of Scotch that I've spent the night with and drain the remains.

I glance out at the morning creeping into the dark.

Foo Fighters' "Best of You" is playing on a loop. It's been playing for hours. It's stuck on repeat. But I can't be fucked to get up and change it. And, honestly, it's pretty fucking apt for me at the moment, so I've just left it playing.

My cell starts to ring. I glance over at it on the coffee table.

Tate.

I leave it to ring out.

My cell's been ringing all night. Vaughn. Julian. Gil. Donna. My publicist. And a bunch of other people I don't give a shit about.

This is the first time that Tate's called though.

He must've just seen the news.

Jesus. The thought of my baby brother knowing what I used to do to make money . . .

I squeeze my eyes shut and breathe through the pain.

I should have called him to give him a heads-up, but I just couldn't bring myself to call him.

Well, he knows now.

The whole world knows.

My cell starts to ring again.

A number I don't recognize.

"Fuck off!" I yell at my phone, like the person on the other end can hear me.

I should turn it off.

But Speedy might call.

Pathetic, right?

She's betrayed me. Fed me to the sharks in return for a cash bonus. And I won't turn my phone off in case she calls.

Not that I would answer. I just want to have the satisfaction of knowing that she called.

She sold you out, you pathetic piece of shit.

I laugh out loud. The sound echoes around my empty apartment, reminding me that I'm alone.

And alone is how I should be. It's how I should have always been. I should never have gotten involved with her.

I can't believe how fucking stupid I was. I told her everything. Spilled my guts out like a little bitch. When what I should have done is gotten rid of her. I should have tossed her out on her ass the second I fucked her.

Needing a smoke, I grab my cigarette pack off the floor, but the box is empty.

"For fuck's sake." I crumple the box in my hand and toss it aside.

Then, I drag my sorry ass off the sofa and go in search of some smokes. I think there are some in the kitchen drawer.

I go into the kitchen and stop dead, hit with a barrage of memories of her in here, cooking.

I can almost see her here, at the counter, cutting up vegetables for that fucking goat. And that time when she was making pizza, and I moved behind her and slid my fingers inside her—"Fuck!" I roar.

I shove everything off the counter with my arms, the items crashing to the floor. Then, I'm grabbing anything I can get my hands on. The cups on the rack go smashing into the wall. The pan sitting on the stove goes flying across the room. I pick up a kitchen stool and start smashing it against the wall until only pieces of wood are left in my hands.

"Fuck!" I grip my head in my hands and slide down the wall to the floor as I start to cry.

I'm fucking crying.

I haven't cried since . . . it's been so long that I can't remember. And, now, here I am, bawling my eyes out like a pussy because of her.

I fucking hate her.

And I love her.

I want her.

I didn't know it was possible to feel such strong conflicting emotions for one person, but Ava's shown me that I can.

The first and only woman I've ever fallen in love with, and she guts me like this.

Why did she do this to me? How could she do this to me?

I thought it hurt when my parents were taken to

prison, leaving Tate and me alone. But this feels so much worse. Ava took my trust and used it against me.

And for what?

Money.

Fuck, if that was all she wanted, I would have given it to her.

I would have given her anything.

Done anything for her.

But it's all just so fucked up. Because she's never been about money. She's never seemed to care about it.

So, why sell me out for cash?

It just doesn't make sense.

But then maybe I didn't know her at all. Clearly, I didn't.

And it's not like I'm known for having a good judge of character. I didn't know my parents were murdering psychos, and I'd known them for seventeen years.

I laugh out loud at my own fucking stupidity, my head thudding back against the wall.

It just . . . fucking hurts so much.

I loved her.

I love her.

It hurts too much, and I need it to stop. I need to stop feeling.

I rub my hand over my face, drying away my pussy tears, and get to my feet. Stepping over the mess I just made, I go to the freezer and get the bottle of vodka from there.

I unscrew the cap and take a long drink. The liquor calms my pounding pulse, chilling my veins.

I retrieve a cigarette pack from the kitchen drawer and go back into the living room.

That fucking song is still playing.

I go over to my iPod system and turn the repeat off. I click forward a song. Fall Out Boy's "Sugar, We're Goin' Down" starts to pump out of the speakers as I flop down on the sofa.

I get a cigarette out, put it between my lips, and light it up. I inhale a long pull of smoke.

I screw the cap off the vodka and take a long drink, letting the smoke out through my nose.

Fuck, that's better.

This is all I need in life—cigarettes and alcohol. Wasn't it Oasis who sang that song? They had it right. I don't need anything else but these two things in my hands right now.

Fuck Ava. And her lies and deceit.

I don't need her. I never did.

And fuck the rest of the world, too.

I don't need anyone.

Everything I need, I've got right here.

Chapter Thirty-Two

Ava

IT'S EARLY MORNING. I'M not sure of the time. I only know it's morning because the sun is up.

Miley is on the TV, swinging on a wrecking ball and singing her little broken heart out.

I feel your pain, Miley. I really do.

Men are assholes.

Maybe I should get a wrecking ball to swing around on. It might make me feel better.

As you can probably guess, I haven't slept all night. My eyes are swollen and puffy, and I'm mentally drained. I've alternated between bouts of crying and then feeling angry and confused to eating my body weight in chocolate to make myself feel better. I'm an eater when I'm sad.

And I'm definitely sad right now, and this song is not doing anything to help my mood.

But I don't turn it off. Clearly, I'm in the mood to torture myself.

I look over at the box of chocolates.

Empty.

I sigh.

I clamber off the bed and go over to the mini bar. There are bars of chocolate in it. But the prices are astronomical, and I can't afford to waste my money on overpriced chocolate, no matter how much I might want it.

"Looks like another trip to the store," I say to Gucci.

She's asleep on the bed. I'm pretty sure she didn't even hear me.

I put my hair up into a messy bun. I pull on my hoodie and push my feet into my flip-flops.

Then, I look down at myself.

I'm wearing my Little Mermaid pajamas.

I consider this for a moment.

Screw it. I'm going out in them. It's not like I'm out to impress anyone right now. And, honestly, I don't give a crap what people will think.

I can just be the crazy lady in her pajamas.

I'm just about to get my wallet and room key when someone knocks on the hotel door.

Gabe.

Don't be stupid, Ava. He doesn't know where you are right now. And he hates you.

I go over to the door and open it without checking the peephole to see who it is, and I find Charly standing there.

"Nice pajamas."

I open my mouth to speak, and I burst into tears.

"Oh, hell."

She wraps her arms around me, hugging me tight, and I sob into her shoulder.

"It's going to be okay." She soothes me, rubbing my back with her hand.

"I'm sorry." I sniffle. Pulling away, I wipe my face with the sleeve of my hoodie.

"Don't be." She closes the door behind herself and drops her bag to the floor. She takes her jacket off and tosses it on top of her bag.

"I know, but you've just gotten here. You don't need me bawling on your shoulder."

"Bawl away." She lifts her shoulder in offering, forcing a smile from me. "That's why I'm here. So, you can cry, scream, and do whatever you need to, to make yourself feel better."

"Thanks," I say, sitting down on the edge of the bed.

Gucci gets up, wanders over to me, and climbs in my lap.

"I'm so glad you're here."

"Me, too." She tosses her cell on the bed and comes to sit by me. "This Gucci?" She reaches out and strokes her.

"Yeah." I smile.

"She's super cute. Aren't you, Gucci?"

Charly scratches behind her ears, and Gucci, the attention whore, climbs off my lap and onto Charly's lap where Charly continues to lavish attention on her.

"Have you slept at all?" she asks me.

I shake my head.

"You need to sleep, Ava."

"I know. I just . . . I couldn't." I rub my hands over my face.

"Have you heard from Gabe since last night?"

As my mouth turns down with sadness at hearing his name, I bite the inside of my bottom lip. "No."

"Vaughn's on his way over there now. He just

dropped me off, and he's going to meet Tate and Julian at Gabe's place. I know you didn't want him to be alone, so I thought you'd want to know."

"Thanks, Charly."

"I saw the news . . . about Gabe."

I glance at her. "It wasn't me. I didn't tell Bradford Digby anything."

"I know that. God, you didn't even tell me on the phone, and you could have because you knew the story was about to drop."

"I would never share Gabe's private life with anyone. I just don't understand how this happened, Charly." My eyes swell with tears, and I blink them back. "There's a recording of our private conversation, which Gabe thinks I did. And a contract with my signature on the bottom, giving exclusive rights to Digby."

"Fucking Digby," Charly mutters. "That guy has his nose in everybody's shit. Look what he did to Vaughn."

Before Charly met Vaughn, he was dating this actress, Piper Watts. Vaughn, Piper, and Cain Acton—Vaughn's best friend—were on Digby's talk show, doing a live interview about their upcoming film. Then, Digby exposed that Piper and Cain had been having an affair behind Vaughn's back. He was humiliated. He took it quite badly for a while, partying and hooking up with multiple women. But that was before he met Charly.

"I just don't get it. How Digby could say that it was me when it wasn't. And it's not like I can call him up and say, *Hey, why the hell are you spreading lies about me?*"

"It fucking sucks, babe."

"The thing I can't get my head around is how he got

a recording of our conversation or my signature on that contract."

"Signatures can be forged," Charly says.

"Yeah, but it was definitely my writing. I recognized it." I sigh.

"Well, have you signed anything recently?"

I shake my head. "No ... oh, wait. I did sign something the other day for Gabe's cleaners."

"What?"

Lifting Gucci into her arms, she shifts around on the bed, sitting Indian-style, and puts Gucci back in her lap. I move on the bed to face her.

"It was this new form. Sadie, one of the cleaners, asked me to sign it. It's something that their boss implemented just to prove that they've done the work."

"And you'd never signed one before?"

"Nope. That was the first time."

"Hmm." Charly taps her lip with her finger.

"What?"

"Just odd that your signature is on a contract that you definitely didn't sign, and only a few days ago, you signed a form that you'd never had to sign before. Did you read the form?"

"Not really," I admit.

"So, it's possible that you signed the contract giving permission to sell Gabe's story without realizing it."

"You mean, Sadie? No. No way. And, anyway, it's Digby who published the story."

"Digby doesn't write his own new pieces. He doesn't need to. He has a team of trashy writers who do that for him. He's the face, but there's a whole slew of rats turning that wheel."

"So, what? You think Sadie has something to do with it? But why use my name? It doesn't make sense. And how would she have gotten a recording of our conversation? She's only at the apartment during the day. And she's not alone. Barb, the other cleaner, is there, too."

"Hang on ... let me think." Charly taps her fingers on her temples.

I can almost see the wheels turning in her head.

"What's Sadie's surname?"

"I don't know."

"What's the name of the cleaning company she works for?"

"Floor-to-Ceiling Cleaning."

"Catchy name."

"Yeah, I thought that."

Charly picks her cell up from the bed and starts tapping away on the screen.

"What are you doing?"

"Getting their number. I'm gonna give them a call."

"Why?"

"To get her name, and while I'm at it, I'll ask about that form you signed."

"Charly, you can't just call them up and ask that!"

"Sure I can."

She grins and puts her cell to her ear. "Oh, hi. I was wondering if you could help me. Sure, yes, I'm in need of a new cleaner, as I had to fire my last one. She was terrible. Anyway, I was just wondering what you have in place to make sure that the cleaners do their job properly. Hmm ... mmhmm. A friend of mine has a cleaner, and she has to sign off on the job to say that the cleaner has done the job to satisfaction. Do you have that? Oh, you don't?" Charly gives me a knowing look. "Okay, that's great. Just one more thing. A friend of mine uses your service and said there's a woman who works for you who is such a great cleaner—Sadie . . . something. Black. Yes, that's right. Oh, she has, has she? Oh, well, that is a shame. Okay, well, thank you for your time. I'll be in touch."

Charly lowers the phone from her ear. "Seems Sadie Black left Floor-to-Ceiling Cleaning a couple of days ago." She taps her nails against the screen of her phone. "She had you sign a nonexistent form a few days before Gabe's story broke, and then she quit her job. Coincidental? Me thinks not."

"Oh my God." My heart starts to pound in my chest. "So, what do you think? That Sadie sold the story to Digby and used my name? But why use my name? And how did she get the recording?"

Charly stares up at the ceiling, thinking. "Where did you and Gabe have the conversation when he told you all that stuff about his past?"

"At his apartment, in the living room."

She brings her eyes back to mine, a light flickering on in them. "Maybe she bugged his apartment."

My eyes widen. "Bugged his apartment? Doesn't that seem a little far-fetched?"

"Maybe. But some people will do anything for a story. She could have bugged Gabe's apartment. Gotten the recording of your conversation. And then sold the tapes to Digby."

"But that still doesn't explain why she used my name. She'd want the glory for herself, right?"

"Not necessarily. Because illegally recording a huge

movie star's private conversation about his personal life and then publishing it in the press would, without a doubt, lead to a huge lawsuit for whoever did it. But if his girlfriend recorded the conversation and she sold the tapes to a journalist and signed a contract to give him exclusive rights to the story of the century? It would keep the journalist's nose clean, and he could run the story without repercussions."

"And, if a lawsuit did happen, it would land back on the girlfriend who recorded the conversation."

"Absolutely right."

"Holy shit." I press my hands to my head.

"Got to give it to Digby; it's clever as hell. If it wasn't so fucking deceptive and it wasn't you and Gabe he was screwing over, I might actually be impressed."

"I just can't believe this." I tug at my hair. "I can't believe he would go so far for a story."

"Digby's a shark with no morals."

"So, we get that Digby's behind the whole thing, but where does Sadie fit into the picture?"

"She probably works for him. So-called journalists like Digby have spies everywhere."

"That's nuts and a lot scary."

"It's the life of a celebrity, I'm afraid." She sighs, knowing all too well what it's like for Vaughn.

"I'm going to look up Sadie online and see if I can find anything out about her." I get my cell, bring up Google, and type in her name, but all that comes up are some Facebook profiles, and none of them are her.

"Check Digby's website. She might actually be a writer for him. He should have a roster of employees on there."

I bring his website up. In the search bar, I type *Sadie Black* and press Enter, but nothing comes up.

"Check Gabe's story. See who the writer is."

"I don't want to. I don't want to see it." I put down my phone. I've avoided looking at the story. The last thing I want to see is the reason Gabe and I are no longer together.

"I'll look then. I want to know who the writer is." Charly starts tapping on her screen. "Hmm. Weird."

"What?" I sit up straighter.

She meets my eyes. "The person who wrote Gabe's story is called Sandy White. Sadie Black. Sandy White. Similar or what?"

I grab the screen, looking at her name, reading it aloud, "'*Sandy White, writing for* Digby's Dirt.' You think that Sandy could be Sadie?"

"Let's find out."

Charly pulls up another search engine and types in *Sandy White, Digby's Dirt*.

A bunch of news stories on other celebrities fill the screen.

"Go on to Images," I tell Charly. "See if there's a photo of her."

Charly clicks on Images. A bunch of pictures of different celebrities come up that link to the stories that this Sandy White has written.

Charly scrolls through the pictures, and one catches my eye.

"There. Stop." I tap on the picture, enlarging it. My heart is hammering in my chest. "That's her. That's Sadie." I jab my finger at the picture.

She's dressed up, her hair down and curled, looking

really glam. Different to how I saw her in her cleaning uniform, but it's definitely her.

"*Chat show host Bradford Digby, actor Chester Handel, and journalist Sandy White at the 2016 Teen Choice Awards,*" Charly reads the text beneath the picture.

"Sadie is Sandy." I cover my mouth with my hands, getting to my feet in disbelief. "I can't believe that she did this. That Sadie or Sandy or whatever the hell you call her and Digby did this to me! What am I going to do?"

Charly looks up at me. "You have to tell Gabe."

"He won't listen to me, Charly." I shake my head. "Right now, I'm the last person he wants to see."

"Then, I'll tell him," she announces.

"What?" I say, surprised.

"Yeah. I'll go see him. I'll tell Gabe what we know about Digby and Sandy, the cleaner formerly known as Sadie."

"Charly . . . I really don't want to put you in the middle of this. Vaughn is Gabe's friend. I don't want to cause problems between you guys."

She takes my hands in hers. "You're not causing any problems. That fucker Digby and his bitch sidekick caused problems when they did this to you and Gabe. Ava, you're my friend, and I help my friends. Ho's before bro's every time, right?"

She grins, and I force a smile.

"Every single time," I say as I give her hands a squeeze.

Chapter Thirty-Three

Gabe

"**G**ABE."

I hear the distant sound of Tate's voice, and then a hand shakes my shoulder.

"What? Fuck off. I'm sleeping," I mumble, rolling away, laying my arm over my eyes.

"Gabe, get the fuck up." That's Julian's voice.

I drag my arm off my face and blink wearily against the morning light.

As I look up, I see the faces of Tate, Julian, and Vaughn.

"Ugh. Jesus. What the fuck do you three want?" I roll onto my side, away from them, facing the back of the sofa. "And how the hell did you get into my apartment?"

"I have a key, remember?" Tate says.

Someone sits on the sofa by my legs.

I open an eye and see it's Tate.

The look on his face. It looks a lot like disappointment. And it cuts right through me.

He knows. They all know.

Of course they do. It has to be all over the news by now.

Gabriel Evans, Ex-Gigolo and Son of Murderers

What a fucking headline. I bet the press have been pissing themselves with excitement.

I pull my anger on and wear it like a protective shield. "Don't look at me like that, Tate."

"I'm not looking at you like anything."

"The hell you are." I sit up, resting my back against the arm of the sofa, bending my knees up so that I can rest my elbows on them, and I scrub my hands over my face. "I don't need your judgment right now, so if that's what you all came here for, then you know where the door is."

"We're not here to judge you." Julian sits on the coffee table across from me. He pulls a pack of smokes from his pocket. Gets two out. Lights one up and passes it to me, and then lights one for himself.

"Gabe, we're here because we're your friends, and we wanted to make sure you were okay," Vaughn says from his spot where he's standing, leaning against the window.

Right where I was standing last night when I got the call that changed everything.

"Or did you just come to look at the freak?"

"Gabe . . ." Tate's voice is a warning.

I spot a quart of vodka left in the bottle I started on last night. I reach down and grab it from the floor. The cap's already off, so I take a good drink.

When I'm finished, three sets of eyes are watching me.

"What?" I put my cigarette in my mouth.

"Should you be drinking right now?" Vaughn says.

"I think drinking is exactly what I should be doing right now."

"Gabe, speaking from experience, drinking yourself into a coma isn't going to help anything," Julian says.

"Advice from the ex-junkie. Just what I need." I roll my eyes and then drain the vodka before tossing the bottle to the floor.

Julian doesn't react. But, still, I feel like a jackass. But I'm too far gone in my own pain to feel anything of real substance right now, so the emotion is gone before it can turn into guilt.

Julian takes a drag of his smoke and flicks the ash into the ashtray. "I'm gonna pretend like you didn't just say that because I know what it's like to be in pain and want to dull it with the nearest substance. And you were the only one who was there for me when I needed help. So, you get a free pass, Gabe. You get as many free passes as you need."

"I don't need free passes. What I need is to be left the fuck alone."

"Yeah, not happening," Tate says, settling back onto the sofa.

"Fine. Then, I'll fucking go out." I stub my smoke out and get to my feet.

"Yeah, you're not gonna want to go out there." Vaughn thumbs over his shoulder. "The paps are out in full force up front. We had to sneak in through the parking garage. And, from the looks of you, you're not in any fit state to drive." He gestures to the empty liquor bottles littering the coffee table.

I drive my fingers into my hair, feeling frustrated and trapped. "For fuck's sake!" I yell. Then, I pick up one of the empty bottles and throw it against the wall. It shatters, shards of glass scattering everywhere.

The silence around me is deafening.

"You feel better?" Julian's voice is low behind me.

"No, I don't fucking feel better!" I whirl on him.

And then all I can see are their faces staring at me. Judging me. As if they know what it's like to be me.

They don't know jack shit about my life!

My head starts to pound like a drum. My blood is hot with anger.

"How the fuck am I supposed to feel right now?" I yell. "Everyone fucking knows! And then you three are here, fucking judging me! And I don't need it! None of you knows how hard it was for me back then! I did what I had to do! And it was my business!" I pound my fist against my chest. "My private fucking business. And I trusted her, and now, everyone knows! She sold me out! She fucking . . . sold me out." My voice drops to a whisper. My legs give out on me. I sink to the floor. I put my head in my hands and squeeze my eyes shut. "I fucking loved her, and she sold me out."

"Jesus, Gabe." Tate is at my side, his arm around me. "I'm so sorry."

I lift my head from my hands and stare at him. "You have nothing to be sorry for. I'm the one who's sorry. I know this is going to come back on you, embarrass you."

"You think I give a flying fuck about what people think?"

"I think you're a kids' doctor who comes from a pair

of murdering drug dealers, and your brother used to let women fuck him for money."

"Stop thinking about how this affects me, Gabe. You don't need to worry about me. This is about you. You're what matters right now. I want to help you. Let me help."

"I don't need help. I'll be fine." I get to my feet, leaving him sitting there.

"You need to stop this." Tate gets to his feet.

"Stop what?"

"Acting like I'm still fucking twelve years old. I'm a grown man, and I don't need you shielding me from shit, Gabe. You should have told me the truth."

I laugh without humor. "What was I supposed to say? *Hey, Tate, remember when Mom and Dad were arrested, and we were on our own, so we moved out here, but I was struggling to make ends meet? Well, I started screwing women for money, so I could pay the rent.*"

He shakes his head. "I could've helped."

"You were a fucking kid, who just had his whole world turned upside down."

"So were you!" he yells, frustrated.

"I'm your older brother." I slam my hand against my chest. "It was my responsibility to take care of you. I did what I had to do. And I'd do it again in a heartbeat."

He's staring at me with a mixture of guilt and anger and frustration in his eyes. He looks so much like me right now that it's terrifying.

I grab my smokes and light another one up. Staring up at the wall, I take a drag and blow out the smoke.

"Have you thought about how you're going to handle this?" Vaughn says.

I turn my head and look over at him. "I'm not going to do jack shit."

"They won't let this go," Vaughn says, like I don't already know.

"They will if I refuse to talk about it."

"I spoke to Gil. He called me when he couldn't get ahold of you. They pulled together a press release. He just needs you to okay it. He emailed it over."

"I'm not sending out any press release. I don't have to justify myself to anyone."

"No, you don't. But you do have to address this with the media and your fans if you want to have a career left at the end of it," Julian says.

"I couldn't give a fuck about my career right now." I walk over to the window and stare out of it.

"You say that now . . ."

I turn back to Julian. "Honestly, all I want to do right now is sleep. Everything else can wait."

I toss my barely smoked cigarette into the ashtray. I walk away from the three of them, leaving them there, and go into my bedroom.

I shut the door. I fall facedown onto my bed and bury my face in the pillow.

But it smells like Speedy.

I roll onto my back and sit up, scrubbing my hands over my face.

As I draw them away, I see a pair of her bed shorts hanging over the back of the chair. Her lip balm on the dresser. One of her hair ties on my nightstand. I push up to my feet. I strip all the bedding from my bed. Then,

I gather it up in my arms. I get the hair tie, lip balm, and shorts. I go over to my bedroom door, open it, and toss it all out into the hallway.

Then, I close my door, climb onto my bed, pull the duvet over my head, and shut my eyes.

Chapter Thirty-Four

Gabe

MY APARTMENT IS QUIET, apart from the low sound of the television in the living room, when I finally drag my ass out of bed.

I go into the kitchen to get a bottle of water.

It's clean. The mess I made is gone, like it never happened. The only signs it did are the missing stool under the breakfast bar and a dent from when I smashed it into the wall.

I walk over to the fridge and get a bottle of water out. Then, I go into the living room.

I see the back of Vaughn's blond head as he sits on my sofa, watching basketball on my TV.

"You still here?"

He turns at the sound of my voice. "You look like shit."

"So sweet of you to say." I unscrew the cap off the water and drain the bottle halfway. "How long was I out for?"

"An hour."

"Is that all? Felt like longer."

"How are you doing?" he asks.

I shrug and walk over to the sofa. I put the water down on the coffee table, pick my smokes up from there, and sit my ass down on the sofa.

"What happened to Tate and Julian?" I ask.

"Tate had to go to the hospital. He got called in. There was an emergency with one of his patients. He'll be back as soon as he can. Julian's gone on a coffee run." He looks at me. "You were out of coffee. And you know how twitchy he gets without it."

"Ava—" I cut off.

"Ava what?"

I drag a hand through my hair. "Nothing. She used to get the coffee; that's all."

He's silent a moment. I light up a smoke and stare at the TV.

"You know, you didn't have to stay," I say low.

I can feel his eyes on me, but I don't look at him.

"I know I didn't have to stay. I wanted to."

I take a drag of my cigarette and slowly blow the smoke out.

"When the shit hit the fan with Cain and Piper, who was the first person to call me? You. Hell, we weren't even close back then. We just knew each other through work. But you were the first to call. You got my ass out of the house. Sure, you took me out and got me trashed, but you were there. The very fucking least I can do for you right now is be here when you need me."

"I'm fine."

"Yeah, you look it. Oh, and I cleaned up the glass from earlier, so you know."

The bottle I smashed earlier. Shit.

"Thanks," I mutter.

"Do you want to talk about it?"

"You mean, me being an ex-hooker?"

I stare at him, wanting to make him uncomfortable so that he won't push the conversation, but the fucker steadily stares back at me.

I look away. "No. I don't want to talk about it."

"And what about Ava?"

"What about her?" I glare at him.

"Do you want to talk about her?"

"No."

His silence weighs heavy for a moment.

"Charly's with her. They're at the Four Seasons. Ava stayed there last night. Charly flew in with me this morning and went straight there to see her."

The Four Seasons, huh? Nice. She must be using the blood money she earned from selling me out.

Hurt and anger squeeze my chest like a vise.

"Why are you telling me this?" I speak the words through gritted teeth.

"I thought you might want to know."

"Well, I don't," I snap. "I don't give a shit where she is."

Silence.

"Charly says that Ava is adamant that she didn't talk to that journalist."

I slide hard eyes to him. "You believe her?"

He lifts a shoulder. "Charly does, and I trust Charly."

"Then, you're both as big of a fool as I was." I stub my cigarette out and toss the butt into the ashtray.

"Gabe"—he sits forward, arms on thighs, hands clasped together—"the stuff that Digby printed. The things from your past. It doesn't matter shit to me. I don't look at you any differently. You did what you needed to, to survive. Fuck, you were barely an adult yourself, taking care of your kid brother. No one will judge you for that."

"Yes, they will." I tip my chin in the direction of the window. "Them out there, they'll judge me."

"So what? Don't let other people make you feel ashamed of who you were. You're who you are now because of your past."

"Yeah, and aren't I just a fucking stellar example of a human being?"

"You can be a moody asshole at times. You drink way too much and smoke like a fucking chimney. But you're also one of the best people I know. You'd give your shirt off your back to help someone. And don't try to fucking deny it because I know you would."

I sit forward, resting my elbows on my knees, and stare down at the floor. "I just wish I hadn't been so fucking stupid."

"You talking about Ava?"

I glance at him. "I trusted her. Spilled my fucking guts to her. And, now, because of that, my past, the stuff I wanted to keep hidden, is splashed all over the fucking tabloids. My career is in the toilet. And not only is my career fucked, but this is going to screw things up for Tate's, too."

"How?"

"He's a doctor for kids. You think people are going to want the child of mob bosses and the brother of an ex-whore taking care of their kids?"

"Tate will be fine. And so will you."

I laugh hollowly. "I'm dead in the water after this. Who's gonna want to hire me now?"

"Gabe, how many actors and actresses do you think have succumbed to the casting couch over the years? Thousands, I bet. The only difference is, they sleep with whomever they need to, to get a part in a movie. You slept with women to feed your kid brother. I know who's the better person in that scenario."

"Yeah, but their stories aren't splashed all over the papers."

"No. But we're all whores in this business. None of us are clean."

"You are."

"I've done things that I needed to, to get to where I wanted to be."

I stare over at him. "The . . . casting couch?"

"Fuck no." Pause. "You?"

"Surprisingly, no."

We look at each other and laugh. And it feels good for a moment. Then, I remember what I'm laughing about, and I don't feel so good anymore.

"That's because you're a great fucking actor, Gabe. Your career isn't done. And neither is Tate's. You don't need to worry about him. Trust me. We've seen worse things happen in this business, and careers have survived."

"Worse than two parents in jail for racketeering, drug dealing, and murder, and me selling myself for money?"

"Okay, well, maybe not that bad. But isn't that what we do now? Sell ourselves, our bodies, to the world for money. Look at Martha Stewart. She did time for fraud, and she came back even stronger. She made more money after that than she did before. It's how the situation is handled that counts. We get your PR team handling this the right way, and it'll be fine."

"I don't know, Vaughn." I lie back against the sofa and let out a tired-sounding sigh. "I just really don't feel like talking to anyone right now."

"Then, let me do it. I'll speak to Gil. I'll handle things for you."

I stare out the window at the view. "Fine." I sigh. "But I'm not speaking to any interviewers or going on any chat shows to talk about my fucking feelings. Got it?"

"Got it."

Chapter Thirty-Five

Gabe

"CHARLY'S HERE," VAUGHN SAYS to me, his cell pressed to his ear. "Is she okay to park in your building's parking garage?"

"Sure. Tell her to put eight-eight-three-nine into the keypad at the entrance, and the barrier will open, letting her in. She can park in bay two. You'll need to go down in the elevator to get her though. Use my key." I point to it on the coffee table.

"Did you get that, Pins? Yeah. See you in a few." Vaughn gets to his feet and swipes the elevator key off the table.

"Charly, she's . . . alone, right?"

Vaughn stops and looks at me. "Ava's not with her if that's what you mean. She's still at the hotel."

"Good."

Vaughn goes to get Charly, and I pick up the coffee that Julian brought back and take a sip.

It's decent, but it doesn't taste as good as Ava's coffee.

And I fucking hate that I miss her making me coffee. God, I'm pathetic.

"What did Gil say?" Julian asks me.

I glance over at him. He's sitting on the other sofa, drinking his coffee.

"Vaughn talked to him. Said I just needed to okay that press release he sent over, and once that's out there, they'll start pulling together a strategy based on the public response to try and stop this shit from completely destroying my career."

"Have you read the release?"

"Yeah." I sigh.

"And?"

"It's just the usual shit that we read all the time. *Gabriel regrets his past actions, and his parents' criminal past is in no way a reflection of him. He does not condone their crimes and has not had contact with his parents since their arrest.* Blah, blah, blah."

"If you hate the release, then have them rewrite it."

"And put what?"

"I don't know." Julian brings his coffee to his lips and takes a sip. "Just think about what you want to say and then tell your publicist and have her write it up."

"Yeah. I guess I could." I take another sip of my coffee.

A few minutes later, I hear the arrival of Vaughn and Charly.

And the first thing I want to do is ask Charly how Ava is.

How fucking lame is that?

I really need a punch in the face.

"Gabe." Vaughn's voice comes from behind me

before he comes into view. He stands to the left of the sofa, Charly by his side. "Charly needs to talk to you. It's important."

I look directly at Charly. "If it's about Ava, then I don't want to hear it."

She presses her lips together, looking like she's really likely to punch me in the head right now. Maybe I should invite her to. Knock some fucking sense into me.

Charly's eyes move around my living room. "Gabe, can I use your bathroom, please?"

I almost exhale with relief that she's not going to try to force me to hear whatever it is she's got to say.

"Sure. You can use the bathroom in my bedroom. It's the first door on your right. Bathroom's off there."

"Could you show me where it is, please?"

"Were my directions not clear enough?"

Her hands go to her hips, her lips pursing into a scowl. "They were just fine. But I'd really appreciate it if you would show me the way." She's staring at me, eyes wide, with a weird expression on her face.

"Vaughn, what the fuck is wrong with your girlfriend?"

"Pins, what's going on?"

Charly sighs, rolls her eyes, and then gets her phone out of her pocket. She starts tapping on the screen and then hands her phone to Vaughn. He reads whatever's on the screen. Then, he hands it over to me.

I read the words she typed into a Note on her phone.

I think your apartment is bugged. We need to talk. It's important. Bathroom is a safe place.

I look up at her. "Are you being for real right now?"

She snatches her phone from my hand. *Yes*, she mouths.

I look at Vaughn for help, and he just shrugs, hands out, palms up.

"What's going on?" Julian asks.

Charly puts her finger to her lips and hands her phone to Julian.

He reads it and then mouths, *Holy fuck*. He hands Charly's phone back to her, his eyes roaming over my living room.

Charly taps me on the shoulder and mouths, *Bathroom. Now*.

"For fuck's sake." I sigh. I could really do without this shit right now.

But I still get up from the sofa and start to follow Charly to the bathroom.

The next thing I know, Julian's beside me, and then Vaughn's on my other side. Apparently, they're coming, too.

I shake my head with annoyance and walk quickly to my bedroom, wanting to get this shit over and done with as soon as possible.

When we reach the bathroom, Charly's already inside.

We file in, and she shuts the door behind us. Then, she proceeds to turn on the faucets on the sink and the shower, leaving them all running.

"What the fuck are you doing?" I frown at her.

"If your bedroom is bugged as well, then they won't be able to hear us over the sound of the running water."

"Really?" Vaughn asks.

"Yeah. I saw it once on TV."

"I think I've seen that, too," Julian chimes in.

"This is fucking ridiculous," I snap. "I'm going."

I reach for the door when Charly barks at me, "Don't you dare open that door, Gabriel."

I look back at her. "And if I do?"

"Then, you'll regret it for the rest of your life. Because I know for a fact that Ava didn't sell you out. She was set up, and I know exactly how, why, and who did it."

My heart starts to beat erratically in my chest. But I keep my expression calm.

I remove my hand from the door and turn around to face Charly. "Is that so?" I lift a brow.

"Yep." She folds her arms over her chest.

"Tell us then," Julian says eagerly.

I shoot him a look.

"What?" he asks innocently. "I'm just keen to know—for your benefit, of course."

"Of course." I roll my eyes at him. "Okay, Charly, I'm listening."

"Okay, so your cleaner Sadie—"

"Who?"

"Your cleaner. You have two of them. They come twice a week."

"Yeah, I know that, but I don't fucking know their names."

Charly shakes her head at me. "Whatever. Well, aside from you, Ava, your brother, and your PA, they're the only people who have regular access to your apartment."

"And?"

"And the conversation that you and Ava had was recorded."

"By Ava."

"No. Not by Ava. I believe that one of your cleaners, Sadie—well, actually, she's not called Sadie, but I'll come back to that—bugged your apartment."

"This is ludicrous." I sigh.

"Just hear me out." Charly frowns. "So, when Ava told me that she couldn't understand how your conversation was recorded and how her signature got on that contract, it got me thinking. So, I asked Ava if she'd signed anything recently. She said no, and then, actually, yes, she did. The other day, your cleaner, Sadie, asked Ava to sign this new form that her boss had implemented to prove that she'd done the work. And Ava, being the lovely, trusting person she is, signed it. Sadie took the form, and off she went.

"But something just didn't sound right to me. Why would a cleaning company have people sign a form to say they did the job? It just seemed weird. So, I called up the cleaning company because I wanted to ask about the form, and I made up some bullshit story about how I was looking for a new cleaner and that Sadie had been recommended to me when the lady on the phone told me that Sadie no longer worked for them. She quit a few days ago. Alarm bells started ringing in my head. So, I asked about the form, and the lady had no clue what I was talking about.

"So, we have Sadie, who had Ava sign a form that she never needed to sign, and Ava told me that she didn't really look at the form when she signed it. This is days before Sadie quit her job, and then your story breaks. It doesn't seem like a coincidence to me."

"Me either," Julian says.

I ignore him and look at Charly. "So, what? You

think the form that Ava signed was actually the con-tract giving rights to the story?"

"Yep. And then I started thinking that maybe she was a journalist who bugged your apartment to get the story and then sold the tapes to the highest bidder."

"But she would know that no news site would touch the tapes because it was obtained illegally, and if they printed anything, they'd be looking at a lawsuit," Julian says.

"Exactly." Charly nods. "But, if it appears that it was the girlfriend who taped the conversation and she signed over the story to Sadie, then she could sell the tapes and story, no problem."

"And, if Gabe did sue, then it'd be Ava who got hit with the lawsuit because it was her signature on the contract."

"You got it, baby." She smiles at Vaughn before look-ing back at me. "So, I decided to Google Sadie, see what I could find out about her. The name the lady at the cleaning company gave me was Sadie Black, so I searched that but came up dry. So, we went to Digby's website to see if we could find anything on there, but there was nothing. Then, I clicked on Gabe's story and saw that it was written by someone called Sandy White."

"Sadie Black and Sandy White." Julian lifts a brow.

"Exactly."

"So, I Google Sandy White and *Digby's Dirt*, and a bunch of stories came up that she'd written about other celebs. So, I went onto Images and scrolled through the pictures. Ava stopped me, pointing at a picture, saying that it was Sadie, and in the picture with her was Brad-ford Digby."

"Fucking Digby," Vaughn growls.

Charly pulls her phone from her pocket, swipes the screen, and turns it around for me to see. "Look familiar?"

I take the phone from her and stare at the picture.

Holy fuck, she's right.

It's her—the chick who cleans my apartment. She looks a bit different in this picture to how I normally see her, but it's definitely her.

"That's her." I grit my teeth. "That's the chick who cleans here."

"That's Sandy White the journalist, who pretended to be Sadie the cleaner, so she could bug your apartment and record your conversations."

"You think her and Digby were in on it together?" Vaughn asks.

"Yeah. I think that Sandy is a staff writer for him, and I think, when he gets wind of a story, he sends her in undercover to sniff it out. She's written all the big exposés that he's done over the last few years. It was her who wrote the story about Piper and Cain," Charly says to Vaughn.

I see his eyes darken with anger.

But all I can feel is my own anger. I blamed Ava. I yelled at her. I said some awful things to her.

I close my eyes, pinching the bridge of my nose, trying to control the anger I feel.

"Gabe?" That's Charly.

I open my eyes and hand Charly her phone back. "What I don't get is how Digby would have known there was a story to be had about me. No one knew about my past."

"Someone always knows," Julian says.

And he's right; there is.

"Maybe Digby heard something on the grapevine," Charly says. "Or maybe he was after a completely different story. If so, then I bet they thought they'd hit the mother lode of all jackpots when they listened to your conversation with Ava."

I tip my head back and cover my face with my hands.

"Gabe, you okay?" Julian asks.

I lower my head, dragging my fingers through my hair. "Yeah." *No.* "I'm just trying to get my head around it all."

"Ava was telling you the truth," Charly says softly.

She was. And I didn't believe her.

God, I'm such a fucking asshole.

"I can't believe you figured this all out," Julian says to her. "You're seriously badass, Charly."

"I can't take all the credit." She shrugs. "It was Ava as well. We figured it out together."

I was here, hating on her, thinking that she'd betrayed me. All that time, she'd done nothing wrong, and she was out there, trying to clear her name.

I've never hated myself more than I do in this moment.

"She wanted to come, Gabe ... to tell you herself, but she didn't think you would listen to her," Charly says.

And that hurts the most because she was right. I wouldn't have listened.

Jesus, I've fucked things up so very badly.

I need to see Ava now.

"Where is she?" I ask Charly.

"She's at the hotel. I can take you to her. I came in Ava's car, so we should be able to get you out without the paparazzi seeing you, as I don't think they'll expect you to be driven around in a Smart car."

"Is that the car that broke your foot?" Vaughn grins.

"Not now," I growl at him. "Can you just call Gil, explain everything to him, and have him call my lawyers? Oh, and we need to get someone to do a sweep for bugs in my apartment as well."

"I know a guy," Julian says, reaching for his phone. "I'll call him now."

"Thanks," I say. Then, I yank open the bathroom door and gesture to Charly. "Let's go."

Chapter Thirty-Six

Ava

CHARLY'S BEEN GONE FOR ages. Well, it feels like ages. It's actually only been just over an hour.

She said she'd call me once she talked to Gabe. But I've heard nothing so far.

What if he didn't believe her, and she doesn't know how to tell me?

Either way, it doesn't matter if he believes her or not. I have the truth now, and I can do something about it. I won't have those bastards using and slandering my name like that.

I should call Jayce. He'll know what I should do. I have no clue what time it is in Japan, but this is an emergency.

I've just pulled up his number to call when there's a knock on the door.

Charly.

Gucci jumps off the bed and runs to the door. She starts jumping around in excitement in front of it. *"Baaahhh! Baaahhh!"*

She can probably sense it's Charly at the door.

It's bad news. I know it is. If it were good news, she would have called me, like she said she would.

She probably just didn't want to tell me over the phone.

I put my phone down and pad over to the door. I scoop Gucci up in my arms and then open the door.

"Gabe." His name comes out in a breathless rush.

The surprise of him being here knocks the air from my lungs.

I only saw him less than a day ago, but it feels like forever, looking at him now.

He looks exhausted. Dark rings under his eyes.

But he's still beautiful.

"Hey, Speedy," he says in that husky, deep voice of his.

And my mouth dries.

He's here, and he called me Speedy. That's got to be good, right?

"Baaahhh!"

Gucci starts wriggling in my arms, so I put her down. She bolts to Gabe and starts jumping around his legs. I've never seen her act this way around him before. Normally, she head-butts him.

The one time she should head-butt him, and she's whoring it up around him.

Traitor.

"Hey, Gucci." He bends down and picks Gucci up, holding her.

I stare at them, my heart flipping in my chest.

He's never held her before. But he's holding her now.

Tears fill my eyes. I don't know why.

He looks at me. Guilt flashes through his eyes.

"What are you doing here?" I try to make my voice sound strong, but it doesn't work.

"Can I come in?" he asks.

"Okay." I stand back, allowing him in the room.

He walks in, and I close the door.

He puts Gucci down on the bed. Then, he turns and walks back to me, stopping a foot away. "I spoke to Charly."

"Where is she?"

"She just dropped me off and went back to my apartment." He rubs a hand over his hair. "Charly told me everything. Fuck, Ava, I'm so sorry I didn't believe you." His head drops in shame.

My heart breathes a sigh of relief. But my chest tightens in pain at seeing him so beaten down like this. "It's okay, Gabe. Honestly. I know the evidence was pointing straight in my direction, and I can understand why you were taken in by it. Do I wish that you had believed me when I told you it wasn't me? Of course I do. But I can understand why you didn't. I think, if I were in your situation, I would have struggled to believe you with the overwhelming evidence."

"You would have?"

"I think so." I nod. "I probably wouldn't have kicked you out of the apartment, and I probably would have at least let you try to prove your innocence. But, yeah, I'd have struggled with it, too."

"You're a better person than I am."

"It's true." I bite back a smile.

"No, you are." He steps closer. "I'm so sorry for everything I said. Will you forgive me for being weak and stupid and for being an absolute jackass to you?"

"I forgive you for the shitty things you said to me. But, as for the other stuff, there's nothing to forgive. We are both victims in this whole thing."

He's staring at me, confusion in his eyes. "I thought . . ."

"What? That I'd be angry?"

"Honestly, yeah. I was expecting you to kick my ass hard. I had this whole speech laid out. I was going to tell you how sorry I am for ever doubting you. That I will never doubt you again. That I love you. So much. Like I've never loved anyone before. And that I need you to forgive me. And I want you to come home, Speedy. I was ready to beg if necessary."

"Really?" I lift a brow.

"Really." He comes close to me, his nearness and the scent and strength of him stealing my breath. He drops to his knees before me.

I stare down at him. Then, I run my fingers through his hair.

His eyes close. Then, he presses his face to my stomach and wraps his arms around me.

I feel his body shudder against mine.

"Gabe . . ."

"I'm so fucking sorry, Ava. For everything." His voice is raw, and it breaks my heart.

I lower down to my knees and take his face in my hands. "It's okay, Gabe." I soothe him, brushing my thumb over his cheek. "It's okay. I love you, and everything is going to be okay. We're together now, and that's what matters."

I kiss his cheek. His forehead. His nose. His lips.

"What those bastards, Digby and Sandy, did to you, putting your past out there for everyone to read about ... it's despicable. And I know you're worrying about what people might be saying ... but it doesn't matter, Gabe. None of it. What matters is you and what an amazing, kind, generous, and beautiful man you are. A man who stepped up for his kid brother when he needed him most and did what he had to do. Not many people would have been able to handle the situation you found yourself in. Most would have stumbled at the first hurdle. But not you, Gabe. You got on with things, and when the chance to escape was offered to you, you grabbed it with both hands and made something of yourself. I admire you so much. I think you're the bravest and strongest person I've ever met, and I count myself lucky to know you."

He's staring at me, his eyes glassy with emotion. "You're wrong," he says roughly. "I'm not the strongest person you know, babe. You are. You're fucking incredible, Ava. And I love you so very much." Then, he seals his mouth over mine and kisses me deeply as he tightly wraps me in his arms.

And I know that, this time, he will never let me go again.

Chapter Thirty-Seven

Ava

GABE AND I WALK BACK into his apartment together, my hand in his, Gucci trotting alongside us, and I'm feeling a hell of a lot better than I did the last time I was here.

Charly, Vaughn, and Julian are still here, sitting on the sofa, and there's some guy I don't recognize.

When Gucci sees Charly, she goes bounding over to her and jumps into her lap. Charly proceeds to give her the attention she was after.

Charly stops stroking her and looks over at me. *Are you okay?* she mouths.

I smile and nod in response.

"Gabe, this is Martin. He's worked security for me in the past. He's one of the best in the business. I called him to come and sweep the apartment for you."

"And?" Gabe says.

"I ran a spectrum analyzer over your apartment, and I found a bug in here. It was under the sofa, just tacked to the base. There was one in your office, under the seat of the desk chair. One in the kitchen, in the light fixture. One in the guest bedroom, behind the mirror, and there was one in your bedroom, tacked to the base of a lamp."

His bedroom.

Oh God. They recorded us having sex.

My eyes fly to Gabe. His jaw is working angrily, his eyes lit with rage.

"Gabe . . ."

His eyes come to mine, and they soften on me. His hand comes around my cheek. "It's okay, baby."

"No, it's not." Tears fill my eyes. "They invaded our privacy. Things between us . . . private things, and they heard it all."

Gabe pulls me to him and presses his lips to my forehead.

"Is there any way we can trace these bugs back to those bastards?" Gabe's voice rumbles through his chest.

"It won't be easy . . . but leave it to me," Martin says. "I know a few people who might be able to help. Are there any other places that could be bugged? Do you have any other properties? What about your car?"

"No other properties. And that bitch, Sandy, didn't have access to my car."

"You'd be surprised," Martin says. "I'll check it out just to be sure." He gets to his feet.

Gabe lets me go momentarily and gets his car keys from the coffee table. He hands them to Martin. "Could you check Ava's car as well, just to be sure?"

"Sure thing."

"Thanks, man. I appreciate you coming down and doing this for us," Gabe says to Martin.

"Anytime," Martin replies.

Charly gets my car keys from her bag and gives them to Martin.

"I'll take you down to the garage," Julian says to Martin.

We watch them leave. I can feel Gabe's silent rage vibrating through him.

"Fucking Digby," Vaughn bites out. "I hate that bastard. I can't believe the lengths he'll go to for a story."

"Nothing surprises me anymore," Charly says. "Ava, you doing okay?" she asks me.

"Yeah." I meet her eyes. "Just feeling ... violated, I guess."

"That's understandable."

"I need a smoke."

I glance up at Gabe. I can see the frustration etched into his forehead, his jaw clenched so hard that it might shatter.

"Okay."

"I'll be out on the terrace."

I watch him walk out onto the terrace. He leans against the railing and lights up a cigarette.

"He's feeling helpless," Vaughn says to me. "I know that's how I'd be feeling right now, and if there's one thing a man hates, it's feeling helpless. If someone had done that to Charly and me ... recorded us doing ... well, fuck. Put it this way, I'd want to tear the fucker apart with my bare hands."

"I should go talk to him," I tell them.

"I'm going to make some drinks." Charly gets up from the sofa. "I think we could all do with a little something strong right now."

Leaving the living room, I go outside to Gabe. I can see how tense he is. His shoulders rigid. His body taut with anger and frustration.

"Hey," I say in a quiet voice. I rest my arm on the railing, standing next to him, and stare out at the sky. "You okay?"

"No." He takes a drag of his cigarette and flicks the ash off the end. "I want to kill Digby. I want to get in my car, drive to his house, and beat the ever-loving shit out of him. And I would never hit a woman." His eyes come to mine. "Never. But that bitch . . ."

"I know." I put my hand on his arm. "I want to kick her ass, too. But getting angry isn't going to change anything."

"I can't help it." He grinds his teeth, working his jaw. "Having sex with you ... making love to you, it was the first time in my life that sex actually meant anything to me. And, now, they've fucking cheapened it." He takes a pull on his smoke, drops it on the floor, and stubs it out with his shoe. He turns to face me. The sadness in his eyes hurts me. "They've made me feel like a whore all over again."

"No, Gabe. No." I take his face in my hands, forcing his eyes to me. "Feeling like that means they win. And I refuse to let them. Those moments with you—you making love to me, you fucking me, all of it—aren't cheap. They're everything."

He lowers his eyes.

"Gabe, if you allow them to make you feel like a whore, that means that I'm one, too."

His eyes snap back to mine. "Fuck no. Never, Ava. *Never.*"

"Then, don't let them make *you* feel like a whore. Because, if you do, they win."

"God, this is all just so fucked up." He blows out a breath. "I feel like this is my fault. I brought you into my life, and then this happens . . ."

"You didn't bring me into your life. I crashed into yours, remember? And the rest of it . . . I came willingly. And so what? They recorded us having sex." I lift a shoulder, letting a smile onto my lips. "We gave them some pretty damn good shows."

Light seeps into his eyes. "We gave some astro-fucking-nomical shows, baby."

"Damn right, we did."

"God, I love you, Speedy."

"I love you, too." I gently kiss him on the lips.

"Sorry to interrupt you lovebirds, but I come bearing alcohol. Bourbon for Gabe. I figured you liked whiskey; you have enough of it in there. And I made a G and T for you, Ava."

"Thanks." I smile at her.

Charly leaves the drinks on the table and disappears back inside.

Gabe is staring over at the glass of whiskey, an expression on his face I've never seen before.

"Gabe?"

"I drink too much, Speedy." His eyes come back to mine. "Way too much."

I know he does. I've always known, but he needs to come to this realization on his own.

"What do you want to do about it?" I ask slowly.

He rubs a hand over the back of his neck. "I don't know. I think maybe I need to slow the drinking down. Or . . . I dunno . . . stop altogether." He blows out a breath. "I think . . ."

"What?"

"I think maybe I use it as a crutch . . . to make myself feel better."

"What are you saying?"

He needs to say this, not me. He needs to admit it to himself.

"I don't know. I just know, when I think about never having a drink . . . the thought scares me."

"Okay. So, what should we do about that?"

He lifts a shoulder. "I think maybe I need help stopping."

"Then, we'll get you help. Whatever you need."

He's silent, and then he lets out a self-deprecating laugh. "After watching Julian struggle with drugs, I was so worried that it could happen to me. I never even realized that I was struggling just with alcohol."

I press my hand to his cheek. "It's going to be okay, Gabe."

His eyes tell me he's not so sure.

"Whatever happens, I'll be with you, every step of the way. I've got your back."

He leans his forehead against mine and breathes deeply. "I don't know what I did to deserve you, but I'm so fucking glad you're mine."

"Right back at ya, babe."

He kisses me again. Then, he takes my hand and leads me over to a lounger. He sits first and then pulls me to sit between his legs. I rest my back against his chest and lay my head on his shoulder. He wraps his arms around me. I can feel his heart beating strong against me.

I glance over at the glasses of alcohol that Charly left

for us. Thinking about what he just said, I ask, "Do you want me to get rid of the drinks?"

He's silent a moment. "No. Leave them there. I'm not saying I'm going to drink it right now, but I know that I won't be able to not drink it either—without some help."

"Then, we'll get you help real soon."

He presses a kiss to the top of my head.

We sit in silence, just being together.

I think about everything. About Digby and Sandy. The bugs in the apartment. Gabe's past out there for public fodder.

"What's going to happen with Digby and Sandy?" I ask him.

He sighs. "I don't know. I guess we wait and see what Martin can find out about those bugs, if they're traceable back to either of them. But I know one thing for sure. I'm not letting those fuckers get away with this. Bugging my apartment and setting you up to take the fall. I nearly lost you because of those bastards."

I slide my hands over his and link our fingers together. "We'd have found our way back to each other; I'm sure of it."

"Once I stopped being an asshole and started listening to you, you mean?"

"Yeah, something like that." I laugh softly. "You're going to need to call Gil and let him know what's going on—about Sandy and the bugs in your apartment."

"I had Vaughn call him to fill him in while I came to see you. But I do need to talk to Gil about all that shit and about the press release. I know he's probably getting twitchy, waiting for my answer on it."

"Press release?" I ask.

"About my past. Gil had my publicist draft a statement. I have to sign off on it."

"You don't sound convinced."

"I'm not."

I turn around and look at him. "Don't you want to tell your side of the story? Get the actual truth out there to your fans?"

"Yeah, I do. But the statement just doesn't feel right. It says nothing about the truth in it. It's just basically an apology for my past."

"So, change it. Rewrite it yourself."

"I'm not exactly a great writer, Speedy. I'm more of a verbal guy, if you haven't noticed."

"So, if talking is your strength, tell them face-to-face from your own mouth."

"I don't want to go on a fucking talk show and spill my guts."

"So, don't. Record a video. Say everything you want to and then put it out there on your social media. That way, you're directing it to the people who matter—your fans."

He stares at me for a long moment. "You ever thought of being a publicist? Because you'd be fucking awesome at it."

"I'm awesome at most things." I give a shrug and a teasing smile.

"You're awesome at everything, Speedy. Except for driving. That, you suck at."

"Hey! It was my shitty driving that brought us together."

Gabe laughs, and the sound is beautiful. "Yeah, and I'm thankful every fucking day for that."

Chapter Thirty-Eight

Gabe

I'VE DECIDED TO DO a live video on Facebook. No fucking around. Just go live on social media and get it over with.

Julian, Vaughn, and Charly left to give us some privacy while I do this video. Martin left straight after checking Ava's car and mine. Thankfully, they were clear. He said he'd be in touch as soon as he had something on the bugging devices.

I also spoke to Gil. Told him to scrap the press release. I told him that I was going to do this myself, my way. He's not too happy with me doing a live video. But it's not like I'm doing a Q&A session. I'm just going on there, telling my side of the story, and then I'm done.

I also told Gil about the bugs in my apartment. He's on with the lawyers right now. And I gave him Martin's contact details, so the lawyers could talk to him directly if needed.

I'm just having a cigarette out on the terrace.

I glance over at the drinks on the table. They're still there.

I've not had anything to drink. I want to do this video with a clear head. But I know I will drink something before the day is out. I can't *not*. I just need to watch how much I drink.

And, first thing tomorrow, I'm getting in touch with whomever I need to, to help me kick this habit I have.

I want to be a better man for Ava. I want to be a better man for me. And cleaning my act up is the first step at that. But the cigarettes are definitely not going. For the time being anyway.

Ava suggested that maybe I could talk to someone about my past. About my parents and the way I used to earn money. She thinks it all contributes to my excessive drinking. A way to dull the memories.

I think she's probably right.

"You ready, baby?" Ava steps out onto the terrace.

"Yeah." I stub my cigarette out and get to my feet.

When I reach Ava, she takes hold of my hand and leads me inside.

"I've got your phone ready to go on Facebook live."

"Okay." I sit down on the sofa.

She sits on the coffee table, across from me. "I put Gucci in the kitchen. I didn't want her jumping in the video or making noise while you did this."

"She won't be happy," I tell Ava.

"I gave her some sliced apples and pears, so that should keep her happy for five minutes."

God, I can't believe I'm about to do this.

I swallow down and rub my hands on my thighs.

I'm shitting bricks. I'm man enough to admit that.

I'm about to go on camera and tell the world things I've been keeping secret for a very long time. But I don't have that choice anymore, thanks to that bastard, Digby, and Sandy, his bitch of a sidekick.

"You okay?" Ava reaches over and squeezes my leg.

"Yeah, I'm good. Let's do this."

"Okay." She smiles gently.

She lifts my phone up to video me. "Just tell me when."

I run my hands through my hair and take a deep breath. "Okay . . . I'm ready."

"It's just counting down. Three . . . two . . . one . . ." She gives me a thumbs-up to tell me I'm live.

Here goes nothing.

"People of Facebook. Hey. I'm sure you know who I am because you're on my social media page. But, for those of you who don't, I'm Gabriel Evans. If you're one of the lucky ones who doesn't know who I am, well, I'm sure you will soon enough. A news story about me went out last night, and that's why I am here. Because I want to address the things that have been said about me.

"I could have done the press release stuff. But I didn't want to hide behind a piece of paper pulled together for me by my publicist. I wanted to talk to you all directly.

"I know what you've all read about me in the media over the last day. And I'm not here to deny any of that. It's true. My parents are in prison. They're serving time for racketeering, drug trafficking, and murder. But I think the piece of news that has probably shocked and intrigued everyone is that I used to sleep with women for money. That is also true.

"But the truth you've been given by the so-called journalist who released this story is a vague representation of what actually happened. There are reasons behind people's actions, and there were reasons behind *my* actions. It's easy to judge based on the initial outlined facts, but when you dig a bit deeper, color in the actual picture with details, those actions begin to make more sense. The story that you first thought you were getting suddenly seems a hell of a lot clearer. A lot more understandable.

"I hope, by telling you the details of my story, you'll see that, sometimes, when you read something in the media, even though the facts stated are the 'truth' "—I air-quote the word—"they're not the whole *truth*. So, here it is." I clasp my hands together in front of me and blow out a breath.

"But, before I get started on the details, I firstly want to apologize to my girlfriend, Ava, who is currently standing behind the camera, filming me for you guys." I look directly at her, our eyes meeting.

"I was led to believe that Ava had betrayed me. That she had recorded a private conversation between us and sold the rights to the story to a vulture of a man who I won't even give the dignity of naming, but I think you all know who I'm talking about. I blamed her. Yelled at her. And told her to leave our apartment— yeah, I did that. But, in my defense, the evidence against her was strong. The people behind this went to great lengths to make it look like it was Ava who had done this. But it wasn't Ava.

"She is a victim in this, as much as I am. Our privacy was invaded, and a private conversation between us in our home, detailing events from my past, was recorded without our knowledge, and then Ava was tricked into signing a release form disguised as something else. This might sound far-fetched, but sometimes, the truth is just that—far-fetched. Because we good people would never do something like that, we find it hard to believe that someone would go so far. Believe me when I say, they would. The lengths these people went to, to get this story, is fucking scary. And something needs to be done about that, but that's for my legal team to deal with.

"My past is mine. But, as it's been made public knowledge, I want to clear some things up. Yes, my parents are in prison. The crimes they committed are in no way a reflection on my brother and me. You can't choose the family you're born into. And my brother and I definitely didn't choose our parents. But having him as my brother is the best thing to come out of it." I take a breath.

"When our parents were arrested, I was seventeen, months from my eighteenth birthday. My brother was twelve. He was, without a doubt, going to be taken away from me and placed with a family. We were all each other had left. So, we ran. Using what little money I had in my savings, I got us a place, and I landed a job. But the money wasn't enough. Before I knew it, I was working three jobs and still barely scraping by. I was just paying the bills and feeding us both.

"Then, the chance to get into escorting was presented to me. It was more money, not tons, but it meant I could work one job during the day and escort on nights. Then, after a while, things changed. I was offered money to have sex with a client. A lot of money. I was young. Getting paid to have sex with a hot older woman, more money than I would have made in a month, was a dream come true. So, I did it. And I carried on doing it. The money gave us a better life, and even though it was—*is* illegal, I don't regret what I did because it meant that I could give my brother a better life.

"Then, I was lucky, and things changed for me. I got the opportunity to get into acting, and my life got better from that point on.

"I won't sit here and say I'm proud of what I did. But, if I were put into that situation again, would I do things the same? If it meant keeping a roof over my brother's head and being able to feed him, then yes. We all do things that we're not proud of, but when you go to judge me for my decisions in life, think about yourself—what you would do for those you love. And then think about me again and see if your judgment would still be the same.

"So, that's it. Thank you for listening to me. And I'll see you guys soon."

I look at Ava, and she ends the video, holding the phone in her lap.

"How did I do?"

"Amazing. Gabe . . . that was . . . perfect. If people don't understand and love you even more after that, then they must be stupid. The views were into the hundreds of thousands, and the comments were coming through thick and fast. I could barely keep up with them, but they all seemed to be comments of support. There were an awful lot of love hearts flying across the screen."

"Really?" That picks me up.

"Really." She smiles.

She comes over and straddles my lap, handing me my phone. "You should take a look, see for yourself."

"I will. In a minute." I put the phone on the sofa beside me. "I just want five minutes with my girl."

I take her face in my hands, bring her to my lips, and kiss her.

"Thank you for being here," I murmur against her mouth.

She leans back, looking me in the eyes. "Where else would I be?"

"After the way I treated you, I wouldn't have been surprised if you had never come back to me." I sigh. "I know I'm difficult and an asshole ninety percent of the time, but I do love you."

"Ninety percent's a bit generous. More like ninety-nine-point-nine percent of the time."

"Funny."

"I'm a comedian, didn't you know?" She grins. "You're being too hard on yourself. Let's just forget everything that happened and focus on the future. You've got a house to build me, remember?"

"Yeah, I do, don't I?"

She nods.

"I'll still have to deal with Digby and Sandy though."

"I know. But we'll do it together, Gabe."

"Together sounds pretty fucking good to me." I tightly band my arm around her, bringing her closer.

"Baaahhh! Baaahhh!"

"Sounds like Gucci's finished her food."

I chuckle, and Ava laughs.

"I'll go let her out." She gets up from my lap and walks to the kitchen.

The next thing I know, the bundle of fur called Gucci comes flying into the living room. She jumps on the sofa and head-butts me in the arm.

"Jesus, Gucci! Nice to see you, too."

"Babe, you want a coffee?" Ava calls from the kitchen. "I'm making one."

"Sure," I say.

Gucci settles down on the sofa beside me.

I pick my cell up and swipe the screen open.

It's still on the video. The comments are filling my screen.

I'm reading through them when Ava comes back in the living room. She hands me my coffee and sits on the sofa next to me.

Gucci gets up and climbs over my lap and onto Ava. Then, she sprawls out, stretching across us both.

We chuckle at her.

"What are people saying?" Ava asks.

"That they think I'm awesome."

"You are."

I turn my phone off and put it down.

"You okay?" Ava asks me.

I look at her, sitting here beside me with Gucci lying on us, and I know that I've never been more okay in my life.

I reach out and cup her cheek with my hand. I press a kiss to her lips. "I'm more than okay," I tell her. "You're everything to me, Speedy. You know that, right?"

She presses her hand to mine. "I know. And I hope you know, the same goes for you."

"I do." I smile.

And I really do.

I know, with her by my side, everything is going to be just fine.

Epilogue

Gabe

One Year and Ten Months Later

TAKING A DRAG OF my cigarette, I stare out at the view of the reservoir and the canyon surrounding it from my spot on our porch at the back of our house.

Speedy and I had the ranch of our dreams built pretty much straightaway, and we've called it home for the last eight months.

I look at Gucci and Donnie running around in the paddock, chasing a butterfly. The sun is shining, glinting off the pool.

It's fucking idyllic.

It's home.

I can't believe I got so lucky to have all of this.

But, most of all, to have Speedy. The girl that dreams are made of.

She's inside, getting dressed to go out for dinner. It's our two-year anniversary of the day she ran over my foot. We class that as the day we got together because that was the day that she came into my life and never left.

Oh, if you're wondering who Donnie is, he's our new pygmy goat. Speedy bought him for me for my birthday six months ago. He's all black with a white patch on his head. He's the cutest fucking thing, not that I'd ever admit that out loud.

I called him Don Corleone. I had to give him a cool name, right? But Speedy said it was too much of a mouthful to say every time. And she said Don sounded like an old man's name, so she nicknamed him Donnie, and it stuck.

Gucci loves her baby brother.

Probably about as much as I love mine. Tate's doing really well. When his residency finished, Presbyterian offered him a permanent job, which he took, even though I offered him money to set up his own private practice. I still offer the money on a regular basis, and he knocks me back every time.

Stubborn asshole.

But, one of these days, he'll say yes. I'm sure of it.

Tate is also heavily involved with the charity that he, Speedy, and I set up.

I came up with the idea for it a couple of days after I did the live video.

It went viral. My story was in every newspaper, and the video was playing on every chat show for weeks after. I received thousands of letters and emails of support. And almost every celebrity came out to support me. A lot of the messages I received were from people whose parents had gone to prison, and they had been left either in the foster system or with relatives. I heard stories that were very similar to Tate's and mine. Kids who'd ended up on the streets. People who had turned to prostitution to feed themselves and their siblings. People who'd had it worse than I had. And I knew I had to do something to help.

So, I came up with the idea of Healing the Breaks.

It's a nonprofit charity designed to help kids and young adults whose parents have gone to prison. Whether it's making sure they have somewhere to live or if they need counseling or support or even money to help get them started, we provide that for them.

Speedy does the day-to-day running of Healing the Breaks. She was running that and still working at the theater where she had gotten the job, but as the charity expanded, she decided she wanted to dedicate all of her time to that. Tate and I do most of the fundraising along with Vaughn, Charly, and Julian, who are heavily involved with the charity, too.

I'm still making movies.

I did the espionage thriller that I'd signed on to do before I met Speedy. I had half-expected the studio to pull me from the role. But, with the positive response I'd gotten from the fans and media after the video, I guess they would have looked bad if they'd pulled me.

Also, five days after I did the live video, I went to a rehab center and stayed there for thirty days.

It was one of the hardest things I'd ever had to do.

The first seven days, going through withdrawal, were fucking horrific. And being away from Speedy made it even harder.

But I did it.

And, when I came out, I got myself a therapist to continue on with the counseling I'd received in rehab, and I joined AA, where they assigned me a sponsor.

I'm now one year and ten months clean.

Do I still want to drink?

Every fucking day.

But I fight the urge.

Because I have too much good in my life now to ever go back to using alcohol to make me feel better.

After rehab, I went home and spent a few days with Speedy, and then I went straight into filming the movie. When it was done, I didn't sign on for any others even though the offers were rolling in, and Gil wanted me to take them up.

Also, I had the issue of Bradford Digby and Sandy White to deal with. While I was in rehab, Martin was able to track down where the bugs had been purchased from and who had made the purchase. Seems Sandy had been stupid enough to pay for them with her credit card. And, with the fact that she'd had access to my apartment, it was enough to contact the police. But, after speaking to the police, they said that it would be hard to make a charge stick, as all they could really potentially charge her with was spying. They advised us to go the civil route and sue her with invasion of privacy. So, my lawyers slapped her and Digby with a lawsuit.

Surprisingly, Digby settled out of court—for both him and Sandy. It shocked the fuck out of me when the offer came through. I'd like to think he grew a conscience, but I highly doubt it. The bastard just didn't want to have the negative publicity, especially after all the support I had been receiving.

Part of the deal with Digby was that he would hand over all the recordings made in my apartment, and he would erase any copies he had.

I received them in the form of five USB sticks, filled to the max. I didn't listen to them. But, that night, Speedy and I had a bonfire on the terrace.

After everything was done, I just wanted to spend some time with my girl. But, first, she wanted me to meet her family, so we flew to New York for a few days, and I met her mom and dad and her brother, Jayce. They're really great people. Her mom fussed over me and fed me some incredible food. And, don't tell Speedy I said this, but her mom's cooking is even better than hers. Her dad and Jayce are really cool, too. They're both Lakers fans, so we had plenty to talk about.

Then, from New York, we flew straight to the Maldives for our first vacation together. We spent two weeks relaxing, eating, and fucking.

It was awesome.

Then, we came home and threw ourselves into getting the ranch built and setting up Healing the Breaks, using the money from the lawsuit and some of my own along with donations from some celebrity friends of mine.

I also started writing a screenplay.

Yeah, I know I said I was a shit writer, but I took some writing classes. Turns out, I'm not as bad as I thought I was.

I'm writing a screenplay about my life. I have a lot to tell. And doing it has been therapeutic.

I'm almost finished writing it. When it's done, I'll

give it to Tate to read. It involves him, so he should be the first to read it.

Whether I'll shop it to any studios or not, I'm not sure. But, for now, I'm glad I'm writing my story.

"Hey there, handsome."

I turn at the sound of Speedy's voice, and I nearly choke on the smoke in my lungs.

She looks fucking beautiful.

She always looks beautiful. But, right now ... she's in a silver satin dress with black lace covering my girls, Pinky and Perky. Her hair is tumbling in waves down her back. The black stilettos on her feet will look amazing while wrapped around my back.

She looks hot as fuck.

My cock is standing to attention, ready to get in on some action with my girl.

I quickly glance at my watch. We've got ten minutes before the car gets here to take us to dinner. That's enough time for a quickie.

I stub my cigarette out, put a mint in my mouth, and walk over to her.

"You look gorgeous," I tell her.

"Right back at ya, babe." She smiles, pressing her hands to my chest. "And we're matching." She tugs gently on my tie.

I'm wearing a fitted black suit, dark gray shirt, and silver tie.

"Yes, we are." I slide my hands over her hips and grab her ass. "So ... we've got ten minutes before the car gets here ..." I raise a suggestive brow as I lean in and press my mouth to hers.

The sound of the buzzer for the gate has me sighing. "For fuck's sake."

She giggles against my lips. "That'll be the driver."

"He can wait." I start to kiss my way down her neck and cup her tit in my hand.

She moans softly.

The buzzer goes off again.

I stop kissing her neck and growl out a sound of frustration.

"We should go. He'll just keep buzzing."

"He'll get his ass kicked, is what he'll get," I grumble. "And the fucker can say good-bye to his tip."

She laughs again. "Come on, grumpy ass." She takes hold of my hand and leads me toward the front door. "We can have sex later."

"You bet your hot ass we will."

We arrive at the restaurant, and the maître d' leads us to the private dining room that I reserved.

It's a new Mediterranean tapas restaurant that recently opened, and it has been getting rave reviews.

We're seated, and the waiter appears, asking for our drink order.

I order sparkling water. Speedy orders a virgin strawberry daiquiri.

"You can have something stronger," I tell her. "Champagne? We are celebrating."

"I'm fine." She smiles.

She never drinks around me, no matter how often I tell her she can. But, honestly, her doing that just tells me how much she loves and supports me.

Our drinks come, and we place our food order.

I start to talk to her about a fundraising idea I have for Healing the Breaks, but I can tell she's not fully listening. She seems distracted.

"You okay?" I ask. "You just seem a little off your game."

"I'm fine. I was just . . . I have your gift, and I was going to wait until the end of dinner to give it to you. But I think maybe I should just give it to you now."

"Okay, sure. But, just to let you know, I don't have your gift with me. I'm giving it to you later."

She cocks a brow. "It's not your dick with a ribbon wrapped around it again, is it?"

I give her a serious look. "No. You know I never give the same gift twice."

I grin, and she laughs, but it doesn't quite reach her eyes, which is weird for Speedy because, when she smiles, she smiles with her whole face.

"You're not disappointed that I'm giving you your gift later, are you?"

"No, of course not." She picks her clutch up from the floor and seems to hesitate. Then, she reaches inside and pulls out a small white rectangular box. She places it in the center of the table between us. "I hope you like it."

"You know I will. You have the best taste. You picked me, didn't you?"

She doesn't laugh, which bugs me.

I pick the box up and give it a shake. It rattles.

"Okay, I'm guessing, watch." I go to lift the lid off and pause when she says my name. "What?"

"Look, if you don't like what's inside that box, it's fine. I swear. I mean, I know we both said in the past that we wanted this at some point, but we never said when, and I don't know when there's ever a right time, but—"

"Speedy?"

"What?"

"Stop talking, and let me open it."

"Okay."

I pull the lid off and stare down at the white stick inside the box.

My entire being freezes.

"You're pregnant?" The words feel like they rush out of me. I lift my eyes to hers.

She bites her lip and nods. "Seven weeks. I had it confirmed at the doctor's a few days ago. I thought I'd wait to surprise you. I just hope it's a good surprise." Her face is screwed up with nerves as she chews on her lip.

"Babe, it's a good surprise. It's the best fucking surprise ever."

"Really?"

"Really." I smile so big that I feel like my face might crack. "Jesus, Ava." I get up from my chair and sweep her up into my arms, hugging her tight. "I'm so fucking happy right now."

"God, I'm so relieved," she whispers. "I was so worried."

I lean back and take her face in my hands. "Why?"

"Because we didn't plan it, and I wasn't sure where your head was."

"You being pregnant with my baby is the greatest thing ever. Babe, it's the best gift I have ever received in my life. It's astro-fucking-nomical."

She smiles big, and my chest feels like it could burst with the love I feel for her.

I move a hand down to her stomach and press my palm to it. "I just can't believe our baby is inside of you right now."

"It's amazing, isn't it?" she whispers.

The waiter appears with our food. I look at it being laid out on the table, and after finding out that she's pregnant, I decide that I don't want to wait any longer to give her my gift.

"Speedy, would you mind if we take this food to go? I really want to give you your gift now."

She looks at me, surprised. "Okay, sure."

"Can you wrap this up to go?" I tell the waiter.

"Of course, Mr. Evans. Would you like any dessert to go with it?"

"Speedy?"

"I could eat some cheesecake."

"Two pieces of cheesecake as well. And make it quick."

The waiter rushes off to sort our food. I reach over the table, get the pregnancy test from the box, and put it in my pocket.

"What?" I say in response to the look on Speedy's face, which is a mixture of disgust and happiness.

"You do realize that I peed on that stick?"

"And your point is?"

"That it's kind of weird and gross that you're carrying around a stick with my urine on it."

"I'm carrying around a stick that says my girlfriend is pregnant with my baby. You're lucky I'm not waving this thing around for everyone to see."

She stares at me, laughter and concern in her gorgeous eyes. "Please don't do that."

"What's it worth for me not to do it?" I grin devilishly.

She leans close and whispers in my ear, "I'll let you do that thing to me that I said I would never let you do."

I lean back and stare in her eyes, my blood suddenly rushing south. "You mean, I can punch the starfish?"

Laughter bursts from her. "If that's slang for fifth base, then, yes, baby, you can punch the starfish."

"God, you're fucking awesome." I grab her face between my hands and press a kiss to her lips. "I don't know what the fuck I did to deserve you, but whatever it was, I'm glad I did it."

"You definitely got lucky, big guy." She pats my hand, grinning at me.

We're back in the car with our to-go food. And I just can't stop staring at Speedy's stomach.

Our baby is inside her right now. A part of her and a part of me. It's fucking mind-blowing.

A thought occurs to me.

"Speedy, does this mean I have to give up smoking now that we're having a baby?"

She turns her face to look at me. "Only if you want to. You've been doing so well with not drinking, and if giving up your cigarettes would feel like too much of an added pressure, then don't do it. The last thing I want is for you to put any unnecessary pressure on yourself."

And this is just one of the many reasons I love her. She always thinks about what's best for me.

"I'll think about it and have a chat with my sponsor, see what he thinks."

"I know you don't smoke in the house anymore, but you can't smoke around me at all now that I'm pregnant."

"I promise I won't." I press a kiss to her soft lips.

I see we're approaching our destination, and my stomach starts to churn with unexpected nerves. And, now, I really could do with a smoke.

I haven't been nervous all day. Every time I've thought about this, I've felt happy and positive. But, now that we're nearly there, I'm starting to shit bricks.

The car starts to slow, coming to a stop outside the studio.

"Why are we at the studio?" Speedy asks me.

"You'll see in a minute."

I open the door and get out of the car, helping her out.

Keeping hold of her hand, I lead her past the studio and to the corner of the street.

I pause before we turn the corner. "Okay, so close your eyes."

"You want me to close my eyes?"

"That's what I said."

She gives me a look and shuts them.

"Are they closed properly?" I wave a hand in front of her.

"Do they look closed to you?" She smirks.

"Funny, smart-ass. Okay, don't open them until I say so."

I take hold of her hands and lead her around the corner and down the street until I stop her on the very spot where she hit me with her car that day.

The street is lit with fairy lights, giving it a romantic glow. There's not much you can do to make a street down the side of a movie studio look romantic, but it has to be here, so fairy lights, it is.

I get the blue ring box from my pocket, and then I get down on one knee in front of her.

Fuck, I'm so nervous.

I feel like I'm gonna hurl. My mouth dries. I take a deep breath and moisten my lips with my tongue. "Okay . . . you can open your eyes."

She blinks her eyes open. I watch her as she takes in the fairy lights and just where we are. A smile ignites her whole face.

That smile. Fuck, it gets me every time.

It takes her a moment to realize that I'm on my knee in front of her, but when she does, her eyes widen, and her mouth pops into an O before she covers it with her hands.

"Ava . . . I had this whole big speech prepared, and then you blew me out of the water when you told me that you're pregnant with our baby. You kinda stole my thunder." I grin. "But, tonight, you've given me the greatest gift ever. And, now, I'm asking you to marry me, with our child growing inside you, on the very spot where we started, and it couldn't be more right." I push up to my feet. "So, Ava Simms . . . soon-to-be mother of my child . . . my Speedy . . . will you marry me?"

I pop open the ring box, and her eyes widen further, filling with tears.

She drops her hands, revealing her gorgeous smiling face. "Yes, Gabe, I will marry you."

My heart explodes with utter fucking happiness. I get the ring out of the box and slide it onto her finger.

"It's beautiful, Gabe." She holds her hand, staring down at the ring.

"You're beautiful," I tell her. "And mine." I take her face in my hands and kiss her, like I plan to kiss her for the rest of our lives.

"I can't believe you're going to be my husband." Her eyes glitter up at me.

"Believe it, baby." I kiss her again. "You're going to be Mrs. Evans."

"I like the sound of that." She smiles. "God, tonight is the best night of my life, Gabe."

"Mine, too." I take her hand in mine, loving the feel of her engagement ring against my finger. "Finding out you're pregnant, you agreeing to marry me, and there's still more good stuff to come."

"More?" She glances at me with intrigue.

"Well, we have food in the car. And then fifth base, baby, remember? I plan to get you home, strip you naked, hit that home run, and then eat cheesecake off your body."

Laughter bursts from her.

"What?" I say, mock innocently.

She stops and stands in front of me, smiling up at me. "Nothing." She shakes her head. "Just ... don't ever change, Gabriel Evans. Always be you because you're perfect, and I love you."

I tightly wrap my arms around her, finally feeling the acceptance that I didn't know I'd been looking for all this time. Full of love for this incredible woman in my arms. A love that I didn't know existed until her.

She might have broken me on that fateful day, right here in this street, when our worlds came crashing together, but she's also fixed me, too. In more ways than one.

I can't imagine my life without her now.

Thank fuck I don't have to.

Acknowledgments

I HAVE THE BEST job in the world. I get to create imaginary worlds with the most amazing characters, and then I get to see you guys enjoy them.

Best. Feeling. Ever.

Or, as Gabe would say, astro-fucking-nomical!

I couldn't do this without a bunch of amazing people. First is my husband, Craig, who goes through every single step of writing a book with me. The highs, the lows—he's there for it all. I definitely won the husband lottery with him.

My gorgeous children, Riley and Isabella, whose daily dose of love and laughter make my already wonderful life perfect.

My agent, Lauren, who continues to bring amazing things to the table and supports every single decision I make. Thank you.

My girls—Sali, Trishy, and Jodi. Best book friends a girl could wish for. I count myself lucky to know you all.

Big thanks to Naj, my cover designer, for yet another gorgeous book cover, and Jovana, my editor, for making this rough-around-the-edges story into something perfect.

And, of course, my Wether Girls—I adore you all and our group. It's the best place to be on Facebook!

Also, a massive thank-you to all the bloggers who work tirelessly to help promote books. I appreciate and adore you all.

And, lastly, to my fabulous readers—Your continuing support makes it possible for me to do what I love. My biggest thank-you of all goes to each and every one of you.